MARRAKESH FILE

A Danny McKenna Novel

PHIL RIBERA

ISBN-13 978-1-7367404-0-8
ISBN-10 1-7367404-0-7

Published by Phil Ribera

Learn more about the author by visiting: www.philribera.com

It was the first Sunday of June. The kind of morning when the sun, the gulls and the sound of a distant train held the promise of another beautiful day in the San Francisco Bay Area.

The parking lot was empty and my office was quiet. I'd been putting off some mundane paperwork and had decided to spend the day getting caught up. Flipping on the coffee machine, I set my things down and poured myself a cup. That's when I saw it...

My secretary had taped the note to my chair, so I couldn't miss it.

McKenna Investigations

From the desk of:
Shanay Moore - Executive Assistant

McKenna~

Some lady collect called us from jail saying they charged her with a murder she didn't do. You know they all say that, McKenna!!

Anyways, she says she's your friend and needs your help, but the lady was crying so bad I couldn't barely understand her. Oh yeah, her name is Aafreen Soltani.

196 Oak Street, Suite 210 Oakland, CA 94607

CHAPTER 1

"McKenna, why you call'n me on the weekend?"

"The message you left on my desk. Is this a joke?"

"Now why would I joke about someth'n like that?"

Slipping on my readers, I looked at it again. "Why didn't you call me right away?"

"I did, but you didn't answer."

I pulled out my phone and saw that I'd accidentally left it on silent mode since Friday afternoon when I'd taken a nap. "Did she say anything else?" I asked.

"Nope, that was it. Got busted for kill'n somebody and wants you to get her out."

"Did she tell you what city or which jail she's in?"

"No, but the operator said she was call'n from Central Detention in D.C." Shanay bit into something that crunched like a piece of toast. "So, who's this chick again?"

"Aafreen Soltani is a Deputy U.S. Marshal, and I highly doubt she killed someone. We worked together on my last case...the missing person. The guy who fled the witness protection program. Anyway, something is definitely wrong with this picture. I should probably go back there and see what I can do to help."

"I thought you had a bunch of work you needed to get done."

"I'll work on it while I'm there."

"Uh-huh."

"Hopefully, I'll be able to clear this up for her in a hurry. It's most likely some sort of mistake."

"Well, good luck, Sherlock. I'll keep everything under control while you're gone."

The cheapest flight on such short notice wasn't until 10:05 p.m. It was a budget carrier out of Oakland, and with a plane change in Salt Lake City, I wouldn't get into D.C. until after 7 a.m.

I looked at the stack of folders that I had hoped to crack into. They were off-shoots from the case I'd just closed—which by coincidence had also taken me to the nation's capital. An envelope tucked into one of the folders held a flash drive and a SIM card—both of which contained data that Shanay had shown me how to access, though until today I hadn't found the time to.

Several aspects of the investigation had been left hanging, and even though I'd been well compensated for my completed work, I don't like loose ends. But as much as I willed myself to get started probing further into the files, my mind was stuck on Soltani.

Our relationship, if you could call it that, had been ambiguous at best. Falling somewhere in the aftermath of an affair she'd had with her boss, Aafreen had been bitter and distrustful toward me—setting boundaries right from the gate in a fiery proclamation that she would never sleep with a guy like me. So far, she'd kept her word.

We'd had no contact during the month since the investigation, leading me to believe that she'd lost whatever interest in me she might have developed. In fact, I'd given it better than 50/50 odds that she'd gone back with Leo Kingsbury—the guy with whom she'd had the fling.

He's an assistant deputy chief in the U.S. Marshals Service—a D.C. heavyweight with powerful connections and plenty of political influence. So, I had to wonder why Soltani called me for help instead of him.

These questions peppered me like gravel from a cement truck, effectively shattering my aversion to travel and violating my doctrine against getting involved in someone else's problems. Especially those of Aafreen Soltani, who hadn't seemed particularly impressed with my abilities as an investigator anyway.

On the other side of the coin was that I'd thought about her every day since Bangkok. She was strikingly gorgeous, with thick black hair, warm mocha eyes, and perfectly white teeth. We had each broken through our personal doubts and distrust to find a middle ground. That had felt really nice, but had also made the lack of contact since then that much more confusing, if not painful.

If I'm honest, my curiosity about Aafreen's feelings toward me took a front seat to every other reason I could come up with to fly back to D.C. and wade into her case. I needed to know if there was anything there.

For kicks, I punched *Aafreen Soltani* into my laptop to see if her arrest had made the news. The page of abundant hits was immediate. Local affiliates NBC4 Washington, WJLA, and Fox 5 DC all carried the story, but the banners numbed me to the core before I could even click on the articles themselves. I sat staring into the screen, horrified.

U.S. Marshal Chief slain; Agent arrested
Deputy charged in murder of Assistant Chief U.S. Marshal
Marshal Chief fatally stabbed; Female Deputy arrested

CHAPTER 2

"Wow" and "holy shit," were the words that came out of me, repeated over and over again as I read and reread the articles. The stories themselves didn't have much more information than the headlines, other than to say that Kingsbury had been stabbed at his home in Oak Hill, Virginia, and that Aafreen Soltani, a deputy U.S. Marshal, had been arrested at their headquarters building in Arlington only hours after the body was discovered.

This thing was going to be sticky and ugly, and unlike my other investigations, this one wasn't *too good to be true*. In fact, it was almost so bad that it had to be true. Yet, I felt compelled to be there for my friend, or whatever Aafreen was to me. I owed her the benefit of my past as a San Francisco police officer and homicide inspector. Putting myself out there again was not something I really *wanted* to do, but it was what I *needed* to do.

Gathering my file folders, I stuffed them into a shoulder bag and then drove back to the boat where I packed a few changes of clothes and some toiletries. I ordered up an Uber and waited in the marina parking lot with my bag. Fifteen minutes later I was in line at the Oakland Airport, waiting to get a stand-by seat on the earliest flight to Washington D.C., regardless of the cost.

As tired as I was, I can rarely sleep on a plane. Besides, my mind had started churning, and that's never a good sign. The case that I had initially left behind in Bangkok still annoyed me like a clothing label on the back of my neck.

The case had begun when a young woman claiming to be Elaina Teagan asked for my help in locating her missing brother. She had charmed me into taking the case against my better judgment, and when I found the man, Teagan and her band of assassins tried to kill him. They were unsuccessful, and the woman ended up perishing under a hail of bullets in a dark alley behind the embassy. I was never able to learn her true identity, and the only photo I had of her did not trigger any matches on a facial recognition search.

I took out my folders, and decided to try doing what I couldn't get done at the office. All of the loose ends were there, staring me in the face. I had written them down on a separate sheet—like bullets on a PowerPoint presentation. The flight attendant brought me a cup of coffee, I put on my readers, and then dug back into the case.

Point #1: Professional hitmen
These two men did not appear to be part of Teagan's team, and had targeted me instead of the missing man. They both died in the same alleyway shootout, and other than having recovered one of their cellphones—vis-à-vis—the SIM card in the envelope—I had almost no information about them. At the top of my concerns was who had paid them to kill me, and why?

Point #2: Mike Prowse
The man was the head of Internal Affairs at the SFPD, and was the police chief's wingman when they ran me out of the department. After ruining my 15-year career, the son-of-a-bitch started dating my wife. When something goes sour in my life, Prowse always seems to be right there. The Bangkok case had brought to the forefront the possibility of his actual involvement in the attempts to kill me. Though the optics may be skewed by my intense loathing of the man, he still remains a possibility.

Point #3: Willoughby-Klehs
The straw company that my missing person once worked for. When he agreed to testify against them, the so-called Elaina Teagan and her hit team tried to kill him. Most of the team are dead, but I ended up in possession of the evidence against them—a flash-drive, presumably with enough information to take down the entire multi-national syndicate.

Meanwhile, the man I was hired to find, and did find, decided not to testify, and is now living the high life on an island somewhere with his Thai girlfriend—both of them under assumed names. I probably would have felt more animus toward the guy had it not been for the money he wired to my bank account at the end of the case. It was enough to reimburse my time and expenses, give Shanay a nice bonus, and keep my private investigations business afloat for another seven or eight months.

My initial thought upon returning from Bangkok was to let sleeping dogs lie. Other than maybe sniffing around Mike Prowse's life a bit, I had no horse in these other races. The Willoughby-Klehs Corporation and the so-called Elaina Teagan meant nothing to me. And since nobody was paying me to investigate them, what the hell did I care?

The question turned out to be rhetorical, as I apparently did care. But just when I'd made the decision to follow the tentacles of my bullet-pointed list, the beast grew another limb. Aafreen Soltani was arrested for killing her lover and boss.

I now needed to start a new file, with new bullet points.

CHAPTER 3

"Hello?" The whispering voice crept into my dreams. "We've landed."

My eyes inched open, expecting to see the mahogany interior of my sailboat. Instead, a line of passengers inched past me toward the exit as a nervous flight attendant gently dabbed at my shoulder.

"Sorry," I said, eyeing the jumble of papers that had somehow ended up on my lap. Some rule follower had apparently taken it upon himself to stow my tray table before landing.

Stuffing the folders into my duffel bag, I shouldered the drool off my cheek and hustled to the tail end of the exit line.

It was dark outside, and I saw that the local time was 9:45 p.m. I'd flown into Ronald Reagan Airport, which is much closer to downtown than Dulles or Baltimore/Washington, and the prison where Soltani was being held wasn't too far. I rented a white Ford Fiesta; the cheapest they had. It wasn't like I'd be charging Aafreen for this, so because I had no paying client the rest of the trip would have to be on a tightwad budget.

My phone showed that Central Detention was only a 16-minute drive, and I jumped on 395 heading across the bridge into D.C. hoping that I'd be able to talk to her at this late hour on a Sunday night. But people were out in droves. Like ants, they appeared out of every hole—crisscrossing the roads as if they all had the right-of-way, and costing me an extra five minutes of driving time.

I finally made it to the place without mowing anyone down, and parked in a quasi-construction area near what looked like the main building. It was difficult to tell, because the structures were all lookalikes; six-stories, pink, honeycombed concrete, with windows of dark glass that looked more like gun ports.

Walking around to the front—which was in the back—I had to get buzzed in and then searched. A heavyset guard with a shaved head sat behind a desk that looked small by comparison.

"Hep ya?"

"Yes, a friend of mine has been taken into custody and--"

"Name?"

"Danny McKenna."

He checked his computer screen. "No prisoners by that name."

"No," I said. "That's my name. I thought you wanted... Forget it. Her name is Aafreen Soltani."

His head shook. "Only men are in the detention facility."

"Okay, then where are--"

A big arm shot out like a side of beef, pointing in the general direction of a janitor's closet.

My head tilted as I stared deadpan back at him. "How about cutting me some slack, big fella. It's my first time here, and I'm pretty sure the women aren't in the closet."

"They're in the correctional treatment complex next door."

I turned to leave.

"But you ain't going to see her tonight," he said. "Only attorneys and investigators are allowed after hours."

"Great." I turned to leave again, barely making it through the door before a string of curse words rattled out of me into the night air.

I walked south along 19th Street SE. On my left was the prison, and on my right were the backs of row houses. The farther I went, the more dilapidated they looked. Lighting was hit or miss toward the end of the block, and suddenly I found myself facing a graveyard. Dark and ominous, the headstones looked ghostlike standing in front of their deep, elongated shadows—as if the prison itself wasn't already creepy enough.

A lighted sign summoned me to the end of an alley where a small building sat across from a series of electronic vehicle gates. By the time I entered the office, I had an idea that might get me inside the prison walls. I wasn't going to let this conversation go like the one next door.

Stepping up to a glass-enclosed counter, I slid two cards into the pass-through: my State of California private investigators license and my SFPD retiree ID.

"Daniel McKenna to see Aafreen Soltani," I said. "Investigator for Ms. Soltani's attorney of record."

"Armed?"

"I'm sorry, what?"

The woman held up my police ID. "Says you're authorized to carry a concealed weapon. Are you armed?"

"Oh, no, not at all." It was a stupid answer. *Not at all*, like maybe she wondered if I was a little bit armed.

"Step through the metal detector." She motioned toward it, and I knew I was golden. Stupid answer notwithstanding, I was inside the prison.

Another guard escorted me to an empty room where two seats were separated by a low wall and a thick glass partition. Intercom phones hung on both sides.

"Wait here," said the guard.

My first thought was that I should have brought an industrial sized bottle of antibacterial spray. As I waited, I wondered how many asses had sat on the seat, how many hands had rested on the counter, how many lips had tried to kiss through the glass, and how much spit and bad breath had been blown into the phone I would soon be using.

The door on the other side of the barrier opened and in walked the woman I'd thought of every day since I last saw her. She hesitated in the doorway as if I was the last person she expected to see, and then she smiled and sat down. The guard went back out and closed the door.

Soltani stared at me through the glass for a long time, making me wonder if she was as afraid of the phone as I was. But it wasn't that. There was a softness in her eyes, a vulnerable aspect to her expression that I'd never seen. Then she began to cry.

Even with the puffy redness of her tears, even with dark circles from worry and lack of sleep, even in the oversized orange jumpsuit, she looked amazing. Beyond amazing. The more she sobbed, the more I wanted to hold her. I almost saw myself kissing the glass.

Pointing to the phone, I eased mine out of the cradle and held it an inch or two from my ear. She wiped her eyes with the sleeve of her coveralls then did the same.

"I wasn't sure you would come," she said in a voice that sounded weak and defeated.

I didn't know what to say. All of the things I wanted to ask her, I couldn't: Did you do it? Did you get back together with him after you left Bangkok? Do you think of me very often? Why did you call me?

"Aafreen," I said, tentatively placing my hand on the thick pane between us. "You are going to be okay. You'll get through this. I'll help you get through this."

She started sobbing again, and I knew this was going to be a long and difficult conversation. I was, however, happy with the words of encouragement I'd found—although they did make her cry again. Finally, she stopped.

"I'm afraid for my life," she said.

"Don't get ahead of yourself. They have to give you a trial first, and then there are appeals..."

"No, I mean in here. Inside the jail. I think someone is going to kill me."

"Did they place you in protective custody? They usually do that when people in law enforcement are arrested."

She nodded, then shook her head. "Yes, but that's not going to protect me."

10

I didn't say anything, hoping my silence would keep her talking.

"I can feel it," she said. "The other prisoners. The guards. The way they watch me. I'm a federal agent, which is an automatic green light for the other inmates. And I'm accused of murdering a high-ranking member of the Marshals Service. Leo Kingsbury was beloved by a lot of people. People with connections. Vindictive people who know how to get things done, even on the inside."

I sat there chewing on the big piece I'd bitten off, unable to swallow or talk. This was out of my league. I didn't know the D.C. landscape—the culture, the people, the politics, the federal system. That didn't even take into account the crime itself.

"Do you have an attorney yet?"

She sighed. "They assigned one at my arraignment this morning, but I think that was just because they had to."

"Wait a minute, today's Sunday."

Aafreen shrugged. "They did it right here at the jail. Judge, bailiff, court reporter, the works."

That told me something, but I wasn't sure exactly what. Unless a suspect is incapacitated or confined to a hospital bed, arraignments are always held inside the courtroom, in public and during the workweek. This sounded secretive to me, almost underhanded. It could have been a simple precaution because of her federal agent status, but I didn't think so. More likely was that the agent-on-agent attack had embarrassed the Marshals Service, and they wanted to keep it out of the press as much as possible. Which also might indicate their rush to find a quick suspect to pin it on.

I emerged from my thoughts to find Aafreen closely watching me. "I'm sorry," I said. "You were saying?"

"The judge read the charges to me, asked me if I'm going to plead guilty or not."

Hesitating, I thought she would elaborate or perhaps even confess the killing to me. But her eyes narrowed and her lips grew tight as she stared back.

"*Not guilty*, is what I told the judge. Because I'm not. So, just in case you're wondering, I didn't do this."

"No, no, of course. That goes without saying." I cleared my throat as if I had an important point to make, which I didn't.

Suddenly, the door behind me slid open.

"Time's up, Sport," said one of two female guards now standing there with crossed arms.

The larger of them said, "You told me you were her attorney's investigator."

I glanced at Soltani, then back at the guards.

She continued, "The prisoner has a court appointed attorney, meaning a real investigator from the U.S. Attorney's Office. Not some washout from California who's managed to get a PI license."

"Hey now, there's no need to get personal," I said, raising my palms in a calming motion,

I hadn't gotten much more than that out before they each took an arm and launched me into the hallway. I thought I was in for yet another night in jail, but thankfully that wasn't their intent. Instead, I was 86'd out of the building.

Glancing at my watch, I realized that I'd been in D.C. less than two hours and this was all I had to show for it. I stood in the eerie parking lot wondering if getting involved in this mess was a colossal mistake. With everything else on my plate, I now had Aafreen's conspiracy theory to consider. Not to mention, her life hanging in the balance.

CHAPTER 4

Sticking to my tightwad plan, I took a cheap room at a place about five minutes from the jail. Lincoln Park B&B was not only a good deal, but also included breakfast each morning and an afternoon *apéritif.* The three-story brick building sat at the corner of Tennessee and East Capital, just across from a nice park—not that I'd have much time to enjoy any of it.

By the time I got settled in, I realized that I hadn't eaten anything. All of the hors d'oeuvres were gone when I got downstairs, along with the apéritifs. I hadn't the energy to go back out in search of a restaurant, so I went to bed with an angry stomach, vowing to take my revenge on the free breakfast the next morning.

Around 4 a.m., I was shaken from my flimsy slumber by a sudden thought. The female guard who had thrown me out of the women's section had planted the seed. If Aafreen had been assigned an attorney, then it stood to reason that an investigator had also been assigned. So even though I was as useless as a blind guide dog here in D.C., I might be able to contact the person and find out what's really going on with Aafreen's case.

The idea was a longshot, but I knew that DA's offices back home hire their investigators from the legions of retired police. My hope was that the East Coast cops would see me as a fellow brother-in-blue and might help me out.

Passing through the dining room, I saw our hostess, if that's what they're called, in the kitchen preparing food. I poked my head in and she sort of waved me off.

"Breakfast is served from seven to nine," she said. "There'll be a choice of strawberry crêpes, shrimp and avocado scramble, or steel cut oatmeal with brown sugar and raisins."

My mouth began watering, and I was afraid I'd salivate all over her lace tablecloth. "I've got an early meeting," I pleaded. "Perhaps you could spot me a little something for the road?"

Another stickler for the rules. The best she would do was coffee in a flowered porcelain cup, which she made me promise to return. There was nowhere to rest the cup in the tiny rental car, and I ended up pouring out most of the coffee and leaving the cup on the front porch.

The district court was only ten minutes in the other direction, then add to that twenty minutes to find parking. The line at the information window would have added another thirty or forty minutes, so I returned to the cops working security at the door. Picked one who seemed to be more interested in his phone than the conveyer belt full of purses, then flashed my SFPD identification. While holding my thumb over the *retired* stamp, I asked if he could direct me to the Public Defender's offices.

He nodded toward the elevator bank. "Second floor, room two-ten."

"Yes?" said the woman behind another plexiglass partition. She eyed me up and down.

Again I produced my identification card, but she didn't fall for the thumb trick. Having me slide it through, she examined it like a forged check.

"I'd like to talk with the investigator assigned to Aafreen Soltani's case," I said. "The arraignment was yesterday."

Not that she needed the arraignment details, but I thought it would give me credibility as someone who's already looped in.

"Case number?"

I started fumbling around in my files, as if I had it but couldn't seem to locate it. "It's in here somewhere."

She sighed and began clicking away to find the number on her computer, thus proving one of my strongly held axioms about people: Most of them are more than willing to let you do their work for them.

"Inspector Leclaire," she finally said. "I'll see if he's in."

After a brief phone call, she went back to whatever she was doing when I came in. I took that to mean she had gotten ahold of Leclaire, and he was on his way out to meet me.

Just as I took a seat, out he came. Curly black hair that thinned on top like mine. His thick eyebrows, wide eyes and rosy cheeks gave him an eager look—friendly, but maybe a little cagey. Carried himself like an ex-cop, and within the first handshake I had him figured out.

"Nate Leclaire," he said. "What can I help you with?"

Ex-cop for sure. Didn't invite me in. Didn't overextend. Just a simple *what can I help you with*, as if I was looking for the men's room. I'd have to play it like he wanted. He was in charge, and I was the out-of-towner who needed something from him.

"Thanks for seeing me." I gave his hand an extra pump. "I know you're busy, so I won't take up too much of your time. I've got some information about a case you're assigned to, and I'm wondering if there's a place we can talk."

"What's the perp's name?"

"Aafreen Soltani."

The eyebrows raised and the cheeks deflated as he evaluated me for a few seconds.

"And who are you?"

I took a breath. Told him my name, showed him my ID cards, and gave him my pedigree—heavy on the *homicide inspector* part. Told him that I was a friend, and that the family had asked me to look into her case for them.

"The parents are confused," I told him. "Don't really understand what's going on. They're from another country. Iran. But they like to be referred to as Persian."

His face wrinkled, and I realized I was trying too hard to sell it. But Leclaire checked his watch—a good sign—and then held the door for me.

"I've got five minutes before I have to be in court."

CHAPTER 5

Leclaire led me through a maze of cubicles into a small conference room. The other investigators eyed me as I passed.

"Coffee?"

Another good sign. "Sure, thanks."

I ogled a pink box next to the coffee pot, knowing what sugary loveliness it held. But as hungry as I was, I didn't want to overplay the chumminess.

"I'll get right to it," I said, setting the styrofoam cup on the table next to my folders. "As you are probably aware, this case is complex. Political. I guess she worked for the guy? The victim?" I scratched my head as if I was just repeating what I'd heard from her parents.

He nodded. "Leo Kingsbury was Assistant Chief Deputy at the Marshals Service."

"Oh, okay." I scribbled a note. "And she worked under him?"

"Bad choice of words." Leclaire made a circle with his thumb and forefinger, then pumped the other forefinger through the hole.

"Uh-huh." I felt my chest tighten. "Still? I mean, was this going on right up to the time he was killed?"

Leclaire shrugged.

"Do you think this is good info about their relationship?" I nodded in deference. "Of course, you're probably an ex-cop and hear a lot of rumors—even from some of the federal agencies, right?"

"First off, it's not a rumor. She gave a statement admitting to it. And number two, I didn't work as a local cop. I'm retired from the Marshals Service. Actually worked for Kingsbury back in the day."

It was the second hit in as many minutes. I wanted to say that it sounded like a huge conflict of interest. He shouldn't be anywhere near this case, especially working on behalf of her defense. But I didn't want to tip my hand and alienate the guy.

"What kind of person was he?"

"Kingsbury?" Leclaire's eyes wandered upward. "Smart, knew all the moves. Was a real comer...in more ways than one."

I scratched my head again. "Not sure what you mean."

"A comer, you know, an up and comer. He had his eyes on the fourteenth floor from the time he started. Moved up pretty fast, too."

"And your *more ways than one* meaning?"

He gave a wry grin. "Kingsbury was a lady's man. Good looking guy, and he definitely used it to his advantage. Inside and outside the Service, he always had something going on the side."

I had to take a breath. "And Aafreen Soltani?"

A shrug. "Just another cupcake from the dessert tray."

"Was he married?"

"Separated. In the process of a divorce. He'd been out of the house for over a year."

"The news said he was killed at home."

"Not the family home. He's got a townhouse over in Oak Hill".

I made some notes. "I'm thinking that with a soon-to-be ex-wife, and so many girlfriends, maybe some married... Seems like a whole load of potential suspects out there. Isn't it possible, I mean, besides the fact that Soltani had a personal relationship with him--"

"Look, I know what you're getting at...McKenna, is it?"

I nodded.

He motioned to three cardboard boxes stuffed with legal files. "These are my cases, just for this month alone. I have to focus on the ones that have a fighting chance. So, believe me when I tell you that Aafreen Soltani isn't one of those files. The prosecution has an air-tight case, and because of who she killed, they'll be balls to the wall. Between you and me, the family would be better off saving their money for a new car or a Caribbean cruise. Their daughter is dead in the fucking water."

With that, he slapped an evidence summary down in front of me. The top third had the basic information: Case number, victim's name, location of occurrence, estimated time of death, and so on.

The rest of the sheet listed the physical evidence that supposedly tied Aafreen to the crime. As I started reading, I began feeling pressure on my chest. The airless room became hot and I could barely breathe.

Besides her fingerprints all over the house, they were also on the murder weapon itself—a steak knife. Soltani's car had been captured on the next-door neighbor's security camera, with Soltani driving. The timestamp in the top corner showed 2210 hours on Friday, June third. I glanced back to the top of the sheet and saw that the estimated time of death was between 2200-2300 hours.

I fell against my seatback and let out a sigh. It seemed more real, now that I'd seen it all in writing. Clipped to the summary was the medical examiner's report. The standard body outline was covered with hand drawn slash marks indicating his injuries. Lines connected each of these stab wounds—twenty-three in total—to notes scribbled in the margins beside the drawing.

"What the hell...?" I handed the papers back to Leclaire.

"I know. According to the first cops on the scene, there had been one hell of a fight. The whole place was busted up, blood everywhere. She even stabbed him in the balls."

From my time in San Francisco, I knew that the more physical and the more personal the attack, the more likely it was to be a case of jealous rage. It still left the door open for another girlfriend, or even one of their husbands. Her fingerprints in the house meant nothing. She'd admitted the relationship. And the car thing wasn't a huge deal; they could have been off on the time of death.

It wasn't necessarily the airtight case Leclaire had implied. Which gave me hope. I gathered my folders, feeling like maybe we still had a fighting chance.

"There's one more thing that isn't in there," said Leclaire. "It just came back from the lab this morning."

I swallowed hard as I eased back onto the chair.

"Blood at the scene and his nail clippings came back positive."

"*Positive*. What do you mean positive?"

He read from a sheet I hadn't been shown. "Tissue scrapings from under his nails came back a positive match with her blood. Same thing with a couple of bloody smudges at the crime scene. And there was her hair."

"She already admitted to having been there."

"The hair was clenched in Kingsbury's hand. It was also a match. Like I said, he must have put up a hell of a fight."

My face probably showed anguish. The information had left me listless, with barely enough energy to lift myself off the chair. The evidence against Aafreen was completely devastating.

Leclaire came around the table to clap his hand on my shoulder. "Look McKenna, if there's anything I can do..."

It was probably just an empty offer, but as I reached the door I turned around.

"Actually, yes, there is."

CHAPTER 6

I headed to D.C. Central Detention, knowing I was *persona non grata* at the women's prison after last night. But thanks to Nate Leclaire, I was now on the official list of visitors approved by the defender's office. What I would say to Aafreen once I arrived there was another story.

A different crew was working, and they buzzed me through with no hesitation. They led me to the same visitation room and left me while they fetched her. It gave me a little time to think, but when the door opened on the other side of the partition I still hadn't figured out what to say.

"You look good," I said. "I mean, better than last night. By better I mean--"

She motioned toward the phone and I let out a sigh of relief.

I picked it up. "Hi."

"Hi. Thanks for coming."

I nodded. "How do you feel today?"

She forced a smile. "Better. It's shower day, so yeah, better."

"This morning I met with the investigator who's assigned to your case. He helps the public defender to represent you in court."

She didn't respond, and I realized she had been to court a hundred times. Knew the drill. Probably knew Leclaire, too.

"So, he ran down the prosecution's case...you know, like their evidence and whatnot. And I was hoping that you felt up to answering a few questions for me."

"Of course." She hesitated. "You know I already waved my rights and answered their questions when I was arrested."

"Only that you told them about your relationship with..."

"Yes, that, and where I was when it happened."

A knot moved into my throat. It was as if I'd swallowed a walnut. Of course, I knew where she was when it happened. They had pictures of her driving her car in the guy's neighborhood. What I really didn't want was for her to lie. I didn't care if she lied to everyone else, but I wanted to be the one person she felt safe enough to be one hundred percent honest with.

"Okay then." I pulled out my notes. The ME figures the time of death to be somewhere between ten and eleven o'clock on Friday night. Is that about what they told you?"

She shook her head. "They didn't tell me. They just asked if I could account for my whereabouts on Friday evening."

"And you told them...what?"

"The truth. I said that I had a migraine headache and stayed in all night."

I forced myself to breathe. Now, I was the one with a migraine. *What could I possibly say to that?*

"Uh, okay." I thought for a minute. "Do you have a roommate who can verify that?"

"No. I live alone."

"Your car. Did you lend it to someone that night?"

"My car? No."

"Did you sell it recently? Buy a new one?"

"No."

"Does anyone else have a set of keys to it? Maybe drove it without your knowledge?"

She frowned and shook her head.

"Can you think of any reason the police would have security video with your car driving around Kingsbury's neighborhood?"

"No. How could they? Is that what they told you?"

"Aafreen, the prosecutor seems to have a lot of evidence—physical and circumstantial. Yes, they have a video of a driver they say is you. Same make and model car, and the license plate on it matches yours."

"What else?"

"What?"

"What else do they have?"

I glanced down the list. "Fingerprints inside his house."

"Okay, well I have been there before."

"And fingerprints on the murder weapon."

She gasped. "What was the weapon?"

"I didn't see it, but they said it's a knife."

Aafreen was quiet. Maybe it was coming back to her.

"What kind of knife?"

I checked my notes. "Steak knife. Why?"

"The guy's a typical bachelor. He ate off paper plates so he didn't have to wash dishes. I don't think he ever even fixed a meal in his kitchen. Always went out to eat, got take-out, or had it delivered."

"What are you saying?"

"Just that I never saw any cutlery at his place."

"Aside from that, they also have DNA trace evidence—your blood, to be exact."

"What? Where?"

20

"Smeared somewhere in the house, is what Leclaire told me. Apparently, some was also recovered from...well...there had been a struggle and they found it under his fingernails. A lock of your hair was also gripped in his hand."

"My hair and blood? My DNA?" This appeared to have shocked Aafreen. Her face turned pale and she slumped back.

"I need to ask you something, and I hope you understand this isn't about me." I paused to get my words in order. "When was the last time you two were, uh, together?"

She rolled her eyes. "Saturday, April 11th was the last time I spent any time with him outside of work. Except for the return flight from Bangkok, which was massively awkward."

"Wait a minute. You didn't get back together with him?"

Aafreen pursed her lips. "I thought this had nothing to do with you."

"Well, maybe only this part. I just figured...I mean, since I never heard anything from you."

"Nope, didn't even think about going back with him. Plus, I was pretty busy trying to hold onto my job. You know, he wrote me up when we got back from Bangkok?" She was becoming more animated now. "Yeah, brought me up on departmental violations for going over there alone, off the books, yada, yada, yada. They docked 80 hours of my pay."

"Sorry to hear that." But I was still back on their supposed last time together. "How is it that you remember the exact date?"

"The bomb," she said. "I was in the middle of breaking things off with him when we got the call about the explosion at the safe house."

"That was two months ago."

"Yeah..."

"So, how does your DNA, your blood, your hair, end up on his body after all that time?"

"It's impossible." She shook her head. "There's no way."

CHAPTER 7

I left the jail on a mission. Like a ping pong ball, I was heading back to the federal courthouse again. Leclaire was still testifying on another case, and the secretary who had busted my chops earlier made me wait in the outer office.

When the courts broke for lunch, Leclaire walked in with a whole gaggle of investigators and attorneys. It was easy to tell which were which. The attorneys told jokes and waited for someone to open the doors. The investigators laughed at the jokes and held the doors.

Leclaire gave me a sideways glance before reluctantly motioning me through with the group. I made sure the secretary noticed, hoping she'd buzz me straight through next time. If there was a next time.

He made an exaggerated show of tossing his big box of files on the desk, punctuating it with a sigh. Then he checked his watch.

"I get it, you're busy. I'll make it quick, I need a little favor."

He tossed his head back. "What's that?"

"A favor is something you do for someone else."

"C'mon, McKenna. Enough with the jokes. What do you want?"

"I need Soltani medically examined, and I need her blood tested.

"That's two favors. Why the medical exam?"

"If her blood was found at the crime scene, then she should have injuries, right? I need them fully documented before they can heal, if in fact there are any. But it would have to be ordered by your office."

He shook his head in frustration, though he wrote it down. I took that as a *yes*. The exam would also document her condition upon entering the jail facility. If Aafreen's fear of an attack while in custody actually came to fruition, I wanted proof of their liability.

"And what is this about her blood?" he asked.

"Yeah, I also need it tested."

"It was tested. I told you there was a positive DNA match."

"I need a different test, something called a Raman spectroscopy."

"A what?"

"It's a non-destructive analysis, so it can be done using existing samples without losing any of it. They use some kind of light to date the blood. It's a new field that's supposed to be very accurate." I had read about it when I was studying for the inspector exam, which was a while ago—hence the foggy specifics. But somehow, it had stuck in my brain.

"Sounds expensive and a complete waste of time. Besides, why the hell would we do that? Soltani's blood was obviously left at the scene when she killed Kingsbury, and we already know his time of death."

"I'm only asking for those two things," I said. "And if any of it is that expensive, I'll pay for it myself."

An eyebrow popped up. "You sure you're not banging her too?"

"I give you my word, that's not happening." Which was essentially true. "I meant the family would bear the cost of the tests." Which was a lie. Right now, I was on my own. I had a hunch. Not an absolute, for certain, can feel it in my bones kind of hunch. But it was something I felt strongly enough to push for.

"I'll see what I can do."

"I won't bother you with anything else." That was also a lie.

In fact, I'd already thought of another thing I wanted. I gave him my cell number and asked that he call me if anything else came up. He closed his eyes, took a breath, then gave me his number—which is what I was really after.

Sitting in my car, I was too exhausted and hungry to drive. I eased back against the headrest and closed my eyes.

Hair. Could have come from the bathtub drain, or her hairbrush. It would be a farfetched defense, but all we needed was a reasonable doubt. The blood under the nails would be tougher. And her prints on the knife that killed him... *We're so screwed.*

I must have sat in the car for hours, going over and over the facts. They seemed to unpack in three different ways:

1. She killed Kingsbury.
2. It's a Marshals Service conspiracy to frame her.
3. She's actually innocent, and I have a shitload of work to do in order to prove it.

On the way back to my B&B, I stopped at a little Chinese carryout. I'd wanted to be good and have the broccoli and brown rice, but I figured that fate already owed me the calories from last night's missed dinner.

I walked into the drawing room, if that's what it's called, with my bag of fried egg rolls, packets of soy sauce, wooden chopsticks, and container of General Tso's Chicken.

Judging from the three couples making small talk around the table, it was apéritif time.

Avoiding their conversations, I maneuvered past them to the bar. There were a half-dozen tiny crystal glasses and a bottle of sherry. Shaking my head at the pathetic offering, I managed to slug down two quick ones before heading up to my room for the night.

CHAPTER 8

My little room was on the top floor. It must have been an attic at one time, because I kept hitting my head on the steeply angled ceiling. It was decorated in pinks and light blues, and had a view of the garden out back. It was the kind of place Doris would love, but I would never have taken her. I thought about that as I sat there eating my dinner, felt bad for having always structured our activities around the NFL and college football schedules, and decided to give her a call.

"Hello?"

"Hey Doris, it's me."

She paused as if we weren't cozy enough for her to automatically know who *me* was. I let her pretend, realizing that after 14 years of marriage she knew exactly who it was.

"Sorry to call so late," I continued.

"It's not late."

I'd gotten the time difference confused. Eastern time was ahead of the West Coast. "What are you doing?"

"I'm eating a salad and watching a special on Gloria Steinem."

I rolled my eyes.

"He's not here, if that's what you're wondering."

"No, I wasn't wondering that." We both knew I was lying.

"Bridget's having a friend over. They're in her room practicing for a school play. I won't even bother telling you when it is, just to save you from yourself."

"What's that supposed to mean?" We both knew what she meant.

"If you don't know the date of the play, you won't have to come up with an excuse to miss it. Or more likely, you won't have to disappoint Bridget after promising not to miss it."

It hurt. I sighed. It was a fair kick in the balls, if there is such a thing. "Look Doris, I didn't call to fight with you."

She was quiet, which was better than another comeback.

"You got my check," I said.

"Yes, thank you."

"And Bridge got the birthday gift I brought back from Thailand."

"Yes, it meant a lot to her."

"Good. So, how about we start from there?"

"Okay," she said. "Not to be smart, but why are you calling?"

I took a breath and let it out. "I was...I'm staying in a place that reminded me of you. That's all."

There was quiet on the other end.

"And, well, I wanted to apologize for watching so much football and not taking you out to places more often."

I could hear her swallow. "You are full of surprises tonight," she finally said. "Thank you for saying that, but you don't have to feel bad or guilty about anything."

She did not add that I was a piece of shit husband and father whom she expected nothing less from. And when she left it at that, I wasn't sure how to respond.

"Anyway," she said, "tell me about the place."

"Oh, it's a room in a little Bed & Breakfast with a nice view. You know, they have snacks and sherry and free breakfast."

"Are you there with somebody?"

"Uh, no. I'm on a case. This place just happened to be close to..." Then it occurred to me. How did I know she wouldn't go and tell the boyfriend? For all I knew, Mike Prowse was right there, spooning her so his ear was right up to the phone. *Why was I telling her anything?*

"Where is it?"

"Huh?"

"Where is it?" She repeated. "The B&B?"

I wasn't about to make the mistake of telling her where I was, or worse, let her think that I was sharing the details of a charming little spot that she and Prowse might enjoy.

"Milpitas," I said. "It's kind of close to the freeway, and you can smell the sewage evaporation ponds, but it wouldn't be a bad little getaway for you and Mike."

"Sounds thrilling."

"So, where is he, by the way?"

A long sigh. "Michael was called away for work, not that it's any of your concern. You and I are no longer together, remember?"

Tit-for-tat. She wanted me to answer her questions about my whereabouts, but wasn't giving up anything in return. Doris was like dealing with the FBI.

"Called to work, eh?" Our conversation was suddenly beginning to crumble, but I had to get in one last zinger. "I'm guessing that you'll be just as understanding about his job as you were with mine."

"Right. Nice talk, Danny."

"Tell Bridge that I love h--"

Click—the call ended.

I tried to sleep after that, but couldn't. Something told me that responsibility for the conversation's poor outcome was mine. About to call back again, I figured it would only make things worse.

Also having a poor outcome, was my attempt at falling asleep. I'd been exhausted, but after talking to Doris I was too keyed up.

The folders I'd brought to work on were piled on a chair next to the dresser. I knew there wasn't much I could do for Aafreen at such a late hour, but thought I might make some headway on the loose ends from Bangkok.

Shanay had gone through the dead guy's phone for me, and had printed out a table chart of the numbers that had been called and received—including his text messages. My *executive assistant* was turning out to be worth every penny I was paying her.

I had hoped something might jump off the page, but nothing on his call log meant anything to me. All but one number were outside of the United States—each beginning with an unfamiliar country code. They were 7, 852, 66, 91, 212, 49, and 46. The U.S. area code was 718. I googled them to find where they were located.

The first, country code 7, had incoming and outgoing calls, and a single text message. It turned out to be the international phone code into the Russian Federation. Shanay had not included the text conversation in her table, and I realized that the words were probably Russian and neither of us would understand the text message.

Each of the remaining country codes had only one incoming call. They were from Hong Kong, Thailand, India, Morocco, Germany, and Sweden.

The last was the only number in the United States. I put the entire phone number into the computer and hit enter.

I sat back, rubbing my eyes. There was no rhyme or reason to the locations. It was as if someone had thrown a handful of darts at a world map. Eastern Europe, Western Europe, Asia, North Africa. It was nuts to think I could decipher any practical investigative leads from them. Not only was all this way over my pay grade, but my experience conducting international investigations amounted to a single case when I was with San Francisco, involving a diplomat in the Latvian Consulate.

The number popped up on the screen, drawing me back to the present. A street view photo in the upper left of the screen showed Brutka Jewelers, a tiny shop packed between a 99-cent store and a delicatessen. The jewelry store was located on the 500 block of Brighton Beach Avenue in Brooklyn, New York—a crowded street in the shadows of overhead metro tracks.

It was late, and I was finally getting tired. Figuring I'd do one last search before bed, I focused on the number with the most activity. Putting in the Russian country code, I searched for the location of the area code that followed. It turned out to be in the Solntsevo District on the outskirts of Moscow.

Again, it meant nothing to me.

"I'm going to bed," I said aloud to my laptop as I closed the lid.

CHAPTER 9

"Danny McKenna, investigator for the defendant Aafreen Soltani."
Taking out my ID, I pressed the cards against the plexiglass partition.

They buzzed me through, and again I waited in the visitors' room.

The door opened behind me and I turned in surprise. A petite
woman in a dark pantsuit stood facing me. An ID card of some sort
was tethered to her lapel and a handheld radio was clipped to her belt.
I assumed she was a supervisor.

"Inmate Soltani is not available for visitation."

"But I've been approved to be on the list of--"

She held up her hand. "No, it's not that. She has been moved to...
Inmate Soltani has been transferred to medical custody."

I stood. "What does that mean?"

Having finally run out of meaningless buzz words, the woman
sighed. "She was rushed to the hospital early this morning."

"Why? What happened to her?"

"Apparently, the inmate tried to take her own life. She was found
unconscious in the shower with a makeshift noose around her neck."

I leaned back, steadied myself against the chair. Staring at the
supervisor, I couldn't put words to the questions flooding my head.
Suicide is often the act of a guilty person. But I still had trouble
imagining Aafreen killing anybody, much less herself.

"Where? What hospital was she taken to?"

"Uh, no, unfortunately that's not something we, I mean, for the
safety of the inmate, we can't release that infor--"

"Get real, sister!" I thrust my ID cards in front of her face. "I'm
working on behalf of her defense attorney. I have the legal right to
know, and you have a legal obligation to tell me. Now where the hell
is she?"

Within minutes, I was on the 395 heading across town to MedStar
Washington Hospital—a level 1 emergency trauma center.

Security was tight, and the guard working the metal detector
wasn't interested in who I was or why I was there. He just wanted to
make sure I wasn't carrying a gun. After setting off several alarms, he
asked for my keys, then my phone, then my pen. Finally, after
sweeping the wand over me for the fourth time, he waved me past the
squawking walkie-talkie on the table and into the main hospital
lobby. From there, I followed the signs to the trauma section.

Aafreen was in an emergency treatment bay when I found her. Pale and half out of it, her lips looked like the salt flats at low tide. A faded yellow gown loosely covered her, and tubes and wires ran in every direction. A monitor next to the bed beeped rhythmically, giving me confidence that her heart was still beating.

As I peered at her through the partly-drawn curtain, I became aware of another person crowding my space.

"Can I help you with something?" asked the officer.

He was a tall, lanky kid, dark skinned, with a gold stud in his left ear. His uniform patch said D.C. Metro, but I guessed he was fresh out of the academy to have drawn hospital guard duty.

"Danny McKenna," I said, forcing a handshake. "Ex-cop, thirteen years on the job, now working on behalf of her attorney." I thumbed behind me toward Soltani.

The cop nodded, but didn't seem completely sold.

"The attorney wanted me to check on her condition." Then I shrugged, playing to our shared status as lowly plebes. "Probably too busy playing golf or having lunch with the judge to do it himself."

He forced a snicker. "Got some ID for me?"

I flashed my police retiree card, but he saw that it wasn't from a local agency. He asked to see it again, studying it more thoroughly.

"Out here from California, huh? How'd that happen?"

I shrugged again, trying to feign modesty. "I've had a few major cases like this one. Got a call from the investigator, Nate Leclaire. You know him?"

The cop nodded, but I knew he didn't.

"Anyway, they needed some help and I agreed to fly out here and do what I could." I gave it a beat to sink in. "I'm on the attorney's list of approved visitors, if you need to check with them."

"No, I'm good. Long as I keep her in sight."

I gave him a swat on the shoulder. "Thanks, man."

Stepping through the curtain, I noticed that Aafreen was licking her lips even in her semi-conscious state. I pushed the nurse's buzzer for assistance, and one showed up right away.

"She said she's thirsty," I said.

The young woman frowned, but went ahead and got a cup of water with a straw and held it to Aafreen's mouth. She took a few mouthfuls, which seemed to bring her around a bit.

"She needs to take it easy," said the nurse. "Only a few questions."

Figuring me for a police detective, the nurse didn't sweat me for being in the room. When she left, I leaned over Soltani.

"Aafreen, it's McKenna." I kept my voice low so the cop couldn't hear me. "Aafreen?"

Her eyes struggled to open, and finally inched apart. "Danny?"

I wanted to rub her arm or squeeze her hand, but the cop was watching from the hallway.

"What happened?" She asked. "Where am I?"

"Uh, you're in the hospital." I tilted my head to get a better look at the ligature marks on her neck. A fair amount of redness was visible across the front where the skin had been rubbed raw, similar to a rug burn. "Do you remember what happened?"

"No." She reached to the side table and took another sip of water. "I think I was in the shower."

"And then what?"

She closed her eyes. "I was knocked down, or pulled down. I just remember crawling, trying to get up. I couldn't breathe."

"They think you tried to kill yourself."

Aafreen stared back at me, her eyes wide and glassy. "No, it's not true. I would never..." Her voice trailed off. "I knew something was going to happen."

I took a breath, stretched my neck, and let it out.

"You believe me, don't you Danny? Please say you believe me."

"Yes, of course I believe you."

A chill came over me as I said the words. Not that I didn't believe Aafreen, but I wasn't sure that I did, either. I wanted to, but there were so many things working against it. She was charged with the murder of her ex-lover, a man she worked for and who had also come after her professionally. In other words, she had plenty of motive.

And there seemed to be no shortage of evidence against her. The video recordings of Soltani in her car, the physical evidence at the scene, and the forensic DNA evidence. They were all the type of proof that led juries to guilty verdicts.

My friend was in a situation that made suicide seem a reasonable option, and I had nothing to go on but her word. For the first time in my life, I didn't trust myself enough to know the difference between my heart and my brain.

If it were anyone besides Aafreen, I would have staked my life on the fact that she had tried to kill herself because she stabbed Leo Kingsbury to death. Everyone else believed that to be the case, and I wasn't sure whether or not I did too.

I took out my cell phone.

"Lift your gown up over your legs," I said.

"What?"

"I want to take a look at your knees."

CHAPTER 10

The flash from the camera bounced around the room and into the hallway.

The cop who was guarding the room turned. "What's going on? You can't take pictures in here."

"Quick," I whispered to Aafreen, "Sit up so I can get some shots of your neck."

Another flash, and then another, and by the third flash the cop was on me.

"What'd I just say?" He puffed his chest into me. "No pictures."

I apologized, blaming it on the attorney who would have my ass if I didn't bring back proof that his client was still alive.

The kid eased off a bit, but was now on high alert.

As Aafreen settled back against her pillow, I tried to remember any other questions I'd forgotten to ask. Though there were more, I could only think of one.

"The news said you were arrested at the Marshals headquarters building."

"That's right."

"So, they asked you to come in and surrender yourself?"

She frowned. "No, I was there working. I'd spent so much time on disciplinary suspension that I'd fallen behind on my cases."

I'm not sure why I had assumed the self-surrender scenario. "Wait a minute. Who kills their boss and then goes into the office on their own time to get caught up?"

Aafreen shrugged.

I scrolled through the photos on my camera and felt the cop's eyes on me. The picture of her knees showed bloody scrapes, just starting to scab over. It proved nothing, since the injury could have happened anytime, but at least it supported Aafreen's memory of being on the tile floor.

The injuries on her neck were even more telling. I knew that hangings generally followed a distinct wound pattern created by the body's weight. As gravity pulls a victim down, the tightening noose inches upward creating vertical striations just above the ligature impression. There were no such marks on the back of Aafreen's neck where they would be most prominent, in fact there was no ligature impression at all.

Interestingly, a 4-inch horizontal burn mark on the front of her neck showed the reverse. Several small striations were visible *below* the original injury, indicating that whatever had been tied around her neck had been yanked downward in opposition to a normal hanging. To me, it was another factor that supported her being attacked from behind while in the shower.

None of this was vindication of the murder she was accused of, but it did shed some doubt on the suicide attempt. It was enough confirmation to convince me that Aafreen's life was in danger, and that someone had tried to kill her inside the prison. To return there would be her death sentence.

I leaned close to Aafreen. "Close your eyes and pretend to fall into unconsciousness. Give me about 15 minutes, and then be ready to get the hell out of here."

Her beautiful brown eyes gazed back at me with an equal mix of apprehension and faith. Then she settled back and closed her eyes.

"I guess she's had enough for one day," I said to the cop on my way out. He glanced in then took a seat just outside her examination room.

Making my way through the hospital lobby, I passed the security station and went out through the main doors. Once I was outside and away from the crowd, I called the inspector on her case.

"Inspector Leclaire," he answered.

"Nate, it's Danny McKenna. Don't know if you heard, but Soltani was taken to the hospital."

"No, I've been in court. What's the matter with her?"

"Suicide attempt is what they're saying."

He let out a chuff. "But you don't believe it."

"Look, I could really use a couple of things from you."

I heard a loud sigh. "Go on..."

"Could you text me a photo of the murder weapon?"

"It'll have to be a picture of a picture. It's all I have in the folder."

"That'll be fine. And if it's not too much trouble, I'd also like to see the security video of Soltani's car near the victim's house."

Another sigh. "Yeah, it is too much trouble. That's going to be a big data file. I'll have to get someone to do it for me, so don't hold your breath."

"Thanks Leclaire, I sincerely appreciate it."

"I just sent the blood evidence to your *hocus pocus* analysis lab this morning. Now you're asking me for all this other shit. If I send you those two things, will you finally back off? I've got a hundred more important cases to work on."

"I will, I promise. Thanks again."

A line had formed at the main entry. The walkie-talkie on the desk squawked and the pass-through metal detector was beeping like a smoke alarm—which gave me an idea.

This time I remembered to put all my metallic objects on the tray. The flustered guard waved me through and I stepped to the end of the conveyer belt to gather my things. As I did so, I quickly reached across to the table and swept the walkie-talkie into the pile with my belt, keys and phone, then moved on before anyone noticed.

My eyes scanned from door to door as I hurried down the hallway. Toward the far end, next to the men's bathroom, I spotted the signage I'd been looking for: NO ADMITTANCE – EMPLOYEE'S ONLY.

It was some sort of breakroom, with lockers lining one wall, and a table and empty chairs scattered here and there. Throwing open the lockers, I grabbed a couple of sets of scrubs and protective face masks.

As I turned to leave, I noticed a pack of cigarettes with a lighter stuffed in the cellophane sleeve, so I grabbed that too. I poked my head out, saw nobody, then made a quick right and ducked into the bathroom to don the scrubs.

Sliding the aluminum trash can into one of the stalls, I centered it just beneath a fire sprinkler head. Paper towels were already heaped inside the can, but some were wet. So I took another dozen or so from the dispenser and bunched them to the top. Then I angled a cigarette across the corner of the can's lip, so that it would drop into the papers as it burned down.

Locking the stall, I lit the cigarette then crawled under the door. And as I hustled to stand, I felt my knee pop.

CHAPTER 11

Smoke was beginning to waft from the stall as I struggled to get to my feet. Gripping the stolen walkie-talkie in one hand and the second set of scrubs in the other, I limped out of the restroom.

My cell phone buzzed in my pocket. It was a text from Leclaire—the photo of the knife. I stuffed it back into my pocket and threw the mask over my face. Just then the fire alarm sounded.

Besides the incessant ringing, several things happened at once. Strobe lights flashed from overhead and wall-mounted devices, and an intermittent audible buzzer began to sound. Heavy hallway doors suddenly released and swung closed.

My phone kept buzzing, and I assumed Leclaire was sending me the security video of Soltani's car. With no time to check it, I held the walkie-talkie to my facemask. "Code Red—second floor," and then repeated it several times. *Red* was the universal code for fire in California hospitals, and I hoped it was the same on the East Coast. Knowing that the cop guarding Aafreen would be scanning the same frequency, I hoped to draw him away from her and up to the second floor.

The place was in chaos despite the staff's valiant efforts to restore calm. Over the heads of people in the hallway, I caught a glimpse of the cop. He looked into Soltani's exam room, hesitated for a second and then slid the door closed—undoubtedly figuring she was asleep or unconscious. Knowing time was of the essence, I made my move as soon as he hit the stairwell to the second floor.

She was already out of the bed when I swept back the curtain and hobbled in. With a hand grasping her open gown, she used the other to free herself from the half-dozen probes that stuck to her. I couldn't resist lifting my eyebrows as a swath of her caramel colored skin flashed by. Aafreen rolled her eyes, trying to hide a grin.

"Put this on," I said, tossing her the other set of scrubs.

Giving her some privacy, I held the curtain closed and faced the glass partition while she changed.

"What happen to your leg?" I heard her ask from behind me.

"Old injury and bad timing."

"Maybe *you* should put this on." She tossed me her gown.

It wasn't the worst idea I'd heard. Once they realized she had escaped, hospital security would be looking for a lone female patient—not a doctor helping a male patient.

Quickly changing into the yellow gown, I grabbed a wheelchair from the hallway and sat in it with my head slumped forward. Aafreen pushed me toward the main entrance, which I was fairly confident would be clogged with fire fighters and other safety personnel by now.

The parade of fire engines and ladder trucks couldn't have helped mask our escape any better. Nobody even gave us a second glance as *Dr. Soltani* strode straight through the crowd, wheeling her decrepit patient with the bad knee.

"Now where?" she asked.

"My rental is in the parking garage, 2nd floor. They have cameras in there so keep your head down."

I directed her to my car, then we ditched the wheelchair before getting in.

"Fiesta," she said with a smirk. "Cozy."

"I can tell you're feeling better."

"Thank you for what you did back there." Several police cars sped into the roundabout in front of the hospital and a puzzled look crossed her face. "Come to think of it, what *did* you do back there?"

She already knew about the jailbreak, but I confessed to the arson and the walkie-talkie theft.

We were both quiet as I headed back to my room at Lincoln Park. By this time, they must have realized their prisoner was missing. Security cameras would lead them to me, and it wouldn't take long to follow my credit card charges back to the B&B. Leaving Aafreen in the car outside, I gathered my belongings and used the same credit card to pay for two additional nights. I figured that would keep them busy staking out the place for my return.

I stopped at an ATM on Pennsylvania Avenue SE, withdrawing as much cash as it would give me. We then crossed the Anacostia River and hit the 395 heading north.

"Where are we going now?" she asked.

I shrugged. "Not sure, but I know we have to get away from here."

Aafreen's eyes narrowed on the odd bulge beneath my sweatshirt. "Whatcha got there?"

I pulled out the bottle that I'd snatched, and handed it to her.

"You don't seem like a sherry man to me," she said, appraising it.

"I'm not, but they still owed me for breakfast and some apéritifs that I never got."

Soltani's heavy sigh fogged the side window as she stared out. "Do you realize how much trouble we are in?"

"It's only a bottle of sherry."

She shook her head. "You know what I mean. Law enforcement agencies up and down the East Coast will have our photos soon."

My mind did summersaults as we drove along, panicking every time a trooper passed us. Stopping for gas in Baltimore, I was happy that it was daylight, and even happier to get back on the freeway without being robbed or shot. It changed to the 95 somewhere around there, which took us to the outskirts of Philadelphia.

Aafreen had been sleeping on and off since we left D.C., and I worried that this was all too much for her.

"We should probably think about stopping before the afternoon traffic," I said. "You must be tired and hungry by now."

She smiled back, as if it was me who must be tired and hungry.

I pulled off the highway in a place called Mt. Laurel, which was actually part of New Jersey. An inexpensive motel near the off-ramp boasted color TV and coffee maker in every room. This next step, however, was going to be a little bit sticky. I was still wearing a smock over my clothes, which would be easy enough to discard, but Aafreen only had her scrubs.

"Should we look for a clothing store?" I asked.

She shook her head. "Too tired. Maybe we can look tomorrow."

I checked us in while she waited in the car. The desk clerk pointed out a McDonald's and an Applebee's—both of them just beyond the parking lot, and both of which he highly recommended.

I'd paid cash for a single room with two double beds. It was a last-minute decision based purely on money, and I hoped Aafreen would be okay with it. I helped her up the stairs, as much as I could with my bum knee still throbbing.

She didn't seem to balk about the room, so either she didn't mind or was just too tired to care. I took out my phone and sat at the end of one of the beds. Along with the knife photo, Leclaire had sent me the supposedly incontrovertible video evidence of Aafreen's car at the scene of the killing. I was about to view it when a dismal thought sank to the pit of my stomach.

"My phone!" I said.

"What about it?"

"Leclaire, the defense investigator, has the number." My heart pounded. "By now he'll know that I helped you escape. They can use it to track us all the way here. They may already be outside!"

CHAPTER 12

"We need to get out of here," I said, removing the data card from my phone.

Aafreen went to the window and peeked outside. "Are you sure? Maybe you're just being overly cautious. I don't see anything out of the ordinary. Why don't we leave for a bit, get something to eat, and see if anything happens?"

Just to be on the safe side, I took all of our things that I had just humped up the stairs, and put them back in the car. Then we drove the hundred yards across the lot to Applebee's.

Taking a table with a south-facing view, we gazed across the parking lot to our second-floor room while we waited for our ice water and menus.

Aafreen ordered grilled chicken and I asked for a burger. We each had a beer, which tasted amazingly good after the amazingly crappy day. By the time our server returned with the food, I began to wonder if I had overreacted. The parking lot was virtually empty, and there had been no unusual activity around the motel.

She ordered us two more beers.

An hour had passed—plenty of time for anyone so inclined, to track my phone's location. This could only mean one of two things; either Leclaire hadn't figured it out, or he had figured it out but for some reason hadn't blown the whistle. The guy was no dummy, and I was pretty sure he knew enough to follow the bouncing ball. This confused me.

"Leclaire should have alerted the locals by now," I said. "Even if he or the Marshals people wanted to take us into custody themselves, they would have at least had the local cops keep the motel under surveillance until they arrived."

Aafreen gazed out at the quiet parking lot as the last bit of daylight receded into an overcast sky. "But there's nobody."

"I know." I frowned into my glass of beer as I tried to figure out how a guy as sharp as Leclaire could slip up on the phone thing.

"What are you thinking?"

"I'm not certain, but it he may have given us a head start."

"You mean, intentionally?"

I shrugged. "Kind of seems like it. But I can't figure out why."

"Ask him."

"What, like, just call him up?"

"Sure. Why not?" She fingered a water ring left by her glass on the table. "If he's doing something to help us, what's the risk?"

"What if I'm wrong?"

She smiled. "Then I guess we'll know soon enough."

Slipping the SIM card back into my phone, I fired it up and hit Leclaire's contact number. It was late enough that he'd probably left the office, but early enough that he'd likely still be awake.

"Inspector Leclaire." He'd answered an all-business intensity.

Right away I recognized the frantic background clamor of a command post or multi-agency briefing.

"You know who this is?" I asked.

"Yes, I have caller ID. Just a moment..."

I heard Leclaire excuse himself from the group, then the sound of him walking as the background activity slowly melted to silence.

"I'm in the middle of a strategy meeting," he said. "Apparently, some ex-cop, private eye from California absconded with one of our homicide suspects."

"Hmm. Sounds like they would be fairly easy to find." I said. "You can probably just track his cellphone, right?"

"Right. But so far only *one* person has his cell number, and that person hasn't shared that information with his office...yet."

"Can I ask, why not?"

Leclaire cleared his throat. "Because some new information has come to light, and that person is trying to figure out its significance."

"Can I ask what that new information is?" I looked across the table at Aafreen who leaned forward with an eager expression.

"It has to do with the suspect's blood evidence collected at the scene of the stabbing. It was sent to a special lab in upstate New York, the only place around here that can conduct this *very expensive* bodily fluid dating called Raman spectroscopic analysis."

I smiled. "And?"

"Her blood was dated at over 1,000 hours."

"Huh?"

"It was 1,128 hours old, to be exact."

I tried to do the math in my head, but it made no sense. I was overwhelmed.

Leclaire helped me. "That's forty-seven days, McKenna."

The air left my lungs and my tongue turned to a lifeless slug in my mouth. I didn't know what to say. My face must have turned sallow.

"What?" asked Aafreen. "What is it?"

I held up a hand to pause her. "Wait a minute, Leclaire." I leaned into the phone. "Kingsbury's murder only happened Friday night. That's just four days ago. And you're telling me that the blood, Aafreen's blood, recovered at the scene, was forty-seven days old?"

"Apparently so."

"What about the blood under his fingernails?"

"Same," said Leclaire. "I had three different samples tested; from under his nails, from a spot on the floor, and from a smudge on the wall. The dates of all three were exactly the same." Then Leclaire lowered his voice. "That's only the good news, McKenna."

"Go on," I said.

The bad news is this process is so new that it's not automatically accepted in the courts yet. Case law on the subject is very limited, almost non-existent. But I'll be honest with you, it kind of makes me wonder about the integrity of the rest of this evidence. Enough so that I'm willing to give you a little more rope."

After the attack on Aafreen, I winced at his metaphor.

"Meaning?"

"Meaning, I'll continue to play dumb. Nobody has to know that I have a way to locate you, at least for now. But I'm only one person. The rest of the world will be hunting you two like Bonnie and Clyde. I assume she's still with you."

I told Leclaire that we were still together, and I thanked him for going out on a limb for us. He warned me to keep him updated, which was a reminder that his generous offer could be rescinded at any time. Especially if the evidence started tipping the scales in the opposite direction again.

After the call, I sat there staring at Aafreen. She had understood enough of the conversation to know that the news was mostly good. My brain was still trying to play catch-up though. I couldn't figure out exactly what had happened; how her weeks-old blood came to be smeared around the homicide scene, or how it ended up under Kingsbury's fingernails.

"I need to ask you something, Aafreen." I leaned over my beer. "And you have to be one-hundred percent honest with me."

She drew forward too, until our faces were only inches apart.

"Do you remember where you were or who you were with forty-seven days ago?"

"Of course." She gave me a silly grin. "Forty-seven days ago, I was in Bangkok...with you."

CHAPTER 13

We returned to our motel room, fairly certain that we were safe there. At least for a while. I knew that the blood analysis might throw a monkey wrench into the prosecution's court case, but alone it wasn't enough to clear Aafreen. The crime was particularly heinous, and the feds would be using every resource at their disposal to track us down.

"Do you have any extra clothes I could borrow?"

Her words snapped me back. "Uh, nothing that will fit very well."

She laughed. "Anything, really. It's just for tonight."

Rummaging through my duffel bag, I came up with a long sleeve t-shirt bearing my college logo. I handed it to her then dove back in for the sweatpants. But she had already turned away.

"This works," she said, closing the bathroom door behind her.

The shower was running and so was my mind. It was as if the beer, the long day, and the imagery of Aafreen in my shirt had all teamed up against me. Then I glanced at the mirror and my own image shook me out of whatever fantasy was in the works. The skin under my eyes sagged from lack of sleep, and I needed a shave. Probably a shower too. If there was ever a time to stay focused, this was it. Inspector Leclaire had given us the gift of time, but it wasn't indefinite. If I couldn't come up with a logical explanation for the blood analysis, or for the rest of the physical evidence for that matter, Aafreen was toast and so was I.

The door opened and I turned to see a mirage. Before a hazy backdrop of steam, Aafreen stood towel-drying her thick brown hair. She had rolled up the sleeves of my shirt, which had never looked so nice on me. It hung to mid-thigh, leaving the rest of her olive-skinned legs unfettered.

She saw me with the laptop and asked what I was looking at. Then she joined me at the foot of the bed to see for herself.

"It's the security video footage," I said. "Leclaire sent it to me in three parts because of the file size."

The first one began with the timestamp reading 2203 hours. It was dark out, and showed headlights approaching on what looked like a small private drive. As the vehicle got closer, an enhanced photo of the front license plate appeared and I paused it.

"Is that your car?"

She studied the grainy video without answering. The car was a newer Range Rover, gray or black, it was difficult to tell. The clip stopped after the car parked at the curb and its lights went dark.

"I have a Range Rover Sport like that one," she finally said. "Mine is slate gray."

I clicked the next clip without mentioning the license plate. She was upset, and I didn't want to come off sounding like an interrogator.

The second video started with the timestamp indicating 2209. The vehicle had apparently remained parked there for six minutes without anybody getting in or out, and in the interest of brevity, and probably file size, Leclaire had edited out the dead spaces.

As the Range Rover's lights came back on, it pulled away from the curb—turning directly toward the camera as if heading into the driveway. The video paused just as the timestamp turned to 2210, and simultaneously an enlarged inset image appeared—obviously enhanced by the FBI's photo lab. The sub-frame contained a frontal view of the driver—the same photo that Leclaire had shown me in his office. It was the spitting image of Aafreen.

I turned to her in silence. No way was I going to stick my foot in it by asking if it was her—even though it clearly was. Again, she intently examined the photo. To my eyes, it was an exact match. The hair, the face, the build, the car, all of it. And to a jury, the picture would be as good as DNA or a fingerprint.

Starting the third of the three video clips, I hoped it would contain some controverting facts. Anything that might cast doubt or question the credibility of the first two clips. No such luck.

It began with a timestamp of 2232, which meant that the subject and the vehicle had been out of camera range for twenty-two minutes. Ample time, as a prosecutor would certainly point out, for Aafreen to enter the victim's home and stab him to death.

The same vehicle came into view, this time heading away from the camera. There was no real shot of the driver, although her outline from the rear was similar enough. As the entire back end of the Range Rover filled the screen, the video paused again. An enlarged inset of the rear license plate appeared, and it was an exact match of the front plate—both of which were registered to her car, according to Leclaire.

My hands found my face and rubbed downward as if trying to pull the skin off. I felt dizzy, sick, and out of my head with fear that this time it was too much for me to fix. I didn't think I was up to the challenge of solving this thing. In fact, as much as I wanted to believe that it wasn't Aafreen, I couldn't will myself to distrust my own eyes. Evidence was evidence and facts were facts—the life blood of every cop. *How do you argue with your own lifetime of experiences?*

She closed the laptop and stood. I was still wallowing in my own internal debate, not sure what any of this meant. When Aafreen turned around, I saw anger in her expression. Her eyes blazed with intensity.

"That's not my car in those pictures! I don't care what the license plate says." She glared at the folded laptop, her finger pointing at it. "And that woman driving the car...that's not me!"

CHAPTER 14

I nodded as if I agreed, though it lacked the enthusiasm of conviction. Doris says I can be condescending at times, so I wasn't about to try calming Aafreen.

"How about we switch gears?" I said, pulling up the knife photo Leclaire had sent me. "Does this look familiar?"

It was a one-piece, serrated steak knife, about 10 inches in length, stainless steel, with a hefty barrel grip.

Aafreen sighed as she flicked the screen to enlarge the image, then shrugged. "No. Yes. Maybe. I don't know. It's a steak knife. Do you remember every steak knife you've ever touched?"

"No. I just thought..." I clicked off of the picture and shut it down. "It's been a long day and I need a shower."

She said nothing. As I took my things into the bathroom, I was aware of her tossing back the blankets and launching herself into her bed. She pulled the bedding tightly around her and turned toward the wall. I reminded myself not to take it personally. I'd been in dire situations before, accused of murder, jailed, the whole bit. So I knew she wasn't angry at me in particular, she was just mad at the world.

My duffel bag was bereft of sleepwear, and I emerged from the bathroom wearing only my sweatpants. Aafreen was still facing the wall under a clump of blankets, which was just as well. As much as I tried to suck in my gut, I couldn't hide the extra pounds I'd yet to lose.

I clicked off the light on the nightstand between our two beds, and slipped into mine. The room fell dark, except for a faint glow peeking through a crack in the curtain.

"You went to Cal?"

"Huh?" It had been almost a whisper. I wasn't even sure I'd heard the question.

"UC Berkeley. Did you go there?"

"Oh. Yes."

"Thanks for loaning me the shirt."

"Sure."

I couldn't tell if that was the start of a conversation or what. I'd played football for a half-year before blowing out my knee, and I would have liked to brag a little. But her breathing changed after that, and it sounded like she had fallen asleep. Maybe that was Aafreen's way of apologizing or making up. That was okay with me.

Just about to nod off myself, I was startled upright by my phone. The caller ID showed it was Shanay.

"Shanay?"

"Yup."

"It's late. Is everything okay?"

"It ain't late where I'm at. Anyways, how come the FBI been call'n the office? They act'n like you done somethin'. 'Course they won't tell me what you did any more than I'm gonna tell them where you're at."

"Good, just act like you don't know."

"That's easy, 'cause I don't—which is fine by me."

"It's probably better that way, believe me. Is there anything else?"

"Yeah..."

"Well, what is it?"

"Some dude called for you a couple of times, says it's important. Name is Shawn Foster, kinda has a sexy voice, like he probably looks fine."

Aafreen stirred and I lowered my voice. "I wonder why he didn't call my cell."

"Says it was out of service."

I'd forgotten that I'd removed the SIM card for a few hours. "Okay thanks, I'll give him a call back."

"So, does he?"

"Does he what?

"Does the brother look fine?"

"I don't know. We'll talk later."

"Why you whisper'n, McKenna? You got someone with you?"

"Yeah, but it's not what you think."

"Uh-huh. Well, good for you anyway. 'Bout time you get even with that wife o' yours."

I disconnected, and took my phone into the bathroom so that I wouldn't wake Aafreen.

Shawn Foster was a Marine Corps sergeant stationed at the U.S. Embassy in Bangkok. As might be expected, he was tactically skilled and fiercely loyal. He was also the best friend of the missing man I'd located there, and he had helped me immeasurably during that investigation. Still, I had no idea why he'd be calling me now.

I dialed his number, which was still programmed in my phone.

"This is Foster."

"Foster, it's Danny McKenna calling back."

"Evening sir, thanks for getting back to me. I'll get right to it; it's about the ambush that took place behind the embassy six weeks ago."

I had orchestrated it with the intent to turn corrupt cops and two teams of assassins against each other. It had worked perfectly, and we fled Thailand immediately afterward.

"Right. How could I forget?"

"I have kept up on the investigation," Foster said. "Even though we are not *officially* involved. I have sources. I hear things."

"And?"

"I wanted to let you know that there were a couple of survivors."

"Really."

"Colonel Boontam for one, though he'll be lucky if he ever walks again. I doubt that he remembers his own name, much less what happened that night."

"Can't say I feel too badly for him." The guy was a corrupt police colonel who had bought girls for forced domestic labor at his estate.

"And the other survivor is a woman. She was apparently with the group of four who went after Johnny."

"She went by the alias, Elaina Teagan," I said. "And I could never figure out her true identity. Was she injured?"

"Not bad enough," he said. "Good gunshot wound to her thigh, but she was not hospitalized here. Escaped from the ambulance on the way to the ER and went MIA after that. Nobody knew who to look for since we were never able to ID her."

"Figures." Of all of them, she was the most devious in my opinion. Not only had she pretended to be the missing man's sister, but she used me to find the guy so she and her crew could kill him.

"Then a CIA intelligence communique came across my desk late yesterday, that I thought you would be interested in."

"Go on..."

"The woman, whose identity we still don't know, was airlifted out of Thailand on a private jet belonging to a Latvian company, Gaisma Pharmaceuticals. She was brought to their consulate in Ho Chi Minh City where we assume she received medical treatment for her wound. We have no information about her after that."

"Latvia..." I couldn't even imagine the odds of investigating two cases involving that country. My first was part of what got me kicked out of the San Francisco PD. This was apparently the second.

I thanked Foster for passing along the information, and told him he could call anytime should he hear anything else.

Leaning against the vanity, I tapped the phone against my lips as I considered all of this. That case was ostensibly closed, since the missing man had been found. So there was really no reason that this new information should even matter. It was of no real interest to me. *But if it was of no interest, then why was I so interested?*

45

I tiptoed out of the bathroom to find Aafreen sitting up in her bed with her bent legs tucked under my t-shirt. She looked into me with those beautiful warm eyes, and it was clear that she'd heard enough to be curious. "Go on," she said. "Tell me…"

CHAPTER 15

We sat until well after midnight, discussing the new development in the old case. Aafreen had as much curiosity as I did, since she had been the missing man's witness protection handler, and as such, had been equally involved in the Bangkok case. But, like me, it was behind her now and she had more pressing problems to be concerned about.

It had to be two or three in the morning when we finally fell asleep again. Waking to the sound of cleaning carts rolling on the concrete landing outside our room, I dressed before Aafreen even stirred and then I left the room to get us some coffee.

When I got back, she had my laptop open and was watching the security tapes again.

"Look!" she said, pointing at the screen. It was the second video, frozen at the frontal close-up view of the driver. "What do you see hanging from the rearview mirror?"

I squinted at the frame. "I don't see anything."

"Exactly." Aafreen closed the laptop. "I live in an area of restricted residential parking. My Range Rover has a Fairfax County parking permit hanging from the mirror. I pay annually for it. But the car in this video doesn't have one."

My face twisted into a question mark. They were like handicap placards, weren't they? Easily removed and stowed in the glove box? To me it proved nothing, but in Aafreen's fragile state it was the smoking gun that would set her free.

"We have to call my attorney," she said. "Or your friend, Leclaire. They need to know that the Range Rover in the video isn't mine."

She wasn't thinking right, and this wasn't a call I wanted to make. Leclaire had gone out on a limb for us already, and each favor I asked of him was like spending money from an empty goodwill account. But this was Aafreen's life and freedom we were talking about, so I figured she was the play caller in this game.

"Leclaire." He answered as if already annoyed.

"It's me."

"I know."

"Aafreen reviewed the security video and her car actually has a residential parking permit in the window." I left out the part about it being removable.

He was silent.

"The Range Rover in the video didn't have one," I said.

More silence. "Is she right there?"

"Yes."

"Can she hear me?"

"No."

"Good." He took a breath. "Now McKenna, you know as well as I do that the parking tag doesn't mean shit. Which tells me that this call was her idea. She's making you call me, which tells me that you're listening to her against your better judgment. Which tells me that you're probably head over heels for the broad and that you're probably banging her, just like I thought you were."

Only part of his deductions were true. Most, I guess. All of them except one. But there was enough legitimacy in his unsubtle point to make me wish I hadn't called.

"I understand what you're saying, though your assumptions are not completely accurate. I just thought--"

"Forget it," he said, cutting me off. "But I was going to call you anyway. The feds got your credit card usage, figured out your rental car and are sending the *descript* out to police agencies along the Eastern Seaboard. The first place they'll be checking are little, out of the way motels close to the interstate."

"How long do we have?"

"Two hours at best."

I thanked him for extending more goodwill credit.

"Oh, and one more thing." He waited a beat. "She might actually be able to help with this one. When the FBI was combing through Kingsbury's computer, they found an encrypted file. They were able to get into it, and it consisted of only a single document. It doesn't make sense to any of the investigators. Doesn't appear to be related to Marshals Service work."

"What is it?" I asked. "What does it say?"

Paper clattered in the background. "The file was labeled OPG. Mean anything to you?"

"No." I told her what they'd found on her boss's hard drive, and she shook her head. "It means nothing to Aafreen either."

"What about the word *Laskin* or the name *Mohammed V*?"

They didn't ring any bells for either of us, but I wrote it all down just the same. I asked if there was anything else of interest in the file.

"Nothing that anyone can figure out. A photograph of a young man in an airport, and what looks like a bunch of dates and times."

"Why don't you just have the feds send the picture through their facial recognition system?"

Leclaire groaned. "I'll be honest with you, McKenna. They are all convinced of Soltani's guilt, and they're going all out to track you guys down. I highly doubt they'll be busting their asses to do her defense team any favors."

"Yeah, I get it." I cast a sorrowful look across the room at Aafreen. "If you want to send it to me, I'll see if she knows the guy in the picture—though I doubt she does."

"Don't be so sure."

Why is that?" I asked.

"Because this encrypted document was a sub-file in Soltani's disciplinary action folder."

"It's unlikely to have anything to do with her," I countered. "She and Kingsbury haven't had any contact in a couple of months."

Leclaire snickered. "With the possible exception of last Friday night."

"Whose side are you on, anyway?"

"Hers obviously, otherwise I wouldn't be risking my job by tipping you off that the feds are closing in. Which reminds me, the clock is ticking, McKenna."

We ended the call, and I relayed as much of the conversation as I could while we drank our coffee and got ready to leave. Since we hadn't had time to go shopping for clothes, Aafreen had to wear the hospital scrubs from the day before.

I found a Ross Dress for Less store a mile from the motel, and we bought Aafreen a few things to wear. From there, we drove to the Trenton Transit Center, dumped the car off in the parking lot, and paid cash for bus tickets to New York City.

CHAPTER 16

All the way up through New Jersey, I thought about what Leclaire had said. It wasn't that I gave a damn about anything they'd found on Kingsbury's computer, but I did care if Aafreen's contacts with him went beyond what she had told me.

It was a quiet ride. Our bus stuck mostly to the highway, but detoured into every town along the way. I worried that we might be recognized, and I worried even more that I was a fool for trusting Aafreen's stories; the one that she was innocent, and the one that she hadn't been with Kingsbury since her return from Bangkok.

"Is anything bothering you?" Aafreen asked as we pulled into the Hoboken Terminal. We kept our heads down while some passengers got off and others boarded.

"The FBI found a file on Kingsbury's hard drive," I said. "The folder is titled OPG. It was a sub-file in your disciplinary folder on his computer."

"I told you I don't know what it means," she said. "And if it was part of my misconduct accusation, I should have been furnished a copy of it—which I wasn't. The personnel rules are very clear about that."

I swiped a hand through the air. "The bigger issue is why he would have a special file, an encrypted file, relating to you. I mean, *if* you haven't had any contact with him."

Aafreen seemed disappointed. Probably in me.

For some reason, she looked innocent and more vulnerable since changing into her newly purchased clothes— aqua blue sweater and loose fitting jeans. I thought she would protest, get angry, become defensive in the face of my comment. But she seemed to turn inward, staring out at the Hudson River as we continued out of Hoboken.

"It must be about the case," she said, suddenly turning toward me. "The document in that file has to be about the case."

Her words caught me by surprise. I hadn't realized she was trying to figure it out. "What case?" I asked.

"Our investigation in Bangkok." As if she'd had a shot of espresso, Aafreen seemed suddenly energized. "I had laid out the facts of our case in my report and also, during my recorded deposition. I gave them a verbal rundown of what happened over there."

"I'm not really following."

She turned all the way toward me, grabbing my hands in hers. "Don't you see? Leo was probably trying to help me. He had taken my defense—the attempted assassination of our protectee, the attack on us, the shootout near the embassy—and he was trying to help me prove that my unsanctioned actions overseas were justified."

It seemed a stretch to me. More likely, Kingsbury had been part of it. He probably wanted me dead because I was developing my own relationship with *his* girl. Maybe he himself had been compromised, was corrupt, somehow being paid off by whatever criminal organization was behind it all.

"Yeah, sure." My words had come out doubtful, even sarcastic.

Her disappointment returned. "Why else would he have such a file?"

She wouldn't take what I had to say very well, so I decided not to answer.

We were in Weehawken, approaching the Jersey side of the Lincoln Tunnel. Gazing through the bus window, I saw the Manhattan skyline looming tall and gray under the cloudy afternoon sky.

"Humor me," said Aafreen. "Let's think about the names in his document. I mean, let's really think about them. They must mean something."

"Okay," I said in a conciliatory tone. "We'll start with the filename: OPG. Could be anything from someone's initials or a business of some type to the latest urban hip-hop singer. Same thing with Laskin. Might mean anything. And what about the name Mohammed V? There are probably Mohammed Vs in every terrorism database from here to Los Angeles."

Her frown told me that I'd come off the wrong way again. To be honest, the revelation of this *secret file* had left me unconvinced that her fling with Kingsbury had actually ended when she told me it had. *And if that was a lie, then what else was?*

"OPG," Aafreen repeated, ignoring my cynicism. She gazed out at the darkness of the tunnel. "Why do I feel like I've heard that somewhere before?"

"Uh, because I just said it?"

She flashed a face at me, which I couldn't see in the dark.

I let out a long sigh, resigned to play along. "Okay, I give up, where have you heard it?"

"I don't know, but I'm picturing a court reporter and a translator. Must have been a witness protection interview."

"Seems like you'd remember if it was one of your own cases."

"Definitely. Which makes me think this was someone else's. I'm trying to remember..." She snapped her fingers. "Russians."

"Russians?"

"Yeah, it was a Russian criminal enterprise case. I was new, sat through the witness interview. We had to have a translator because the guy's accent was so heavy. Anyway, I remember him referencing OPG. It had something to do with a Russian crime syndicate."

I sat there feeling a little foolish. Another coincidence that could not be a coincidence. Stretching my neck, I closed my eyes, thought back to the phone records.

We had emerged from the tunnel, and when I opened my eyes Aafreen was watching me through discerning eyes. We turned left onto 8th Avenue and I knew the Port Authority Terminal was only a few blocks farther.

"You know something else, don't you?" she said. "I can tell that the Russian thing struck a chord."

I glanced behind us, to the sides, and around at the people sitting near us. "Can't talk here."

"Oh no." She gripped the crook of my arm. "You're not getting off that easy. What is it?"

"One of the guys who tried to kill us in Bangkok," I whispered. "His phone records had calls to and from Russia."

"See?" Aafreen swatted me on the arm. "Leo was looking into it for me. That can't be a coincidence."

I was nowhere near as certain as Aafreen that her dead boyfriend had been trying to help us. I decided not to remind her that the man who phoned the two assassins in Bangkok was also called Leo.

In any case, it seemed increasingly likely that we had been dealing with Russian mobsters in Bangkok. But as far as Aafreen's murder case, I still didn't see any connection.

We passed a half-dozen parked police cars as we turned into the underground bus terminal. NYPD and Port Authority cops were everywhere, and so were security cameras.

"This place is going to be a big problem for us," I whispered to Aafreen. "Nowhere on earth is likely to have more CCTV cameras than here. And I'm sure they'll have facial recognition capabilities, so we need to keep our heads down."

My own words triggered something in my head. It was too vague to pin down at that very second, but I knew it was important.

We were the last to exit the bus.

"Where to now?" Aafreen asked.

I didn't have an answer. All I knew was that we had to get away from the bus terminal. We headed back down 8th Avenue, avoiding Times Square and all the cops and cameras that came with it. The cameras. My thought, or revelation, whatever...it had something to do with the cameras.

"Look," said Aafreen.

We had just turned onto W. 35th Street. She stood pointing across the street toward a wig store. I waited outside while she went in and paid cash for a wig to use as a disguise. Another couple of blocks later, we ducked into the Americana—a tight little inn that boasted "European style" lodging.

Definitely for those on a budget, we were able to grab their last Twin-Twin room—a tidy rectangle with a window and two twin beds. Each floor had a shared bathroom and a shared kitchenette.

Aafreen tried on her blondish wig, which was called the Mariah, and turned for me to see. As I sat on my bed evaluating her new look, the light hair contrasting with the dark eyebrows, it came to me. It was as if all my disjointed thoughts and musings had finally coalesced into a rational notion.

"You think it looks stupid?"

"No, not at all. In fact, you don't even look like you."

"Who does it make me look like?"

"Doesn't matter." I shook my head, trying to stay with my thought. "Where do you live?"

"In Fairfax."

"I mean, where exactly? What's the address?"

CHAPTER 17

I logged into the hotel's Wi-Fi to get my laptop up and running. Bringing up her address on my mapping app, I entered the words *photo department* into the *"search nearby"* box.

There were two stores within a mile of her condo; a CVS and a Walgreens, both on Nutley Street in Fairfax.

Aafreen watched me through eyes that were made even darker by her blond wig. "I'm not getting any of this."

I hadn't explained anything to her because I still wasn't 100% sure of where I was going with all of it, and I didn't want to go off half-cocked like the last time I called Leclaire. When I turned to interpret my mind's tangled reasoning to Aafreen, she was already heading out the door.

"I'm going down the hall to check out the amenities."

By amenities, I knew she meant the "shared bathroom"—which was likely to be a big problem for her, because it would have been a deal-breaker for Doris.

With an over-the-shoulder wave, I went back to my internet research. After another half-hour, Aafreen returned just as I realized I was onto something.

I dialed Leclaire's number.

"I know you're busy," I said, before he could get a word out. "And I wouldn't have bothered you again if it wasn't important."

"What's important to you, McKenna, may not even make it onto my radar."

I gave him a charity chuckle, hoping it would help pave the way. "I need you to check with the photo department at the Walgreens Store on Nutley Street in Fairfax," I said, probably a little too bluntly. "We're looking for a woman who came in on or around May 30th, the day of the murder."

"McKenna..." He exhaled a windstorm into his phone. "What are you trying to do to me? There must be at least a thousand--"

"Listen," I cut his complaint short. "She would have picked up and paid for two items: a custom face mask made from a photograph, and an enlarged image of a D.C. license plate."

Leclaire was quiet for a second, as he tried to digest my request. "Christ sakes McKenna, are you trying to make a defense that the car and the woman were imposters? Give me a freak'n break."

"How hard would it have been?" I asked. "They started offering these masks as a gimmick when the pandemic hit. You send in a photo of yourself or someone else, and they make it into a mask. Now you can have them made anywhere. The internet is filled with places that'll manufacture them. There are even instructional DIY sites on how to create your own mask with a photo editing program, paper, glue, and scissors."

"If you can buy them anywhere, then why am I wasting my time at Walgreens?"

"Because they offer a short turnaround. Imagine, she buys a dark wig to go with the mask and she's the spitting image of Aafreen."

"And the car's tag number?"

"All someone would have to do is upload a photo of Aafreen's license plate to the store's site, have it enlarged, then trim it to fit over the existing plate."

"Why that particular Walgreens? Why not Costco or some other online outfit?"

"Like I said, she would have needed it in a hurry. Same for the license plate photo. And this Walgreens does both masks and photo enlargements, and they'll do rush jobs. Like within a couple of hours. Also, it happens to be less than a mile from Soltani's condominium."

"Don't tell me you two are shacked up there."

"Don't be ridiculous. But there's another thing."

Silence.

"The car. A car to mimic Aafreen's would be too expensive to buy just for the night of the killing, so she would have rented it. And Range Rover rentals are not easy to come by."

"Go on..."

"There are three major airports in the D.C. area, but you can only get a Range Rover at Dulles and Reagan. And of those, only Sixt Car Rental Company at Dulles carries the Sport model."

"Uh-huh."

"I'm guessing it was rented on the day of the killing. Easy to track down."

"Yeah, easy. Right."

"Think about it. The woman rents a car exactly like Aafreen's, covers the license plate with a photo of hers, and then wears a wig and some type of face covering to look like Aafreen. She makes sure to get herself and the car into the camera's field of view during the timeframe of Kingsbury's murder."

Another sigh.

"How did this mystery woman come up with Soltani's blood? Even if it is dated, it was there at the scene along with her hair."

"I haven't quite figured out that part yet, but I'm working on it."

Leclaire did a final sigh, a sure signal of his surrender.

"McKenna, you're either the sappiest, most gullible man on the planet—which is what I've got my money on—or you're one hell of an investigator."

Now I sighed. "I guess we'll see soon enough."

CHAPTER 18

Leclaire's email landed in my inbox that afternoon. It contained the single document and single photograph found on Kingsbury's hard drive.

I turned the laptop toward Aafreen. "This guy anyone you know?"

She examined it and shook her head. "Is that the man on Leo's computer?"

I nodded. The guy's lean build and green military fatigues fit with his buzzed haircut. He carried a matching duffel that seemed almost as big as he was.

Aafreen shook her head again, then motioned to the file doc.

We studied the entries; OPG, which Aafreen was convinced meant Russian Syndicate involvement, and on the same line next to it, the word Laskin.

I googled the word with paltry results, including a guitar maker, a professor of chemistry, and a skincare product spelled *LaSkin*.

Next to the word Laskin was a question mark—which Leclaire had not mentioned. Realizing that he hadn't read me the document in its entirety, I suspected he had mentioned only the portions he thought were germane.

Lastly, I noticed the name Mohammed V—also on the same line— followed by the parenthetical letters (STL).

"Any clue what STL is?" I asked Aafreen.

"St. Louis?"

"Could be." I scratched the two-day-old whiskers on my chin. "But St. Louis doesn't really fit with anything we've found. Can you think of anything else?"

She gave it a long look. "Our fugitive detail uses acronyms like that in their case notes sometimes. You know, like, when they're tracking somebody."

"What do you mean? Can you give me an example?"

"I think there are four of them," she said. "STH means *subject's trail is hot*. STW is used when the *subject's trail is warm*—like a day or two old. STC would indicate *cold*—when the investigation is a week or so behind the subject."

"And STL?"

"STL means that the *subject's trail was lost.*"

More chin scratching. "So, this would mean that the investigator lost Mohammed V's trail?"

When she didn't answer, I realized she was as confused as I was. The name Mohammed seemed to suggest an Islamic inclination, yet nothing in my investigation even hinted at a Middle East or Muslim connection. If Kingsbury had been conducting his own off-the-books inquiry, it was unlikely to be connected with mine. It was also doubtful that someone named Mohammed had played any role in Aafreen's alleged violation of Marshals Service rules and regulations, which made his presence in her disciplinary file even more of an enigma.

Something drew me back to the image of the man in an airport, and I wasn't sure what it was. There was something both familiar and unfamiliar at the same time.

I donned my readers and carefully examined the photograph. It was a feeling more than an articulable fact; a sort of incongruity that gave him an imbalanced appearance. It was the man's features—his cheekbones, his skin tone, the line of his brow...

"This is a woman," I said, turning the screen toward Aafreen.

She squinted into the image. "How can you be sure?"

Taking out my phone, I said, "Because I've seen her before. We both have."

I flipped through the photos, stopping on the picture of Elaina Teagan—the young woman who had claimed to be the sister of my missing person. I had taken a picture of her holding a photo of her brother at the onset of my last case. After learning that she was actually one of the assassins, I had my friend Sarah Brooks run it through the Customs and Border Protection's facial recognition. Unfortunately, the angle and lighting were bad and they couldn't make a match.

"I think you're right," said Aafreen, comparing the two pictures.

Texting the new photo to Brooks, I wrote:

Brooks—I suspect this is the same (female) suspect you ran for me a couple of months back. Might be associated with "Mohammed V." (also unknown). Please run through CBP's facial recognition system and let me know. Thanks, McKenna

I checked my watch. "It's early enough on the west coast that Brooks might get back to us today. In the meantime, I need to let Leclaire know about this latest development."

He didn't pick up and I left a message for him to call me back as soon as possible.

I gazed at the street below. Towering midtown buildings blocked the light into our room, but I could see the rush hour traffic starting to congeal on the roadway, as taxis, busses, and all manner of pedestrians scurried beneath neon lights to get home.

I wanted a steak and scotch, but the risk of being recognized outweighed the desire.

Aafreen joined me at the window and together we watched the action on W. 38th Street while waiting for Leclaire to call back.

"I'll put on my little disguise and go across the street to get us some takeout."

Following her line of sight, I saw a Sushi & Bento Box Restaurant on the opposite corner. Though I'm not a fan of dead, uncooked fish and seaweed, it was the only eatery visible from our room.

I watched Aafreen cross the street below me, blending into the mass of humanity. Just then, my phone rang.

"Yes?" I answered.

"It's Leclaire." He sounded busy, as if he was still in his office. "We may have gotten lucky with the license plate swap. I talked to a clerk at Walgreens who remembers printing a photograph enlargement of a Virginia license plate, but described the customer as a man. She's going to research the receipts for a name, but doesn't hold out much hope."

"That's good!" I said. "We may actually have something then. The guy in the picture you sent...the one from Kingsbury's file...it's a girl. A woman. She's a suspect in a case I just finished working."

"And you know this, how?"

"I can tell by the photo. I'm like, 99% certain it's her."

"Okay, I give up. Who is she?"

"We don't know for sure." I stretched my neck. "This girl claimed to be the missing guy's sister and we were never able to ID--"

Leclaire's sigh drowned out the rest of my sentence. "So, what does all this have to do with the license plate photo, or with Soltani's defense, for that matter?"

"Well..." I gazed up at the cobwebbed ceiling. "I'm thinking that this woman posed as a man, and that's who printed the license plate pics at Walgreens. Maybe she's the same one who--"

"Where was this case you worked?" Leclaire asked, cutting me off.

"Bangkok."

"Bangkok, Thailand? You're shit'n me, right?" He suppressed a belittling chuckle. "And you think this chick came all the way over here to pay you back by killing the guy your friend was sleeping with?"

"Actually, yes, I do." Although Leclaire's way of saying it made the whole idea sound less probable.

"Seems like a pretty big leap for a jury to make." Leclaire paused as he thought. "Not saying you don't have something. This is all good evidence to discredit the prosecution's theory, but we're going to need more. A hell of a lot more."

I went to the window and watched Aafreen come out of the restaurant and cross the street carrying a couple of takeout bags under her arm. It had started raining, and she used a free hand to cover her blond wig.

"What about the rental car?" I asked.

"Sorry. No joy on that inquiry. Their two vehicles in that model have been sitting on their lot, and never moved during that time period."

"Are you sure?"

"McKenna...not my first rodeo. Got it?"

"Yeah. I didn't mean to..." I scratched my head. "Got it. But I think we need to follow up with the Walgreens clerk. If we can get a name, or any other identifying info..."

"Uh-huh. By we, you mean me?" Leclaire was silent, and I thought he was scratching some notes. Finally, he said, "I'm not sure what it all means, but in any case, the feds are coming hard. I think you've uncovered enough to cast doubt on Soltani's guilt."

"Meaning what?"

"Meaning it's time to turn yourselves in and trust the justice system to do its job. From this point on, you and Soltani can't do any more good unless you submit to custody."

My phone buzzed and I saw that Sarah Brooks was calling me back.

"I'm getting a call that I have to take," I said. "Okay if I call you right back?"

"Is it okay? No." Leclaire didn't seem to feel the same urgency as me. "It's not okay to call me back. I'm heading home, and I'm planning to have a drink and watch a movie on TV. I don't want to be interrupted for anymore of this shit tonight."

"Please stay on the Walgreens angle." I pleaded. "The license plate photo means something. Why else would they have printed it, if not to frame Aafreen?"

I clicked off and took Brooks' call.

"The fuck, McKenna?" Brooks' voice cawed in my ear. "We got a match on the photo you texted me. The woman is listed on an Interpol Red Notice. What the hell did you stumble into?"

CHAPTER 19

She came in as Brooks started to tell me what she had uncovered. I signaled Aafreen with a raised hand, and she went about setting out the little plastic trays of food.

"Russian organized crime operative," said Brooks. "She has used the name Viktor Orlov when traveling as a male, and is known by half a dozen female aliases. CIA believes she is actually Natalia Laskin, daughter of Nestor Laskin—former head of the Taganskaya Crime Syndicate."

"Whoa!" I hadn't exhaled a breath since she began talking. "Okay, the name Laskin figures into this already, only we didn't know that it was a name."

Aafreen's eyes became fixed on me when she heard *Laskin.*

"And you were right about the photos," said Brooks. "Laskin was the same one in both images. Confirmed by both CIA and NSA."

It felt like I was finally getting somewhere, only I could barely believe that it was actually happening. "Anything on Mohammed V?"

"Seriously? *Mohammed* is the most commonly used name in the entire world. No, I didn't find anything useful on him. But I'm warning you," Brooks added. "You need to tread lightly with these soviet assholes. The Russian Mafia has connections all over the globe."

We disconnected and I sat down on the corner of my bed. My mouth was open and I felt like the blood had drained from my head.

"Tell me," demanded Aafreen.

"You were right about OPG being Russian organized crime." Opening the laptop, I pulled up Natalia Laskin's picture again. "This is who murdered Kingsbury," I said. "And then she framed you for the crime. I have to get the first photo of her to Leclaire. He needs to submit it as evidence right away, before they..."

"Before they what?"

Aafreen probably knew the answer to her own question. She had worked for the Marshals Service, and she knew how hard they'd press to find their boss's killer.

"Leclaire wants us to come in," I said.

"Just give up?"

I nodded. "Reading between the lines, he thinks we have enough to clear you. Especially once he's got the photo and hears who we're dealing with."

She sat across from me and gazed at the floor. "I... I can't go back to jail. I can't just wait there for this to go to trial. There must be another way."

I took a deep breath and slowly let it out. "He feels like we're only hurting our chances by staying on the run. If he presents all of the evidence we've gathered, it might be enough for them to release us." Either way, I've got to let him know what we've learned."

I dialed Leclaire's number and it went to voicemail. As his greeting played, I wondered who else might have access to his phone messages. "Damnit Leclaire! We need to talk, in fact, we need to meet right away. I know you told me to stop calling, but I've got something for you, something big, and it needs to be in person."

"Not answering?" Aafreen's gaze was still downcast. "What now?"

I snapped my fingers. "The phone records!"

She looked up.

"The assassin who crashed his motorcycle. I have his phone's SIM card. There were calls and texts to and from someplace in Moscow. This is all starting to come together. More evidence to tie these people to the case in Bangkok, the attempted murder of your protectee, and of us too."

She nodded slowly, still deep in thought. "But why Leo? He had nothing to do with the Bangkok investigation. Someone went to a lot of trouble to kill him."

I shrugged, but there was a logic to her question. Had their sole objective been to frame Aafreen, or was that only a bonus?

"Let's assume that he, Leo Kingsbury, had been looking into your claims of a larger criminal element at work to take out your protectee. If he was getting close to identifying Laskin, maybe she knew it. Think about it; Kingsbury had a photo of her and her real name on the file in his computer—which probably means he was using intelligence channels to get it. Maybe even utilizing foreign intelligence services to poke around in Laskin's background."

"Pull up the document again," said Aafreen.

I moved over to her bed, holding the screen on my knees so we could both see it.

She said, "Maybe we should be trying harder to identify this Mohammed V."

I shook my head. "According to Brooks, there are just too many possibles. She kind of implied that the name search was a waste."

"Then, what now?"

I looked at the array of cartons on the tiny table. "I guess we eat our sushi before it gets cold."

"Ha-ha."

We didn't talk much, as I think we were both examining ourselves as much as we were thinking about the case. Aafreen clearly did not want to turn herself in. I felt similarly, but for different reasons. Not having the same fear of being killed in prison, I was more bothered by the investigative leads left unexplored. As much as I tried to will myself to give up, I wasn't ready to trust someone else to clear Aafreen of the charges against her.

"Thought you'd like the California Rolls," she said.

"They're good. I nodded as I took another bite. "The Land Rover still bothers me," I added.

"I almost forgot." She took two Kirin Lagers from one of the bags. "If they took pictures of my license plate and had them enlarged, then the only reason had to be to put the photos on a similar car, right?"

I nodded again as I dipped another roll into the salty soy mixture. "It's the only reason I can come up with."

"That's hot."

I glanced down to my plastic tray.

"The green stuff," she said. "It's wasabi. Too much at one time will burn your sinuses." She opened the beers. "But Leclaire struck out at the airport car rental, right?"

I grabbed my lager and took a long pull. The wasabi warning had come a second too late, and I sat waiting for my eyes to stop watering. "Yeah. Said Dulles was a no go. And nobody else around here carries your Sport model."

She took the last roll and held it out as an offering. I declined with a shake of my head.

"Something worth considering," I said.

She had taken it all in one bite and could only urge me on with a raise of her eyebrows.

"Sooner or later, they're going to track us down. And them finding us holed up in a seedy hotel isn't going to infer the same sense of innocence as us turning ourselves in."

Aafreen didn't respond, but I could tell she was thinking about it as she stuffed the empty cartons into the wastepaper basket.

The room had grown dark, save for the flashing lights from outside that bounced off our ceiling. She sat down next to me on her tiny bed and we both leaned back against the wall, enjoying the last of our beers.

CHAPTER 20

Aafreen fell sound asleep sitting next to me on the bed. I took the time to enjoy the aura of her closeness, the scent of her hair, the sound and rhythm of her breathing. I played with it, imagining the two of us together, falling asleep every night entwined in each other's arms and legs. Then I eased her over so that her head was on the pillow, and I covered her with a blanket.

Only two feet away, I lay on my back, arms folded across my chest like a corpse, staring up at the kaleidoscope of reflected lights, the din of the city insinuating itself among us with its honking horns and tires splashing across wet pavement. It reminded me of San Francisco, but on a grander scale.

The sound of a siren cut through my quiescence, bringing me back to the present and its attendant problems. Glancing at my phone, I realized that Leclaire still had not returned my call. Unsure of what that meant, I worried that I was the boy who had cried wolf too many times and was no longer being listened to.

Then I thought of his warning about the feds, and the intensity with which they were trying to find us. Suddenly the cell phone felt heavy in my hand, as if it were a beacon transmitting our location to the FBI. Surely by now they would have figured out its identifier and begun tracking it. The tiny green light of my laptop charger suddenly seemed to grow brighter—another signal and another way for them to locate us.

Unplugging my laptop, I shut it down and then did the same with my cell phone. I knew they were tenuous countermeasures, and that eventually they would find us. I tried to sleep, but tossed and turned on my tiny bed, encumbered by question marks in my mind.

For the next several hours, I went over everything, taking it apart and putting it all back together, piece by piece. Having made some headway on proving Aafreen's innocence, I realized that it was still very speculative. The license plate photo supported my scenario, and in my heart I now knew that Natalia Laskin was behind it. But we had no real evidence to convince a jury that the plate was only a photo, or that Laskin was the customer who procured it. Worse, was the fact that nobody in the D.C. area had rented a Range Rover Sport during the time of the murder.

I wondered if I had done myself a disservice by limiting the rentals to only airports near the Capital. Guessing that Laskin would have arrived and departed the same day, I may have wrongly assumed that she would have traveled to and from an airport nearest to the crimes. Why not Philadelphia, or even New York, for that matter? I had never checked that far when researching car rental companies.

Wanting to fire up the laptop and expand my car rental search, I was now too fearful of giving away our location to the feds. I was also anxious to turn on my phone and see if Leclaire had called, but was afraid for the same reasons.

It was almost 5 a.m., and I couldn't wait any longer. Aware of NYC's reputation of a Starbucks on just about every corner, I also knew they offered free Wi-Fi. I gathered my things, quietly slipped on my shoes and sweatshirt, and left the room without waking Aafreen. A Starbucks was just opening for the day, less than a half-block up 6th Avenue. After buying coffee and a warm cinnamon roll, I slid into a comfortable upholstered chair in the back, with a panoramic view of the street outside.

Once I figured out how to link up with Starbucks' system, agreeing to be deluged with their online ads and all that, I expanded my search to the three New York area airports; JFK, LaGuardia, and Newark Liberty in New Jersey. Unfortunately, all three had the same rental company that offered the Range Rover Sport. More work for Leclaire, once I got a hold of him.

I bought another cup of coffee and was suddenly stopped by a thought. The phone records that Shanay had printed out for me. I'd never really looked into them because the guy who owned the phone was dead, and I hadn't ever connected him with the Laskin woman. But his calls, at least a couple of them, had been to Moscow.

I took the printout from my folder and put on my readers. As I sipped my coffee, I was reminded that one of the calls had been received from a New York number. In fact, it was the only call within the United States—the rest being scattered around Europe and Asia.

Looking at it again, I saw in my notes that the phone number came back to a jewelry store in Brooklyn. On my mapping app, I saw that the closest airport to it was JFK. In fact, the Q line of the NYC's transit system ran along Brighton Beach Avenue, which was right in front of the store. Tracing the route along the map, I saw that a short subway ride could take anyone to or from the airport in no more than fifteen minutes.

The jewelry store seemed like an odd place to be calling a trained killer. A hotel, a friend, maybe a gunsmith, but why the jewelry store? There had to be a connection that I was missing.

I knew that the chances of Natalia Laskin being connected to the Brooklyn address were slim. But so were the odds of both she and the dead assassin being Russian—yet, it turns out they were.

Then, as I queried Google for information about the Brooklyn Jewelry Store, something nearly jumped off my screen and hit me over the head.

An article about Russian organized crime in New York identified Brooklyn as their hub. In particular was the neighborhood of Brighton Beach, which the article said has become a Russian enclave where over half of the residents were born in Eastern Europe. So many of them speak an Indo-European dialect that the entire area had been nicknamed "Little Odessa."

Excitedly, I scribbled down notes that I was certain would become the linchpin of Aafreen's defense.

"This is all good stuff," I said to myself as I transcribed highlights of the article onto my file notes.

I needed to get the information to Leclaire. It was imperative that he not only check the car rentals at JFK, but also contact NYPD's Russian gang experts and connect the dots from that angle.

Leclaire still didn't answer his phone. I checked the time and realized that he was probably on his way in to the office. I was giddy with energy, and I wanted to share what I'd learned—if not with him, then with Aafreen.

I bought another breakfast pastry and a large coffee to bring back for her.

As I started down the block, a flurry of activity clogged the street in front of our hotel. Lights flashed and pedestrians were forced to walk into the street to avoid the commotion. There were cops. And then I saw the black sedans, the men in suits, and the windbreakers with the initials stenciled in yellow.

Between two of them was Aafreen, her head bowed forward with her beautiful black hair now matted and tousled down over her face. She was still wearing the Cal t-shirt I'd lent her, though mercifully they had allowed her to put on a pair of my sweatpants. They hung sadly over Aafreen's bare feet as a woman agent eased her into their car.

My God, I thought. She must have woken up alone, afraid, with feds pounding on our door. She wouldn't have known where I had gone. My stomach had been struck with a battering ram. I dropped the bag that held Aafreen's breakfast. Heard the coffee splash onto the sidewalk beneath my feet.

Would Aafreen think I had fled? Saved my own skin at the expense of hers? Or worse, would Aafreen wonder if I had turned her in to the feds?

Dialing Leclaire's number again, I listened with a sickening feeling as it rang and rang and rang. Finally, it stopped and someone came on the line.

"Leclaire!" I spat into the phone, my voice cracking and my lungs out of breath.

The sound on the other end was muffled, and I wondered if he was in a meeting. Covering the phone with his hand until he could get to a quiet place and talk privately.

Uncovered now, the background noise was clearer. People talking in hushed tones.

"Leclaire? It's me..."

"I'm sorry," came a voice that didn't fit. A woman's voice, and she sounded like she was crying.

"Who's this?" I stuttered into the phone.

"This is Nathan's ex-wife, Bonny. I'm sorry, but Nate Leclaire is dead".

"What do you mean he's dead?" The woman's words had been clear enough, and I suppose I understood them on some level. But with all that Leclaire had done to help us...the background details, all of the evidence that was finally coming together...the evidence that only he knew about...and now with Aafreen's arrest. It was more than I could fathom.

"He was found this morning in his apartment," Bonny said. "Apparently, he took his own life sometime during the night."

I drifted off into some sort of catatonic haze. People on the street shouldered past me, oblivious to what was happening, concerned only with their lives.

"No, Nate didn't take his own life," I said to Leclaire's Ex. "He was murdered."

CHAPTER 21

Disconnecting from the call, I turned away, leaving the Starbucks bag and its contents to be trampled under the heels of a thousand rushing New Yorkers.

I walked like a zombie through the streets, too discouraged and too exhausted to figure out how the feds had found us. Aafreen was back in prison, her most feared scenario, the place where she had already been assaulted and nearly killed. And Leclaire was dead. The defense investigator had been our one ally and the only person privy to the exonerating evidence we'd uncovered.

Already wanted as an accomplice in Aafreen's jail break, I was now alone and being hunted in an unfamiliar city. My credit card charges were being watched, and I had no idea if I could trust the privacy and confidentiality of my cell phone or laptop. Giving myself up to the feds seemed like the most logical choice at that moment.

Turning back, I cut diagonally across 6th Avenue, midblock. Amid honking horns and cursing drivers, I continued unfazed toward our hotel. The car containing Aafreen had left, but the rest of the federal slick-tops were still parked outside with their red and blue grill lights flashing.

I walked up to one of the city cops, a redheaded kid who was as tall as me but weighed half as much. He leaned into the wedge of his open car door, waving one hand in a halfhearted attempt to clear the sidewalk of onlookers.

"Excuse me," I said, looking him in the eye. "I'd like to speak with the person in charge."

His head tilted as if the request itself was an affront. "Just keep moving along. You can complain later about the inconvenience."

"I have no complaint," I said. "My name is Danny McKenna and I'm here to--"

Another wave cut me off. "I'm sure you're an important man, but you need to move along so we can keep the sidewalk clear."

I realized that the BOLO for me hadn't yet trickled down to the street. At least not in New York, 200 miles from the scenes of the murders and the suspect's subsequent escape.

Frustrated, I schlepped along with the rest of the working stiffs. Except that I had nowhere to go.

At W. 35th Street I sat down on the raised stone border in a tiny park where a clock tower monument stood. The small alcove off of 6th Avenue held food carts and flower vendors, and it provided a place where I could try to gather my thoughts.

My phone buzzed and I almost ignored it. "Hello," I said listlessly.

"Dad!" Bridget said. "Are you all right?"

"Uh, hey Bridge. Yeah, I'm okay. Why?" I glanced up at the tower above me. It was 8:20 a.m., which equaled 5:20 a.m. in California. On a normal weekday she would still be asleep.

"The cops were here," she said shakily. "They came in the middle of the night. I think they had a warrant or something because they came inside even though Mom said they couldn't, and they looked all around for you."

I pressed my free palm into my forehead. "Shit."

"They said you helped a killer escape or something. Is that true?"

"No, Bridge. I didn't help a *killer* do anything." I took a long breath and let it out, wondering if Doris knew our daughter was calling me. "It's a long story, but not anything for you to worry about."

"If you're in trouble, of course I'm going to be worried."

There it was. Bridget was one person, maybe the only person who was worried about me. Of everything that had happened to defeat me, only her words gave me hope.

"What did your mom say?" I asked.

"I don't care what she says, and I don't care what Mike thinks about you either."

Mike. I had tried to put Michael Prowse out of my mind, but here he was, back again. "Are he and your mom still seeing each other?"

"Yeah." Bridget sighed. "Shanay says not to trust him."

"Shanay is right."

I was still suspicious of Prowse, and not convinced that he wasn't somehow involved in all of this. The fact that the asshole was still seeing my wife only added to my distrust.

There was a sudden clatter on her end, and I heard Doris's grating voice in the background asking Bridge who she was talking to. It sounded like the phone was being wrestled away from her, and my wife abruptly came on the line. "Who is this? Is that you Danny?"

"Yes Doris, it's me."

"Haven't you already done enough? Are you really going to drag everybody through this again? The FBI has searched our house because you've done God knows what. And now you're calling our daughter in the dead of night on a school day?"

I didn't want to get Bridge in anymore trouble, so I let Doris think that I was the one who had called her.

"Do you have any concept of the humiliation?" Doris continued. "The neighbors? My friends? All of them reading about you in the newspapers? And Mike says--"

"Stop!" I yelled, causing people around me to look up. "I don't give two shits about Mike Prowse. You haven't even asked if I was okay, or to hear my side of what happened. You get all of your information from that idiot Prowse, and you gobble it up with a goddamn spoon!"

She was quiet for a second or two. "The only reason I brought him up is because this situation impacts *others* as well."

"You want to tell me how my private life impacts Mike Prowse's?"

"I'm not supposed to say anything, but he's under consideration for the police chief job."

"In San Francisco?" I nearly fell over. "You gotta be kidding me! Instead of working his way up the ladder, Prowse kissed ass all the way to the top."

"Excuse me?" She took a breath like she was about to go on one of her point-counterpoint rants.

"So, what happened to Dowd?" I asked. "He hasn't even been in the chief's job a year."

"Greg Dowd is running for mayor," she said. "And if things go well for him, they might also go well for Mike. Anyway, what I was saying is that neither Mike nor Greg need to have one of their ex-cops on the front page right now."

"Wow. Never mind what I'm going through. So long as I don't tarnish the stellar reputations of the two shitheads who screwed me right off of the force."

I clicked off, as hard as one can push the disconnect button. When things seem like they can't get any worse, a conversation with Doris always reminds me that they can. I gripped my phone and reared back with it, ready to launch the thing all the way to the East River. Then I thought of Bridget.

The purpose of her call was to check on me. She wasn't going to let her mother, or Prowse, or the news media, change her mind about her dad. She trusted me, and I wasn't going to let her down. I'd figure this thing out if it killed me, and one way or the other I'd prove Aafreen's innocence and clear my own name.

Walking another block down 6th Avenue, I saw a subway sign at 34th Street. It was the Q line to Brooklyn and Brighton Beach. I needed money and I needed to make another call, but I wanted to accomplish both before the feds could hone in on my location.

I found an ATM and made a maximum withdrawal, and then I dialed Linh Phú's cell phone.

CHAPTER 22

Linh was a newly promoted inspector, partnered with me after Lou Cassidy's heart attack. The assistance she gave me during my final days at SFPD had cost Linh her spot in Homicide. Last I'd heard, she was running a Bay Area wide drug task force.

"Inspector McKenna, you're up early."

I smiled at the *inspector* reference. "Actually, Linh, I'm on the East Coast working on a case. I hope I'm not calling too early."

"Not at all. Is there something I can help you with?"

"I'm wondering if you have any contacts with the New York PD. This case has thrown me a curveball, and I'm beginning to smell the involvement of Russian gangs. The only stateside phone number that my suspect has called comes back to a jewelry store in Brooklyn. I'll text it to you along with the address I have."

"I can't think of any New York connections, but I can definitely reach out on an official level. They're usually pretty helpful."

"Yeah, unless you're trying to turn yourself in," I mumbled.

"What's that, sir?"

"Nothing, nothing." I thanked her again before disconnecting.

If the FBI or Marshals had been tracking my cell location or watching my bank transactions, I figured I'd have only a few minutes to clear out before they deployed into the tiny park to search for me. People would remember the weird guy arguing with his wife on the phone, but I wanted potential witnesses to remember me leaving.

"The hell with you!" I yelled into my phone as if still on the call. And then I stormed out into 6th avenue, crossing to the Victoria's Secret Store on the other side. In through the front door and out the side door I went, before skittering down into the subway without being noticed. By the time the feds talked to witnesses and searched the store for me, I'd be long gone.

With my phone shut down, I boarded the Q Train into Brooklyn. The landscape changed once the train emerged from the bowels of Manhattan onto an elevated track. I watched out the window as the scenery transitioned from a mostly white suburb to a multi-ethnic mix. After crossing the Shore Highway, it changed again, this time taking on an almost exclusively Eastern European quality. Russian shops with Cyrillic script signaled my arrival in *Little Odessa*.

I got off the train at the Brighton Beach Station, where I glanced over the platform railing at Brutka Jewelers just below me. Without even leaving the station, I could stand and monitor the place and still be completely unnoticed. The ease with which one could blend in was definitely a surveillance advantage in the city of over 8 million people.

It was 9:50 a.m. when I began watching, though I was still unsure of what I was watching for. It was a jewelry store for Chrissake. What did I really expect to find?

By noon, I was realizing the futility of my plan. The sun had come out, making my eyes water and the top of my head burn. I was also hungry and had to take a leak.

There was nowhere to pee, so I descended the stairway to the street and slipped into a construction site porta-potty. I picked up a ball cap and sunglasses at a discount market across the street, and then got a sandwich called the *Belly Buster* at the deli directly next door to Brutka Jewelers. Sitting on the steps to the metro, I ate half my sandwich while continuing to watch the shop.

It was a little after 2 p.m. when I spotted a Land Rover Sport. It was charcoal gray, just like Aafreen's. Its windows were so dark that I couldn't see the driver as it drove slowly by me on Brighton Beach Avenue. After circling the block, it came down the street again. The driver was either looking for a parking spot or watching for police.

I wanted to get a picture of it, but I knew that turning on my phone could have dire consequences of its own. It was a toss-up, especially since the car I was watching could be completely unconnected to the one used to frame Aafreen.

The Land Rover came to a stop on the street, directly in front of the jewelry store. With the emergency lights flashing, the driver's door opened and I quickly turned on my cell phone.

A young woman stepped out, paused, and looked around. It was Natalia Laskin.

Wearing a cap and sunglasses, much like mine, it was clear that she did not want to stand out or be recognized. To me, her counter surveillance measures were also further evidence of her guilt.

Raising my phone, I used the zoom feature to magnify the scene. I wanted to get both her and the car together in the same shot. I had to lift up my sunglasses to see the screen, but I didn't want Laskin to notice what I was doing. She would recognize me in a heartbeat.

The sudden buzz of an incoming call startled me, causing my saved half a sandwich to roll off my lap and slide down the stairs. I snapped a quick shot in Laskin's direction, not even knowing how well the camera was aimed or focused.

"Yes! Hello?" I answered, not even taking time to look at the caller's ID.

"It's me, Shanay," she said. "Linh Phú been try'n to get in touch with you."

I held the phone away and squinted to see that I had three missed calls. "My phone was off so the feds couldn't track it."

"Yeah, I heard you had to hot step it out of D.C. in a hurry."

"How did you know about--"

"Li'l Bridget told me," she said. "Black suits been search'n your house. And they been sneak'n 'round here, too. Anyways, Linh was try'n to get word to you that...hold on, gotta get my notes...okay, she says that Brutka Jewelers in Brooklyn is a front for the Russian Mob. Weapons, money laundering, women—stuff like that. The cops that Linh talked to in New York said they were 'up on the place,' whatever that means."

"It's a cop term," I said. "They're probably talking about a wiretap. Means NYPD investigators are probably listening to their phone calls. That's a good thing for us, but we can't wait for their investigation. We need them down here now, before this chick is gone forever... Hold on. Shit, she's leaving!"

Laskin had run into the jewelry store, and exited just as quickly. Tucking an envelope into her handbag, the woman jumped back in the Land Rover, turned off the flashers, and started the engine.

"Can you follow her?" asked Shanay.

Slipping in the slop of my sandwich, I mumbled and cursed as I made my way into the street. Unlike Manhattan, taxis were not as plentiful in the far reaches of Brooklyn.

"I'm trying to find..." I was talking more to myself, though Shanay was still on the line. "Here comes a..."

It was a Subaru with an Uber sticker in the window. I pulled my retiree badge from my pocket and stepped into the street to block it. "Police!" With a hand on the hood, I rounded the front of the car and got into the passenger seat. "I need you to follow that gray Range Rover."

My driver was an older man, black with short cropped white hair. The smile lines on the corners of his eyes made me like him right away. "That's no New York City badge," came the deep resonance of his voice. "But I'm always willing to help someone who's doin' the right thing." His words had the slightest hint of a Caribbean accent. "You doin' the right thing, my man?"

"I'm trying to."

CHAPTER 23

I unslung my duffel bag and buckled the seatbelt. "You still there, Shanay?" I pressed the phone to my ear.

"I'm here," she answered. "You still got eyes on her?"

"Yeah. A few cars ahead." I turned to the driver. "What's your name?"

"Clarence," he said with a calming thrum. "Clarence Eubanks."

"Glad to know you, Clarence." I awkwardly patted his hand, which was still gripping the wheel. "I need to know if anyone else is in the car."

He glanced back over his seat. "Nope. Just me and you."

"No, no, I mean inside the Land Rover. We need to pull up to the passenger side so that the driver doesn't see me. You'll have to tell me what you see."

Clarence put on his turn signal and moved up in the right lane. Pulling my hat low over my sunglasses, I kept the phone to my ear and turned away.

Shanay asked, "Do you need me to call the cops for you?"

"Not yet." I slunk in my seat as we came abreast of the SUV. "I'm still..." I continued in a whisper so Clarence wouldn't hear. "I'm still wanted. They would take me in before they'd even look at Laskin."

"Just one person that I can see," said Clarence. "Looks like a young white girl." Both of our cars had stopped side-by-side for a red light, and Clarence was still gazing over at Laskin. Then he waved at her.

"No," I said. "We don't want to draw attention--"

Clarence's throaty laugh filled the car as the light changed and her Range Rover accelerated through the intersection. "Way I see it is, she's a pretty girl, and old men wave at pretty girls. I couldn't look much more normal than that, now could I?"

He had a point. And the fact that Laskin had sped away without so much as a smile, sort of proved it.

"I guess someone could have been in the back of her car," he said. "Couldn't see much 'cause of the dark windows. But she was definitely talking to someone."

Shanay's voice squawked, "Put me on speaker, McKenna!"

I raised up my sunglasses and held the phone at arm's length to see the tiny buttons. "Okay, can you hear me?"

"Yeah," she answered. "Hey Mr. Clarence, I need to axe you if that girl was talking into her phone?"

"No, ma'am. I didn't see a phone."

"Okay McKenna, that means that she's paired."

I glanced at Clarence and then at the phone in my hand. "Not sure what you're saying, Shanay."

"She's *hands-free* on her phone, which she most likely has paired up with Bluetooth. Specially if she's using the navigation system to find her way around."

Clarence motioned toward the map on his dashboard-mounted phone, and nodded in agreement. I, on the other hand, wasn't grasping the significance.

"Listen up, McKenna. My friend used to hack peoples' personal stuff all the time by getting into the car's *infotainment system*. Once someone's paired, all the shit from their phone gets loaded into it."

The Land Rover made a right turn onto the Belt Parkway onramp, heading east. Clarence signaled, then calmly moved over behind her.

"You're saying her phone's data stays in the car's system?"

"Yup."

"You're sure?" I asked.

"Yes, McKenna. It's all stored in the system's cache. Even if she only plugged it into the port to charge it up for a minute."

"Exactly what information does it store?"

"Everything," she said. "Address book, web searches, phone calls, texts, even the directions she got off the GPS."

It was a goldmine. My heart raced and I felt flush with adrenaline. "How can I get it off the system?" I asked. "Can I download it on a disk or something?"

"A disk." I heard Shanay laugh. "Yeah, after you tie your horse to the hitch'n post."

Laskin was picking up speed, and I got the impression that my driver wasn't comfortable outside of the slow lane.

"That's the bad news," said Shanay. "To get the stuff off the car's system, I think you gotta have a special program on your computer. Black suits got 'em." She was quiet for a minute. "Unless..."

I motioned impatiently for Clarence to kick up the speed.

"Unless what, Shanay?"

"Unless you can get at it while this chick's phone is still paired to the car. Once she's outta range, the system gonna lock you out. All that stuff you try'n to get will still be there, but you ain't gett'n to it."

"How am I supposed to do that?"

"I don't know, McKenna. You supposed to be the detective."

"Son of a bitch," I said as the Range Rover moved to the exit lane.

Clarence frowned, and I realized that bad language was another thing he was not comfortable with.

"Laskin's about to take the off-ramp toward JFK. If that car's a rental, she's probably going there to return it."

Shanay said, "If I was her, I'd dump it off right before gett'n on my flight outta there."

She was probably right. It would be a hurried car return, and then Laskin would hustle through security just in time to board her flight. There would be no opportunity for me to hack into her car's system, or even arrange for the cops to stop her.

The Range Rover eased into the rental return lane, and Clarence gracefully swung over behind it. "You're going to need a distraction," he said, "if you want to keep the lady's phone in range."

I took a deep breath to steady my racing pulse. "I'll need more than that. What do I do, Shanay?"

"You ask'n me?"

"No, I mean, what do I do if I get into the system before her phone goes out of range? How do I find the information?"

We were on Federal Circle, following Laskin onto Cargo Service Road toward the Enterprise Car Rental. It was coming up on our right, not more than 100 yards ahead.

"You still there, Shanay?"

There was a staticky response, and I was losing our connection.

The Range Rover slowed as it made a right turn into the lot.

"Shanay?"

More static over the phone.

Laskin came to a stop, third car in the drop-off line.

Clarence pulled his Subaru right up behind the slick gray SUV. "What should I do now?" he asked.

CHAPTER 24

I'd lost connection with Shanay.

Clarence's smiling brown eyes never changed. Reaching up to the dashboard, he unclipped his own phone. "Here, use mine," he said.

Laskin stepped from her car without glancing back. Wearing her cap and sunglasses, she quickly removed a single shoulder bag and her phone. I could see it in her hand as she stood waiting for one of the employees to check in the car.

Quickly dialing Shanay's number, I could hear her answer—still a little broken up, but better than it was on my phone.

"It's me," I said as I watched Laskin stroll toward the front of the line. "Stay with me. I'm moving up now."

I jumped out and hurried to the passenger side of the Range Rover, using the car itself to block Laskin's view of me. She'd left the driver's door open and the key in the ignition, and as I peeked over the hood I saw that she was a good 30 feet away. Far enough that she probably wouldn't see me, but I hoped not too far to stay connected. A clerk was checking in another car, and it appeared that Laskin was trying to jump the line.

Slinking down, I slithered into the Range Rover and turned on the key one click in order to activate the car's electrical systems. The touchscreen lit up.

"Okay Shanay," I said into the phone. "You're on."

"First, look for *System Settings*."

"Got it." I hit the button and a new set of options appeared.

"You see *Bluetooth Setup*?"

"Okay, yeah." I pressed that and a few more choices popped up. Glancing over the dash, I saw Laskin trying to flag over the attendant. If she was successful in jumping ahead of the others, he would be coming to check the vehicle's gas and mileage.

"You're looking for phones that have been connected to it," said Shanay. "Should be a whole bunch of 'em."

"Uh, here, *Paired Phones List*."

I touched the screen and a new page came up. Just then I heard voices. They grew louder as they approached. Laskin's phone was still connected via Bluetooth, but I was going to be caught before ever gathering the evidence I needed.

Suddenly, there were squealing tires and a horn honking. I sat up just enough to see over the dash, and Clarence's little Subaru had shot out from behind and whizzed past me. Gunning his engine, he sped forward, nearly taking off the Range Rover's door. With his horn blaring and headlights flashing, Clarence came to a screeching stop next to Laskin and the employee—both of them only feet from the front of the car I was in.

"What was that?" asked Shanay.

"Clarence, running interference."

"Okay McKenna, you should be in. Find her phone number on the paired list and open it. Should give you at least some of the stuff you try'n to get."

I didn't know her number, but figured it had to be the most recent on the list. Quickly pressing the number, I watched an entire record of activity populate the touchscreen. I used Clarence's phone to take a photo, then scrolled to the next page for another shot, and then another. There were three pages in all.

Clarence was yelling something in a voice that had lost its smooth tranquility and increased in volume. There were accusations that the woman—Laskin—had cut him off on the expressway. Not that the lot attendant could have done anything even if it had happened, but it had been enough to stall their return to the car. But my time was up, and I heard them getting closer.

About to slink back out, I suddenly saw the GPS icon on the screen. Somehow, I had accidentally disconnected with Shanay when I took the pictures. *Son-of-a-bitch!*

Just a few more seconds. My thick fingers fumbled furiously to bring up the mapping app. I mistakenly hit the button for Satellite radio, and music blared from the speakers. *Shit!*

I back-buttoned my way out to the homepage, and started again. Finally working my way back to the navigation function, I opened it. The most recent location inputted was the Brutka Jewelers address. Continuing to scroll, I was looking for the address that would stand out above all others. Then I saw it.

Footsteps on the pavement were fast approaching. My phone was like a banana in my sweaty hands, and my heart was pounding so hard that I trembled. Lying sideways across the seat, I cocked my head to see the address through the phone's viewfinder. *One more second,* I prayed.

The driver's door sprang open with a gusto, and I was suddenly bathed in blinding sunlight. With the light behind them, I squinted up at two silhouettes looking down at me.

CHAPTER 25

Peering up at the two figures, I felt like a teenager caught sneaking through his girlfriend's window. I shielded my eyes and saw the lot attendant and my driver, Clarence.

I grunted and turned back to the touchscreen. Aafreen's address was there, but I passed it up for the bigger fish. As I raised my phone to photograph Leo Kingsbury's address, the entire screen suddenly went black—except for three words: *Bluetooth connection lost.*

Natalia Laskin had moved out of range and I was now locked out. Through the windshield, I saw her heading across the lot toward the steps leading up to the *AirTrain*. I wanted to run after the woman, tackle her to the ground and snatch her cellphone.

"What's going on?" asked the attendant. "Did you leave something in the car?"

Clarence saw the disappointment on my face and led the kid away, "Yeah, he lost something," said Clarence.

Climbing out of the Range Rover, I saw that Shanay was calling me back.

"Missed it," I said into the phone. "I got a few of the numbers she'd called, but Laskin went out of range before I could get a picture of the navigation info."

"What was on it?"

I groaned. "Aafreen's Fairfax address, and Kingsbury's townhouse in Oak Hill. It proved Laskin was at Kingsbury's on the night he was killed."

"Why would she go to Aafreen's house?" asked Shanay.

"Probably to take a picture of her car's license plate. It's a long story, but it doesn't mean anything at this point."

"Send me all them phone numbers you got, and I'll try to help ya from this end."

"They're mostly foreign," I said. "I doubt you'll be able to track them down."

"Maybe, but the way I see it we got nothin' to lose. Just send 'em to me anyways. And don't sweat this, McKenna. We'll figure out another way to get that bitch."

Shanay clicked off, and for some strange reason I felt as if I had let her down—in addition to Aafreen, who I knew I'd let down.

I returned Clarence's cell phone after texting Shanay the photos of Laskin's phone calls, and then I retrieved my things from his car. It had been an Uber ride that I doubted he would ever forget. The guy had risked a lot for me—someone he didn't even know—just because I had assured him that I was trying to do the right thing. For that, I paid him handsomely before he drove away.

I was left standing in the lot with a shoulder bag containing my computer, the Bangkok files, and my passport. I'd also begun a file for Aafreen's defense, and had I been able to capture the Range Rover's data, that evidence would have gotten her case dismissed. Without it and without Leclaire, the prosecution's case against Aafreen was going to be a slam dunk. And after springing her from federal custody, the case against me was just as strong.

Clarence's little Subaru rambled out of the lot, and I wondered if I should have gotten back in and left with him. There wasn't much more for me to do here but try to follow the Russian murderer who had framed my friend. The woman already had a substantial lead on me, and without the ability to use my phone, I was working at a huge disadvantage. Activating it for any reason was essentially sending out a GPS signal to the feds of my location.

I walked up the steps toward the AirTrain and stood at a window in the stairwell overlooking the rental car lots, then I waited. Having already used my phone to talk with Shanay, I anticipated a legion of federal agents swarming in at any minute.

It took almost ten minutes, but they eventually arrived in their slick-top cars, their starched white shirts, and their dark glasses. It appeared that my phone's signal hadn't been precise enough to pinpoint my location, so they sort of fanned out among the half-dozen or so rental companies. My hope was that they'd think I'd rented a car rather than dropped one off. If they suspected the latter, they would assume I was catching a flight—which could present a whole new set of problems for me.

My takeaway from all of this was that I had to find another way out of the airport before the feds locked down the entire system and maybe even the airport itself.

On the upper platform, I realized that I'd just missed an AirTrain by one minute—probably the one Laskin had taken. Now, I'd have no way to know at which terminal she got off. The map on the train showed six of them, but as I stared at it I realized the sheer futility of trying to tail Laskin. I had some cash, but not enough for an airline ticket. And using my credit card to purchase one would immediately alert the cops. My investigation was pretty much dead in the water.

On the wall of the train beneath the map, there were a number of travel posters. They each included beautiful photos of exotic places that could be reached via direct flights out of JFK; Aer Lingus to Dublin, Royal Air Maroc to Casablanca, Icelandair to Reykjavik—all of them great vacation spots for anyone other than me.

Glancing back at the AirTrain map, I realized the lines also ran in the opposite direction of the airport and could take me to Howard Beach or Jamaica Station—both of which had access to the subway and other public transportation.

I tucked myself against the wall, hoping my hat and sunglasses were enough to prevent a camera from recognizing me. Being in such a public place made me uneasy, but there was suddenly something else gnawing at me. The feeling had come on quickly, and it felt as if an answer was knocking on the door of my consciousness but I wasn't allowing it in. Hovering in the recesses of my brain, it frustrated me that I couldn't pull it out.

We reached Jamaica Station and I saw signs directing departing passengers to the subway. As I stepped off the train, it suddenly hit me. I'd only taken a few steps. "Wait a minute!" I said, spinning back toward the train.

But I was a tic too late. The doors closed with a swoosh, and the AirTrain started to move.

Peering in through the windows, I focused over the heads of the passengers now sliding past me as if they were on a carnival ride. The system map swept by, and then the travel posters. It was something on one of those posters that my subconscious had seen.

I squinted through the thick glass as the train picked up speed. Suddenly, there was Mohammed V.

CHAPTER 26

I had broken my own rule against making assumptions, and it had cost me valuable time.

The next AirTrain came three minutes later, and I took it back toward JFK's Terminal 1—the terminal handling most international flights. I searched the main rotunda for a departure's status board and checked the evening flights. There was one in particular, and the confirmation of my hunch shot through my body like lightening.

Hunkering down near an abandoned shoeshine stand, I rifled through my shoulder bag for the phone call notes from Bangkok. I ran my finger down the list, stopping at the call beginning with 312—the country code for Morocco.

I needed to call Shanay, but couldn't activate my phone without being located and arrested. Then, an idea came to me; a workaround that I should have figured out sooner.

Swapping out my phone's SIM card, I replaced it with the data card from the Russian assassin's phone. It gave my cell his old number and populated it with his phone history. He had died in Bangkok almost two months prior, and I knew that the cops had no reason to be looking for him.

I couldn't remember Shanay's cell phone number, and wasn't sure she would even pick up for an unknown caller. So, I tried the office instead.

"McKenna Investigations, Executive Assistant Shanay Moore speak'n."

I wasn't sure I'd ever get used to the new title she'd given herself. "Shanay, it's me. I need a big favor."

"Boss, if it's something really illegal you gonna have to pay me a lot more."

"No, nothing like that. I need you to call Royal Air Maroc and get me on tonight's JFK to Casablanca flight. It's scheduled to take off at 8:40 p.m."

"And how I'm supposed to pay for it?"

"That would be the favor," I said. "I can't use my credit cards, so you'll have to charge it on yours. I'll pay you back as soon as I get home."

"Yeah, okay, fine. It might take me a few minutes, so go get yo'self a drink or somethin'."

It wasn't a bad idea, except there were no bars or pubs on my side of the security checkpoint.

After waiting as patiently as I could, I got in line and worked my way up to the Royal Air Maroc ticket counter. "Ticket for Daniel McKenna," I said, sliding my passport across the counter.

The woman wore a pleasant smile as she punched the keys of her computer. "Any luggage?"

"Just this carry-on bag."

Another nice smile as she placed my printed tickets into a folded envelope. "Your flight departs at 8:40 p.m.," she said. "Getting into Mohammed V International at 8:30 a.m."

Now I smiled. I'd seen the airport on the AirTrain's travel poster, boasting a new 76,000-square foot terminal with a capacity of seven million passengers annually. Though I'd skimmed over its name, something had stuck in my subconscious. I'd finally realized that Mohammed V wasn't a suspect, but the name of the Moroccan King's father, after whom the airport was named—the 'V' being Roman numeral for 5, not an initial.

I walked away with my tickets, feeling more pieces falling into place. The notation *STL* on Kingsbury's computer file now made perfect sense. The subject's trail had indeed been lost, but the subject wasn't Mohammed V., as I had wrongly assumed. It was Natalia Laskin whose trail had been lost, and it was after she'd landed at the Mohammed V Airport.

Figuring out this particular piece of the puzzle felt good, although of the two people who could appreciate it, one was dead and the other jailed for murder. As eager as I was, my plight had become much more complicated and more solitary. In addition, I was flying to a foreign country, which I detested doing, and there was a very good possibility that Natalia Laskin was taking the same flight.

The boarding area was packed. From what I could tell, over half the passengers were indigenous and the rest were tourists. I chose not to venture into the waiting area for fear of being recognized by Laskin. Instead, I loitered around a Martini bar—which was more like an alcove—across from my boarding gate.

Keeping my ball cap on, I removed the sunglasses to avoid the pervert look, and ordered a drink. A big screen TV played over the bar, but without volume. I mindlessly watched the local news as I ate a sandwich and sipped my drink. As I got up to leave, the screen cut to a story that stopped me in my tracks.

The video clip was of our Manhattan hotel, and Aafreen being led out in handcuffs. My gut ached, and I suddenly wished I hadn't had the panini sandwich.

Above the shot scrolled the text: *Federal Agent arrested after fleeing D.C. murder charges.*

I watched as Aafreen's bare feet padded across the wet sidewalk, and my eyes began to water. She didn't deserve any of this, and I knew I was the only one who had any hope of getting her out of it.

The TV screen changed to a photograph of me. With no volume, I couldn't tell what the newscaster was saying, though I surmised it wasn't good.

I immediately felt conspicuous, as if I was suddenly dressed only in my underwear.

The first boarding groups were being called for my flight, and families with small children were beginning to board. I hustled over to a newsstand and bought a Washington Post before donning the sunglasses again and schlepping into line.

I flipped to the local news and the first story confirmed my worst fear: besides an accomplice in Aafreen's escape, I was now a "person of interest" in Nate Leclaire's murder.

CHAPTER 27

The aircraft seemed to stretch on forever. The seating configuration was 3-3-3, with the exception of the Business Class section which had already boarded and was sectioned off by a curtain. Being a late addition to the flight, I was seated in the middle seat of the middle section toward the back of the plane.

As much as I dared to look around, I never saw Natalia Laskin—in either the female or male version. Once, after the meal service and the lights were turned down, I ventured a stroll to see if I could spot her. But most people were asleep beneath their eye masks, making it impossible to identify her if she was one of them. Nudging my way back to my seat, I concluded that she was either in Business Class or had taken a different flight. My worst fear was that my hunch was bad, and she had never even left New York. In which case, the trip was a complete waste of time and money.

An hour or so prior to landing, the flight attendants passed out Moroccan Immigration forms. A bolt of fear struck me as I realized that I hadn't applied for any type of visa to enter the country. Filling out the forms the best I could, I suspected they may refuse entry or perhaps send me home on the next flight.

Three buses awaited the passengers, the second of which I was in. They dumped us out at a terminal with signage in Arabic, French, and English. As I stepped off the bus, I caught a glimpse of a young woman who had ridden the first bus. From the back, she looked like Natalia Laskin—formerly Elaina Teagan, who had masqueraded as my missing person's sister.

The woman wore her hair extremely short, which fit with her male impersonation while operating in the D.C. area. Now, however, she was dressed in a cream-colored robe like many of the other Moroccan women. Covering her head with a scarf, she moved quickly through the Immigration line.

I hung back, trying to keep an eye on her while at the same time fretting about what would happen to me once I got up to the window.

"Passport and Immigration card," said the stout man behind the partition.

Handing both to him, I was preparing my plea when he snapped, "You didn't list the residence address where you will be staying while you're here."

"Huh?" I squinted up at the row of fluorescent lights. "Oh, it's 123 Sahara Street."

He frowned and shook his head. "Sahara Tours?"

"Yes, sorry, that must be it."

Scratching off what he had started to write, the man scribbled something illegible and handed it back to me.

My shocked expression was probably a tip-off.

"No visa is required for visits less than 90 days," he said. "Will you be staying longer?"

"Jesus, I sure hope not." I took my papers and scurried into the Customs line, which was a breeze since I only had my shoulder bag.

But the woman I believed to be Laskin was nowhere to be seen. She had gone through the doors only seconds before me, and then disappeared.

Son-of-a-bitch! I had been tailing her all of three minutes and I'd already lost her.

Looking as frantic as a parent who'd lost their kid, I hustled all the way through the airport. A fork at one point went one way to the main exit and another way toward the train. I went toward the train, emerging onto a vast brick platform not unlike the New York Subway.

I spotted the woman, facing away from me as she stepped onto the train. I started running toward the end car, but the doors closed and the train picked up speed as it left the airport.

I hooked the arm of a woman sweeping the station floor. "Where is that train going?"

With eyes like a terrified horse, she reared back taking her arm with her. "I cannot answer your question," she said, now with a look of disgust at the inappropriate American. "The train stops at many places: Berchid, Sidi el-Aydi, Settat, Skhour Rhamana, Ben Guerir, and Marrakesh."

"When is the next one?"

She motioned to the wall, then returned to her sweeping. "The schedule just there."

I thanked her in a plea for forgiveness sort of way, but the woman did not turn back. Collapsing against the wall, I slid to the floor with my head between my knees like someone about to be sick. My plan had become a disaster.

After a while of feeling sorry for myself, I started to get pissed off. My anger was at myself as much as at the Laskin woman and the people she represented. Maybe I'd end up giving up, but I wasn't ready to do it yet. I was stuck in Morocco, at least for a little while, and realized that I should try to make the most of it.

Taking out the page that Shanay had put together of the phone calls from the dead guy's SIM card, I looked over the list again. The single call received from Morocco is what had tipped the scales in favor of me following Laskin here, though I still couldn't see any logical connection between her and the country of Morocco.

The Russia and Brooklyn calls could easily be explained by Laskin's organized crime connection, but like Morocco, the rest of the foreign calls still made no sense to me; Hong Kong, Thailand, India, Germany, and Sweden. None of them seemed to have any relation to the others, or to my investigation. The whole damn thing was giving me a headache.

Posters all around the airport boasted free Wi-Fi for sessions up to 30 minutes. I wasn't as concerned about the feds tracking me down on the other side of the world, so I took a risk and logged in.

Entering the entire Moroccan phone number, I hoped the search results would be telling...perhaps something like *Assassins for Rent*, or *Natalia Laskin's residence*. But instead, what came back was more of a head scratcher. *Alshahn Marrakesh-Safi* was listed as a shipping company located in the Marrakesh-Safi Region—an area stretching about 170 miles from east of Marrakesh to the Atlantic.

Like everything else I'd uncovered, it meant nothing to me. For all I knew, it could have been a telemarketer calling the dead Russian's number. So meager was the lead that it didn't even rise to the level of a clue. There was no *gut feeling* to support further investigation of it. In fact, my continued effort in Morocco was nothing more than a drowning man grasping at straws along a treacherous shore.

The next train pulled in and announcements were given in Arabic, French, and English. Passengers disembarked while I debated going back into the terminal and buying a ticket home.

I logged off and gathered the papers scattered across my lap. As I stood there weighing my options, perspiring travelers flowed past me. I had all but made up my mind to return home.

Then, just before the train doors closed, I made a mad dash for the last coach.

I was in, and the train was departing, but I had no idea where I was headed.

CHAPTER 28

I ended up with a ticket in the First-Class coach, which amounted to little cubes of four seats that faced each other. The hideous odor inside was an odd combination that I couldn't immediately place, until I saw the bathroom symbol over a door near me. Just then, an employee whose sole job it was to spray a deodorizer, walked the length of the train pumping madly on his sprayer. His apple-scented mist hung in the air, merging with the toilet odor and allowing me to reconcile the mysterious blend that assaulted my senses.

The terrain outside was not what I expected. A semi-modern city with a working-class texture whizzed past my window as a smoky sky hovered overhead. There were no camels, no Bedouin tents, and no windswept desert.

Eventually, its topography flattened to a more arid stretch that could have easily been Arizona or New Mexico, though a quick glance around our coach was a reminder that I was in a Muslim country.

"British?" asked a woman seated behind me.

Turning in my seat, I faced two pleasant looking ladies—both of whom had a good 25 years on me.

"American," I said. "Danny McKenna." I extended my hand.

They both smiled widely as they eagerly took turns squeezing the tips of my fingers. "We're Bella and Sophie."

Bella, the talkative one, was roundish with light skin and freckles. The other woman had similar features but wore eyeglasses and had an unspeckled complexion.

"We're sisters," said Bella. "Traveling from Ryton-on-Dunsmore." Then with a practiced pause, "It's a suburb of Coventry."

The accent told me more than the towns she'd cited, but it was nice to meet fellow English speakers. We talked briefly; them telling me that one was divorced and the other widowed, and me lying that I was a teacher on sabbatical. As they tried to circle back to my lonely, companionless travels, I got the impression that they fancied having a man along on their journey. Not for any other reason than allaying their security fears. It wasn't in the cards however, as my mission here was narrowly focused on finding Natalia Laskin.

"We've both spent our adult lives raising children and keeping our homes in order," Sophie said.

"And taking care of our husbands," added Bella with a laugh.

"It is now our turn to enjoy life," continued sister Sophie. "We've not traveled outside the U.K., and our hope is that this trip will be our adventure of a lifetime."

"Very brave," I said.

It came out a little patronizing, but I truly meant it. If not for Aafreen's dire predicament, I'd never have had the guts to come to Morocco. As it was, I wasn't sure I'd even be staying.

My new friends, the Elliott sisters, strong-armed me into sharing a cab from the train station to Marrakesh. I found myself crammed into the back seat with the two women because our driver's brother rode up front with him. Why the brother was in the cab with us was never explained.

We left the railway station on a meandering route that the driver told us was to avoid roadwork. I suspected it was to up the fare, which seemed completely arbitrary since he had never started the meter.

After about a mile, I noticed a black SUV emerge from a side street in front of us. It pulled to the side, and after letting us pass it fell in behind us. I suddenly felt my mouth go dry. As the Elliotts blathered on about their tour itinerary, my attention was on the vehicle behind us that didn't fit the surroundings.

On our left was a park with a stadium and event center. I recall it well, because one of the sisters had spotted a British pub and was squealing with delight as the car behind us suddenly drew closer.

The first impact knocked our taxi forward, flinging me against the seatback. I looked over my shoulder and saw the SUV intentionally accelerating to ram us a second time.

Now the Elliotts were both squealing, but not in a good way. Our driver slung a string of Arabic words into the air as the ash from his cigarette flew about inside the car. His brother said nothing.

Several cars in front of us had slowed for road construction, and for a second I thought we were going to be accordioned into them. The people in the SUV would undoubtedly be coming out shooting. Who they were and why they were doing this was a mystery, which was all too familiar to me. It felt as if I was watching the slow-motion rerun of a horror film that I loathed the first time I saw it.

Our driver quickly jerked the wheel to the right, bouncing us up onto a brick sidewalk. As the cab fishtailed around several bicyclists, our driver continued his verbal invective without ever losing his cigarette.

We skittered around the construction barricade, and the taxi slid sideways into the next turn. We were suddenly face-to-face with a police checkpoint. An officer waved us into the queue of stopped cars, as I glanced back to see the SUV hastily pull off.

"Bloody hell!" said Bella, holding a hand to her ample bosom. "What just happened?"

Meanwhile, Sophie had fused herself to my arm.

"Robbers, maybe." The driver's eyes scanned the rearview mirror. "This happens sometimes on the highways."

But his words lacked the certainty I was hoping for, which made me wonder if this attack was more than random. Though there was no way Laskin knew I was even in Morocco, I'd been surprised by her attacks against me before.

The fleeting hope crossed my mind that it actually *had* been an attempted highway robbery. After all, our little threesome could have easily been picked out at the train station as Western tourists with plenty of traveling money. I imagined that the driver and the guy he claimed was his brother might even have been involved. But if that were the case, our driver probably would have stopped and submitted to it rather than bust his ass to get away.

In any event, we had made it through the security check without spotting the SUV again. Our taxi pulled up in front of the gates to the Old City of Marrakesh, which the driver referred to as the *Medina*. The lot was clogged with tour buses, taxis, and vendor carts.

As much as I didn't want to believe it, I finally came to the conclusion that the target of the taxi ramming had been yours truly. Proceeding under that premise, I had only two immediate objectives; jettison the Elliott sisters, and get lost in the teeming masses within the Old City before I was attacked again.

90

CHAPTER 29

What we had driven through while trying to outrun the SUV, turned out to be only part of Marrakesh. The Old City, or *Medina*, was a crowded labyrinth cloistered behind a 30-foot wall in the center of the district. It was the Jewel of Morocco, also known as the Red City, according to the side of a tour bus parked outside.

As I hustled toward the main gate, the shrill of Bella and Sophie filled the air.

"Oh Mr. McKenna," they took turns calling as they fumbled over the uneven bricks with their suitcase rollers.

I couldn't just ignore the women, so I waited impatiently for them in the shade of a fruit vendor's umbrella just outside the gate.

Bella paused, taking her time to admire the entrance. Conferring with her little guide, she took out a camera. "This is called the Bab Doukkala Gate. Isn't it just lovely?"

"Sublime," said Sophie.

We finally entered the Old City, and were immediately swarmed by sellers, beggars, and supposed "tour guides." The sisters asked one of them if they knew where to find their hotel, which she pointed out on her little map. Of course he knew the place, and of course he would be happy to lead us to it, in exchange for a few *dirham*.

I kept my bag tucked tightly under my arm as we pinballed our way through bustling markets and alleyways. The wheels on Bella's rollers had become clogged with dirt, and we had to keep waiting as she dug serpentine grooves in the pasty dust behind us.

Our "guide" stopped abruptly at a massive green door. Its heavy timbers with iron hinges were set inside a stone archway bearing a sign that read: Riad Mwimbi Spa.

"Where are *you* staying?" Bella asked, flushed and out of breath. "Because Mwimbi Spa is absolutely charming, and the Tripadvisor ratings are quite good."

I admitted that I'd yet to make reservations, claiming that it was a last-minute decision to visit Marrakesh. What I didn't say was that I had no desire to stay in the same hotel as them. Besides, anyplace that included the word "Spa" in its name was way above my budget.

Next to me, only chest high, stood the boy who had shown the Elliotts to their hotel. He wore blue jeans, a loose tunic, and a friendly smile beneath his plain white ball cap.

"You are not staying?" he asked.

"Too expensive for me." I said.

"These ladies?"

"No," I laughed. "This place, Mumbai Spa."

"Mwimbi," he corrected.

Borrowing Bella's little map, the boy ran a soiled fingernail from our location to an indiscriminate spot. "Maison El Idrissi," he said. "Very good price for you, and also it is clean."

Returning the map to Bella, I bid the sisters farewell and off I went with the kid.

"I am Hassan." He held out his hand.

"Danny." I reached under my shoulder bag with my free arm.

Pulling back, he grinned. "Only right hand in Morocco."

I tucked my bag around the other side, and we shook properly.

"Never your left hand," he cautioned. "It's only for the bathroom."

"Good to know." I studied my left hand and unconsciously wiped it on my pant leg.

We passed a money exchange near the gate we had entered, and I took the opportunity to buy a bunch of their currency. The dirham came in coin and notes, and was the equivalent of about 8 or 9 to one U.S. Dollar.

Grabbing my elbow, Hassan led me off the main road back into a squirrel hole as I tried to tuck my money away.

With such dimly lit confines and so many characters brushing up against me, my careful vigilance still had to be shared with the uneven stones beneath my feet that several times caused me to stumble. What I really didn't need in this town was for my knee to go out again.

In the narrowest and darkest of alleys, he stopped unexpectedly and held out his hand like a gameshow host. There was no signage out front, only a rusted iron gate with empty flower buckets on either side of it.

The boy called through the gate in an Arabic dialect, and an old woman shuffled out to let me in. I gave my guide a handful of coins and he disappeared back down the alleyway. I wondered if I'd ever be able to find the place on my own. Which was sort of an encouraging thought. If I had trouble finding it, then anyone coming after me would have trouble as well.

As I followed the old woman, I realized that this was not a motel, but a family house. They rented out one room on the top floor, which had a single bed, a sink, and a small terrace overlooking the Medina. The kid had been right on both counts; it was clean and cheap. Maybe a tad steamy, but I was sure I could handle it.

I ventured out around 5 p.m., hoping to find a clothing store and something I could eat. A ten-minute walk revealed a small café and a menu with pictures. I pointed to the chicken leg, which was the only thing I recognized. It came with peas and a few slices of eggplant, but was edible. Afterwards, I found an open-air market that had a good selection of clothing—though most of it had a North African flavor.

Ending up with something called a kaftan, I returned to my room and tried it on. It was a hooded garment, made of cotton. Part pajama and part robe, it was quite comfortable. I only hoped that Moroccan local laws didn't require underwear as Bangkok's had.

The best part was my burgeoning beard. Not having shaved for several days, I was actually beginning to look like one of the locals. As I studied myself in the mirror, my cell phone rang.

I had turned it on at the airport to check the time, and forgot to shut it off. Not that it mattered all that much, since I was in Morocco and was using the dead Russian's SIM card.

"Hello?" I answered tentatively.

"What the fuck, McKenna?"

"Brooks?"

"Yeah, it's me," she said. "You ought to really think about officially changing your name."

"What do you mean? Why?"

She laughed. "Same reason why nobody names their kid Adolph or Osama anymore. You're all over the news out here, and not in a good way. It's like déjà vu. They're saying you not only sprung some honey from jail, but you killed her defense lawyer."

"Partly true," I said. "Leclaire wasn't the attorney; he was the investigator."

"That'll be a great defense." Brooks laughed.

"No, I mean I didn't kill the guy. In fact, Leclaire was a friend. He was actually helping us." I sat on the bed and pinched the bridge of my nose. "Why do they think I did it?"

"Best I can tell, they have you on his voicemail trying to arrange a meeting with him the night he died. Also, some kind of vague threat about having something for him."

"Information! I meant I had information for him!"

"Hey, whatever, let's not kill the messenger here. So, I got these phone numbers that your secretary texted me. She said you needed the addresses that go with them. That right?"

"Shanay did that?"

"I told you she was good. Anyway, these numbers are all over the map. Too much information to text back to you, so I'll email it instead. I assume you can get emails where you are."

"I have my laptop," I said. "And I'm in Morocco. Marrakesh, to be exact."

"Oh yeah, that was the other thing." She paused, and I knew it was more bad news. "The FBI knows you left the country. Apparently, they were monitoring your secretary's credit cards as well as yours."

"Bastards."

"Be that as it may, Morocco has no extradition treaty with the U.S., which has convinced the feds of your guilt and supports their theory that you fled there to avoid going to jail."

"I fled here to find the woman who killed Leo Kingsbury. She's the same person behind the bombing of the Marshals' safe house in rural Maryland, and the attacks on their protectee in Bangkok."

"I get it, McKenna. I know you're helping out my friend, Aafreen. Just thought you'd want to know what the stakes are."

I thanked Brooks and we said our goodbyes.

Once off the phone, I connected to the guesthouse's Wi-Fi and brought up a world map. As I waited for Brooks's email, I punched in the names of the countries on the Russian's call log. There were six of them; eight if I included the Brooklyn jewelry store and the Moscow numbers.

I stared at them for a long while, then closed my eyes and tried to squeeze the answer from my brain. They were in different areas of the world and on different continents. No matter how random the places seemed, there had to be a connection, a commonality of some kind, and it had to be right there in front of me. I knew that I'd want to kick myself once I'd found the link.

Exhausted, I felt myself giving in to the heat, the smell of spices, and the flute music permeating up from the street. With the laptop resting on my chest, I reclined on my bed and gave it one more look before shutting it down.

The map gave me a better visual picture of each country's location relative to the others, but they still appeared unconnected and arbitrary. The only common feature I could come up with was that none of the countries were landlocked; they all had at least one piece touching an ocean.

Closing my eyes, I wondered if that could be the link I was so desperately looking for.

CHAPTER 30

I'd gotten up around midnight to use the bathroom, and booted up the laptop to see if Brooks had sent the phone information from the foreign numbers. It was in my inbox, and I opened the file.

Being unfamiliar with these countries, the cities from which the calls had been placed left me perplexed and wondering if I'd ever be able to figure it out. The second page of the file listed the actual service subscribers, which confused me even more.

The Hong Kong phone number was registered to Hoang Medical Supplies at the Port of Aberdeen. The map showed that Aberdeen was a small port located on Hong Kong Island across from the sprawling Victoria Harbor.

The Thailand location turned out to be a shipping company in the town of Rayong, about 180 miles from Bangkok.

In India, the phone subscriber was a commercial fishing company at the Port of Mumbai.

Next was a freight barge company operating out of Jade-Weser, a small shipping port only a short distance from the Port of Hamburg—Germany's largest and busiest.

Sjögren Petroleum was the source of the phone call from Sweden. The company was located in Brofjorden Port, 70 miles north of the massive Port of Gothenburg.

Last on the list was Morocco. The number was registered to a warehouse in Safi—a fishing village about 2 hours west of Marrakesh. Like the others, it wasn't far from a much larger shipping facility—this one being the Port of Casablanca.

Since each of the phone subscribers were located at seaports, it was clear that my hunch that their proximity to the sea had indeed been the common link. With that said, it still made no sense to me. The man whose phone received these calls was a highly trained killer, not a barge operator, or a fisherman, or a merchant seaman. And he certainly wasn't in the medical supply business.

Whoever was behind these killings was working hard to ensure I didn't uncover their operation, whatever it was. I also suspected that Kingsbury and Leclaire had been killed because they had gotten too close to figuring it out. I had to assume it was also the reason for the attempts on my life and their effort to frame Aafreen.

Perhaps I had found *a* link, but it wasn't *the* link. Now I had to work out how Natalia Laskin and the dead Russian were connected to all of this, and, what *all of this* was. The feeling in my gut told me that the answer to that question would prove Aafreen's innocence, but it would probably put me in a great deal more danger.

As I lay in my room thinking about that, I wondered about my good friend Sarah Brooks. Presumably, she had used an intelligence database to research the phone numbers—possibly the same system that Kingsbury and Leclaire had accessed. *Was that what got them killed? And, had I now placed Brooks in danger too?*

Walking out onto the terrace, I stood in the dark listening to the far-off sounds of the marketplace—still bustling at the late hour. Other noises, more melodic, were string and flute instruments, and the song of a night bird that I'd never heard in the States.

Then came another sound, barely noticeable yet unnatural. It was the creaking of a rusted gate. I often caution myself against becoming paranoid, especially when in an unfamiliar place. But this was one time that I listened to the hairs on the back of my neck—which were all standing at attention.

Tiptoeing back into my room, I gathered my computer, charger, my newly purchased clothes, and my toiletries, and put them into my shoulder bag. I felt around in the dark for my pants, but couldn't find them. By the time I remembered that I'd hung them in the wardrobe, it was too late.

Whoever had come through the gate had now entered the house. The clack of the front door closing and footsteps echoing on the tiled floor confirmed it. Knowing that I was the only tenant, and that the old woman—probably half deaf and dead asleep—was the only other person there, I had to move quickly.

Wearing just my t-shirt and boxer shorts, I climbed over the terrace railing and shimmied down a drainpipe to the ground floor. As I reached the gate, which had been left ajar, I heard the door to my room being kicked in.

As I ran down the alley, stumbling over cobblestones in my bare feet, I remembered that my shoes were also in the wardrobe. Not my best planned escape, but at least I was away. Thankfully, this area of the Old City was not well traveled so late at night, and I was able to take the *kaftan* out of my bag and slip it on.

I somehow managed to navigate my way back to the main gates, with the intention of getting a cab to take me somewhere. Anywhere. But I froze in my tracks when I saw a black SUV idling at the curb just outside the gate.

Whatever I was dealing with, I now knew that it was more than just Natalia Laskin. The good news was that I was not paranoid. The bad news, of course, was that there was now an entire hit team in Marrakesh with me in their sights.

CHAPTER 31

I wandered through the Medina for what seemed like hours, trying to find a hidden spot to rest. In the dark and without my shoes, I looked enough like a beggar that nobody bothered me.

At the southern end of the Old City, I came upon another huge gate through which I emerged onto a paved expanse.

I crossed to the other side where a forest of palm trees provided shelter for the night. I awoke after little sleep, a tad stiff with my head resting on my shoulder bag. Having escaped what I was certain had been another attempt on my life, I had suffered only a minor scratch on the arm from my perilous climb down the drainpipe.

As I sat beneath a palm examining the tacky spot on my forearm, my mind flashed back to Bangkok. There had been a similar incident when, after being shot at, Aafreen had discovered a small cut on her arm that had been caused by the shattered window of our tuk-tuk. It was a momentary flash through my mind, but I grabbed it out of the air and clung to it like a lottery ticket in the wind.

Aafreen had dressed the wound in the bathroom of our rented apartment, right before we were broken into. My mind spun as the pieces that had eluded us, now found their places in the puzzle. The burglars, which had to include Laskin, must have taken the bloody cotton and gauze, later using it to mark the Kingsbury murder scene with Aafreen's DNA. How difficult would it have been to moisten it and splatter in around, even after so much time had passed?

The time sequence! My eyes rolled upwards. That was why the Raman spectroscopy analysis of the blood at the scene had come back 47 days old. Though I couldn't compute the timeline in my thick head, Aafreen was certain that it was during our time in Bangkok.

More pieces fell in line as I realized all of the DNA evidence could be attributed to Bangkok; the blood beneath the victim's nails, the hair in his hand, and maybe even the murder weapon with Aafreen's prints on it.

Reaching back in my memory, I struggled to recall an image. Then I had it. Aafreen had used the knife from the kitchenette to cut the slices of pizza for us. Again, it was just prior to the break-in.

But who could I tell? With Leclaire dead and the feds convinced that I killed him, nobody else was going to listen to a disgraced ex-cop who had fled the country to avoid prosecution.

This conundrum was like a fork in the road for me. Was I to hope for the best and return home with the new theory about the source of the DNA evidence? Or, was I to push forward and try to uncover the conspiracy that Natalia Laskin was part of?

I spent most of the day hiding out in the park, thinking about what to do. After hours of deliberation, I realized that to do the former and head home would feel like giving up on Mt. Everest only 100 yards from the summit. Besides, my theory about how Aafreen was framed was nothing more than that. A theory.

Going back through the gate and into the Medina, I had a renewed determination. Darkness was settling in and I'd finally figured out a way to gain an advantage over those who were hunting me.

The massive open-air market called Jemaa el-Fnaa took up the equivalent of two football fields. It was the beating heart of the Old City, and throngs of people flooded there to buy everything from spices and prepared foods, to artifacts and live animals.

I nearly stumbled over a real-life snake charmer who sat cross-legged with his flute, only inches from a king cobra. The snake was upright, sticking halfway out of a basket, wavering to the melody as if mesmerized by it. A glass terrarium with a lid held another cobra, and people were already lining up to photograph them. As I glanced back, I noticed the snake charmer's assistant moving through the crowd demanding money for the rights to take pictures.

After a short search, I found a market—or what they called a *souk*—selling both hard shoes and sandals. I purchased the sandals, thinking they would go better with the image I was creating. I also bought a round cap the same tan color as my kaftan.

Rubbing some dirt on my face to darken it a tad, I felt that when combined with my beard and my customary clothing, I might now have the advantage of a disguise. It wasn't perfect, but I wouldn't stand out unless I had to speak.

My grumbling stomach reminded me that the guesthouse I'd fled had offered homemade meals. I had not only blown my chance to eat, but I now had nowhere to stay. And if my credit card had led the attackers to the guesthouse, I would now need to figure out how to pay for a room with cash. I had some, but not that much.

As I continued up and down the narrow alleys looking for a decent meal, I found that some of the street food looked a little dicey. Finally spotting a tidy café with outdoor seating, I started toward it. Then I slowed abruptly as I recognized the Elliott sisters at a table, chatting as they photographed their dinner.

I sidled up to the corner of the building so as not to draw the attention of anyone in the vicinity. Luckily, their table was the farthest from the front of the café and from the other guests.

My mouth watered as the women spooned gobs of rice and meat from a tagine onto their plates.

"Psssst." I called from my shaded spot.

They turned and looked at me with contempt, then shooed me like a bothersome gnat. *"Yabtaeid! Yabtaeid!"*

I had no idea of the meaning, but their gestures made it clear enough. The words were clearly a brush-off that Bella had learned in her handy little travel guide.

The women hadn't recognized me, which meant I'd have to break cover and approach them in order to keep from dying of starvation.

"Ladies," I whispered out of the dark. "It's me, Danny McKenna."

The effectiveness of my disguise was evident from their stunned expressions. They remained frozen for several seconds, until Sophie's hand covered her open mouth. Bella blinked a few times then said, "Blimey O'Reilly, it really is him."

I concocted a story that my credit card had been compromised, and was declined by my guesthouse.

Examining my ensemble, Bella asked, "What about your clothes?"

"My clothes?" I cleared my throat. "The guesthouse held my pants and shoes as collateral. It's something they do in Morocco."

"That really takes the biscuit," said Sophie.

"Speaking of," I said. "Is there any way you can order me a little snack? I flipped a few notes onto the table."

"Poor thing," they took turns saying. "You must be famished."

I waited around the corner, and after several minutes they joined me in the dark alley. Handing me a bag of local goodies, they again gazed at me from head to toe before raising eyebrows to one another.

"Where will you stay?" asked Bella.

I told them that I would figure out something.

"Rubbish," she said. "We have a two-room suite. You'll stay with us, and we won't take no for an answer!"

CHAPTER 32

Unfortunately, I had few options. To use my credit card to pay for another room would only lead the attackers to me again.

Staying in the suite where the Elliotts were already registered would save me money while also avoiding the finicky Muslim rules about propriety; no extra bed needed to be ordered up, because the ladies each had their own rooms and I'd be sleeping on the couch. What the management didn't know, wouldn't hurt them.

They were ecstatic to have male companionship. Sitting on either side of me in their living room, they seemed to have years of chatter stored up. Whenever the conversation worked its way around to my teaching job, I deflected to another question about them. The night wore on until I could barely keep my eyes open.

"We had better leave Mr. McKenna to his sleep," said Bella. "We all have a big day tomorrow."

That woke me up. "We do?"

"Oh yes," she said. "We've booked a birdwatching tour and a ride on a camel."

"On a camel..." I looked at the two women. "You're not serious."

Sophie nodded with great enthusiasm.

"You should join us," insisted Bella. "Our tour guide would surely agree to add another--"

"I'm sorry, but no. No birds, and definitely no camel in my future." I shook my head, trying to dislodge the image of it. "Who's your guide anyway, that kid, Hassan?"

That got a laugh. "Of course not," said Bella. "A very nice man who works for a reputable tour company. Their reviews are quite good. You should really think about joining us."

Blaming it on my credit card snafu, I left them no recourse but to accept my refusal.

Their bedrooms were on opposite sides of what they called the sitting room. My billet was there, in the middle of the two bedrooms, on a soft leather couch that I sunk into. With the addition of a blanket, I had no trouble falling asleep and staying asleep. Even as I heard the two sisters scurrying around at sunrise to get ready, I barely stirred. Finally, they left for their camel trip and I snored through two more hours before getting up.

I pulled on my kaftan and skullcap, then slipped into my sandals before heading out to find some breakfast. In the back of my mind was the warehouse in Safi that had appeared on the phone subscriber list. Aside from Natalia Laskin and whoever else was in the SUV, the Safi warehouse was the only investigative lead at my disposal. It was a good two hours away, however, and I'd still have to figure out transportation while at the same time remaining off the grid.

Avoiding the snake charmer in the Jemaa el-Fnaa marketplace, I ventured down a side alley. A smiling man stirring a steaming brew caught my attention, and I motioned him that I wanted some. He frowned quizzically at my outfit, then poured a bowl from a large galvanized can. The man tossed a round of flatbread onto the table, then he tore off a piece and dipped it into my bowl, apparently to demonstrate how it's supposed to be done. He ate it, and with a big grin, motioned for me to do the same.

The hardy liquid was amazing, perhaps the best gravy I had ever tasted.

"It's fava bean soup," came a youthful voice.

I turned to see the boy who had escorted me to the guesthouse when I first arrived. "Hassan," I said. "You want some?"

My intent was to buy the kid a bowl, but in an instant he had torn off a chunk of bread and was also dragging it though *my* soup. As it had now turned into a communal breakfast, I had no choice but to sit back and let the boy eat.

"By the way," I said, "how did you recognize me?"

Hassan tilted his head as he looked me over. Then he smiled and shook his head as if I was wearing a cheap Halloween costume.

"You don't want to ride camels with the ladies?" he asked.

"How do you know that they--"

His head tilted and he gave me the same look again. Apparently, not much happened in Marrakesh that Hassan didn't know about. Which made me wonder... "Do you know how I can get to Safi?"

"You drive 50 kilometers on Highway N7 and then turn left."

"I meant, I'd like to go there."

Instead of the head tilt, he frowned. "Nothing much to see in Safi, Mr. Danny. Mostly just pottery and fish."

"I need to visit Safi on business. Can you get someone to take me?"

He asked me to wait at the Bab Ksiba Gate while he arranged the excursion. It took me a while to find the gate, and we both arrived at the same time. Hassan's eager brown eyes peered up at me from beneath his ball cap.

"My cousin's uncle will drive you," Hassan said, guiding me by the hand to the little brown sedan parked under a palm. "He is a good driver, and also safe."

I pondered why his cousin's uncle wouldn't also be his uncle, or if the man might even be the boy's own father. Not that it mattered.

"Thank you, Hassan," I said, reaching into my pocket for some dirham coins.

Dropping them into the kid's extended hand, one-by-one to make it seem like there were more, I gave him a paternal wink.

He kept his hand out, and I reached beneath my shouldered bag to shake it.

Only then did he pull it back. "Use the right hand in Morocco," he reminded me. "And also, I'm going with you to Safi."

CHAPTER 33

"No way," I said to Hassan. "You will *not* be coming with me. It's too dangerous."

He flashed a crooked grin. "I thought you were sightseeing in Safi for your business. What could be so dangerous?"

I stared back at the boy, realizing I'd probably said too much.

He continued, "Safi is a small village. Many people don't speak English like they do in Marrakesh. I am familiar with the area, and I speak Arabic, French, and English."

Finally, I nodded and we got into his cousin's uncle's car.

"...and I don't charge too much for directions and translation," added Hassan.

I almost laughed at the little deal-maker.

Maybe his language skills would come in handy, particularly with our driver who only seemed to know one word of English: *cigarette*— which he smoked nonstop.

Outside of Marrakesh, the two-lane road droned beneath the car, mile after mile through a landscape devoid of vegetation. After an hour, cars and buses suddenly appeared, parked helter-skelter on the sandy roadside.

"Jamaa D'Mnabha," said Hassan, motioning toward the cluster. "Each week, a shopping mall."

I nodded as we passed a pen crammed with goats. A bit further on stood several dozen tents and a collection of market stalls. There were a few homes of tan brick, a pharmacy, and a mosque. The driver eyed us in his mirror, apparently wondering if I wanted to stop, but Hassan motioned for him to continue.

As the road jogged west toward the coast, the scene again turned dry and barren. Every now and then the low dunes gave way to a house or small village, but the arid landscape remained for another hour or so until we hit the outskirts of Safi.

What I had wrongly imagined to be a tiny fishing village was itself a bustling seaport city. It took the driver awhile to find the warehouse, which was on a dirt road near the docks at the north end of town. No signage on the street or on the building itself helped to confuse us, but after a couple of guttural grunts and a few more cigarettes, my driver came to a stop next to a rusted Audi with no tires.

The stone building had to be as old as the city itself. It was tall and narrow, with a corrugated tin roof and two tiny barred windows 20 feet from the ground. A set of double doors were padlocked at the front, but otherwise there appeared to be no other way in.

I listened at the door, and after hearing nothing I squatted to peer through a gap that was once a working keyhole. The interior was lit only by the slanting rays from the high windows as they illuminated the dirt floor in oblong rectangles. It was empty.

Feet rapidly approaching from behind startled me upright. Turning, I saw that it was only Hassan. He followed me around to the back of the building, his deep brown eyes peering around intently.

"You came all this way for a business?" he asked. "This building? It is the business?"

"Apparently so." I checked the address on the paper again and showed it to Hassan. He nodded, then with his hands on his hips, he stood surveying the surrounding area.

The solid rear wall bordered a dirt alley, and Hassan abruptly started down a small incline toward a cluster of homes. In front of one of them, an old man sat on a stool shaping clay on a wooden potter's wheel. The man stopped as we approached, then dipped his hands in a bucket of water and dried them.

He spoke French, as his thickly scarred eyes drifted skyward. Hassan nodded respectfully, though I knew the man couldn't see him. They conversed for a moment before Hassan turned back to me.

"He is a blind pottery craftsman," Hassan said.

I tilted my head. That much I had been able to put together.

"His name is Adil. I told him why you came here, and he asks what type of business you are in."

"Tell him real estate. Say that I am interested in buying the place."

After another exchange, Hassan said, "Adil says the owners are foreign men who don't come here often. Maybe a woman too."

"Where are they from? Can he tell the language?"

After another conversation Hassan shook his head. "He doesn't know. They are not French, Arabic, or American. He says the girls come to work once a month, and then after a few days they go."

I scratched my head. "How does Adil know all of this?"

Another brief exchange took place and Hassan said, "His ears are not scarred, just his eyes."

I asked a few more questions such as what kind of work was being done and how many girls there were, but the old man did not know. Hassan thanked him for me and we turned to leave.

Another thought came to mind. "Does he know when they will return?"

"Oui," said the man. *"Le milieu du mois."*

Hassan translated, "The middle of the month."

Adil mumbled something else as his potter's wheel began to spin again. Hassan listened to the man before turning back toward me. "They only stay for a few days, he said, then they go to their mother."

"Their mother?" My face twisted.

This was not the clear evidence I had hoped for. It made no sense and it did not fit into any organized crime scenario I had come up with. These girls could have been hired to clean fish for one of the seafood companies in the harbor. As for the foreign owners, Spain and Portugal were just across the Strait of Gibraltar. It was probably commonplace for their residents to own businesses in Morocco and to travel back and forth.

The drive back to Marrakesh seemed longer and more boring. My mind kept going over the Safi warehouse, and what a disappointment it had been. The part about the mother confused me the most.

"Are you going to buy it?" asked Hassan, shaking me from my thoughts. "The building. Are you going to buy it?"

"No, I don't think so." I turned away and stared out the window.

The driver said something to Hassan—his first complete sentence since we got in the car this morning. The two of them conversed in a quick blur of words, none of which I understood. Finally, Hassan addressed me.

"My cousin's uncle asked me what the blind man said."

"And?"

"And, I told him what he said."

I shook my head. *Just when I thought this day couldn't get any more confusing, the kid starts talking in circles.*

The driver said something else, and Hassan shrugged.

"What?" I asked.

"Nothing."

"What did your uncle say?"

"He knows French better than me," said the boy. "He was just correcting me about something."

"Oh." I sat quietly for a few more minutes before it got the best of me. "What was it?" I asked.

"The French words for *the mother* are *le mere*."

"Okay, so?"

"They are sometimes confused with *le mer*," said Hassan.

"Which means what?"

"The sea."

CHAPTER 34

We rode in silence for another few miles while I thought about it. "Wait a minute," I finally said. "So, what the blind man was saying is that some girls are brought to the warehouse in the middle of the month, stay for a few days, and then go to the sea?"

Hassan shrugged. "I think, yes."

"That doesn't even make sense," I said. "Why would anyone trust the testimony of a blind man?"

"What is this *testimony*?" asked Hassan.

Before I could answer, the driver spoke and Hassan repeated in English. "The man's name, Adil. It means wise and honest."

I rolled my eyes and slumped back into my seat. We were passing the big, once-a-week shopping mall, which meant that we were only halfway to Marrakesh.

As we drove by the last of the parked buses, something in my peripheral view caught my attention. A black SUV was parked there, but we had passed too fast for me to see if it was occupied.

Slumping down further, I peeked over the seatback in time to see a swirl of dust as it pulled from the sandy roadside onto the highway behind us. *Son-of-a-bitch!*

I had to calm myself, realizing that not every black SUV carried highly trained hitmen who were out to kill me. And unless Hassan, or his cousin's uncle, or the blind man, had tipped them off...

My mind could go on like that, suspecting literally everyone, if I allowed it to. I forced myself to take a breath and close my eyes.

"Are you ill?" asked Hassan.

"No, just a little carsick."

He said something to the driver, and our car started to slow.

"Don't stop!" I yelled. "Just keep driving like nothing's wrong. Is the SUV still following us?"

The driver glanced in his mirror and Hassan started to turn around.

"Don't look," I said, screwing his head back to the front.

I caught the uncle and Hassan exchanging looks in the mirror, then the uncle said something.

"This is a busy road," said Hassan. "Many tourists hire big cars to take them around. Very common."

"Yeah, you're probably right," I agreed, yet remained hunkered down. "Let's just keep driving without looking back at them though, just in case."

"Just in case what?"

"Just in case."

Our driver fumbled with his cigarettes as he eyed the rearview mirror, but neither he nor Hassan spoke.

The SUV stayed behind us for another hour, all the way to the outskirts of Marrakesh. Since there were few places to turn off of the highway, I kept telling myself not to worry, that it was probably a completely normal occurrence.

"Don't return to Marrakesh," I said to the driver, as if he could understand me.

Hassan translated and the man's Arabic reply sounded angry, if there is any such difference.

"He said that you should have told him sooner. We are nearly at the gate."

"Doesn't matter," I said. "Tell him to just keep driving."

His uncle made a sudden and obvious turn, and I figured the maneuver would up the ante. If they were benign, the big black car would pull off and drop its passengers at the Medina's massive gates. Otherwise, they would reveal themselves by ramming our little sedan into a palm tree and then kill me.

They wouldn't want to do it right in the middle of town, I realized. Instead, they would follow us to a more remote spot before attacking.

"Are they still there?" I asked.

The uncle's saucer eyes seemed to take up the whole rearview mirror, and his stuttered Arabic response needed no translation. Fumbling his lit cigarette onto his lap, he fanned it to the floor and stomped it out.

"The car is still behind us," said Hassan, calmly. "Where do you want to go now?"

"Where does this road lead?" I asked.

"Algeria."

"No, closer. Any towns up ahead?"

Hassan nodded. "Forêt Toufliht. It is not a town, but a large park in the mountains."

"Okay, this is what I want you to do. When we get into the hills, tell your uncle to speed up gradually. Just get far enough ahead for the black car to lose sight of us. Then I'm going to jump out, and you two will keep driving to the park."

"Why would you do this, Mr. Danny?"

"Because those are bad men behind us, and I don't want you and your uncle to get hurt. If they catch up to you, if they question you, don't admit that I was ever in the car. Don't even admit that you know me. I've stayed down since they pulled up behind us, so they can't be sure I'm actually in here. Tell your uncle; no matter what they accuse you of, deny it. I think they'll eventually believe you."

"He is my cousin's uncle," said Hassan.

I sighed and rubbed my temples. "Got it. Tell him anyway."

The greenery around the city turned to brown, then disappeared altogether. Winding our way up the mountain, the wind kicked up and the road narrowed to one lane each way. I was waiting for the occasional clump of scrub brush behind which I could hide, but they were few and far between.

Hassan had briefed his *cousin's uncle*, and I felt the speed of our little car increasing.

"How far back are they?" I asked. "Can they see us?"

"Alan! Alan!" yelled the uncle.

Hassan turned. "He says to jump. Jump out now!"

CHAPTER 35

Thankfully, the uncle had slowed the little sedan just a bit as we rounded a bend in the road.

I launched myself out the door, feet first as if I could somehow hit the ground upright and running at the car's pace. Instead, my body spun and twisted like an Olympic diver in midair. Tumbling onto the sandy roadside, I felt the familiar pop of my bad knee.

As I lay writhing in the dirt, I heard the SUV whizz past. Prone in the desert sand in my tan kaftan, I must have blended into the terrain. In any case, they did not seem to notice me and continued after the sedan. That, of course, worried me for Hassan and his cousin's uncle, and I hoped they would stick to the script if confronted.

I was fearful of being seen on the road, so I turned inland several hundred yards and followed a dry wash created by ancient rainfalls. On the lookout for snakes, I limped slowly along the hard-packed sand in the general direction of Marrakesh.

My mind was still jumbled after my double gainer from the car, and it was difficult to think of anything but getting home. Not to Marrakesh, but home to the sanctity of my little sailboat in Alameda.

The trip to Morocco had been a disaster, and the excursion to Safi even worse. It had gotten me no closer to locating Natalia Laskin or to obtaining evidence to exonerate Aafreen. I had only accomplished being stalked by unknown assailants and blowing out my knee again.

This, I thought to myself. *This is exactly why I hate to travel.*

I was not making good time with my knee, and the afternoon sun was like a broiler. Dust was caked onto my face and had found its way between my lips and into the cracked skin around my eyes. Taking a seat on a dirt mound, I came to the realization that I couldn't walk all the way back to Marrakesh. Shielding my eyes from the sun, I gazed out toward where I thought the road would be. If I could make it back to the highway, I could take my chances avoiding the SUV and try to catch a ride with a passing tour bus.

A wild sound suddenly filled the air, startling me to my feet. It was the angry grunt of a vicious animal. Again came the bleating sound, something like a fight between a moose and a walrus.

I was ready to run as best I could or defend myself with a stick, when over the rise I saw its head. Then came the hump of its back, followed by a dozen of its friends—all with riders on them.

"Yoo-hoo, Mr. McKenna, is that you?"

I couldn't imagine how the Elliott sisters recognized me with all the dirt on my face, yet somehow they did. The chance meeting in the middle of the desert was beyond uncanny.

The camel train stopped next to me—their guide and five other couples. The guide began speaking to me in his native tongue, which got a big chuckle from the sisters.

"He is an American teacher," said Bella, "the man I told you about. He didn't want to join our excursion today."

"You missed a wonderful tour of Forêt Toufliht Park," said Sophie.

The other couples nodded. "Lovely birds," said one man. "Desert larks, finches, and even a Northern bald ibis."

"Swell. Sorry I missed it." I used the sleeve of my kaftan to wipe dust from my eyes. "The car I hired broke down a few kilometers up the highway, and I decided to walk. Please tell me you people aren't riding camels all the way back to Marrakesh."

That generated another round of laughs. "Of course not," said the guide in a thickly accented voice. "Our caravan ends at Touama, just there over the hill. You may ride with me, if you like."

Under any other circumstances, I wouldn't be caught dead on the back of a camel. But these weren't other circumstances. My knee was shot, my face was cracked and blistered, and somewhere out there were deadly predators in a black SUV.

I heard myself thanking the man, and the next thing I knew I was on the hump of a camel with my arms wrapped around a pungent man named Waleed.

Touama was a dusty little place with streets made of packed clay. The center of town was little more than a few *souks* and a well that served as a gathering place for the local tour industry and a watering hole for the animals.

A rumbling sound echoed off the stone buildings, and our caravan paused as a black SUV sped past. This time I was able to see the occupants—two men. The passenger had a map spread across the dashboard and was alternately consulting with it and then pointing the way for the driver.

They clearly hadn't found the person they had hoped to find, which I was fairly certain was me. It struck me that their search was for an American tourist, not a dust-covered Bedouin on a camel.

The car wove a figure eight around the small central square, stopping a few times, and then continued back toward the highway. Seeing them was both good and bad. It gave me hope that Hassan and the uncle had been spared, but it also meant that the men in the SUV were determined to continue their search for me.

Unbeknown to me was that the Elliott's tour also included an authentic Moroccan dinner. Insisting I join them as their guest, the two women sat on either side of me at an extremely low table. Now, besides trying to find a comfortable position for my throbbing leg, my hips were also killing me from the ride there. The dinner, of course, was a no-brainer. I was parched, hungry, and running low on dirham. A free meal was definitely the way to go.

That is, until Waleed stood and asked for everyone's attention. "Excuse me, ladies and gentlemen, I have something important to share with you."

I had a fleeting hope that belly dancers were going to be our entertainment for the night, but it was not to be.

"I was just warned," he continued, "that a dangerous person has been seen in our province. He is a Caucasian man, possibly from the United States or Great Britain. I will pass around a photograph of him."

When the picture got to us, an audible gasp emitted from the sisters, and I immediately felt them inching away on their cushions. Reaching beneath the table, I grabbed each of them by the hand and squeezed just enough to ensure their silent obedience.

"If you know where this person is," Waleed held up a business card, "you must report it to the Office of Special Investigations."

CHAPTER 36

In my mind, silence fell over the group as they all turned to stare at me. The reality was that nobody except the Elliotts recognized my face in the photograph. They had been the only ones to see me prior to my costume and dirt encrusted façade, and now I could actually feel the sisters' eyes boring into me from each side.

Releasing their sweaty little hands, I leaned closer to Bella—the more talkative, decision-maker of the two. "I know what you must be thinking, but just give me a chance to explain."

My free dinner stuck like a blob in the middle of my throat, and what I really needed was a strong drink to wash it down. But this being a Muslim country, the table was wholly devoid of liquor.

The sisters didn't appear to be enjoying their time any more than me. Sophie sat as rigid as a hostage with a gun in her side, and Bella seemed impatient to hear whatever extenuating excuse I had.

Office of Special Investigations, I thought. What kind of bullshit is that? The men in the SUVs weren't Moroccan government, in fact the more I thought about it, they weren't official at all. Their so-called special investigation was probably me.

I leaned into Bella. "You need to get that phone number for me, the one on the card they gave Waleed."

Her brow wrinkled into a deep frown. "My sister and I refuse to take part in whatever illegal activity you are involved in."

"I'll explain everything as soon as we get back to our room, but right now I need you to get--"

"*Our* room?" She recoiled. "I'm afraid that our offer of lodging has been rescinded, Mister McKenna. We will expect you to remove your personal belongings immediately upon our return."

Sophie nodded her emphatic agreement.

Just then our hosts brought out some kind of cookies and sugared peanuts. As they poured us each mint tea, someone began playing musical instruments. I could barely hear my own voice over the pounding conga, clashing tambourine, and the zippy fiddle. When the music finally stopped, our tour group settled into an assortment of quiet sidebars.

The entertainment had given me time to decide how to play it with the two women. I knew I couldn't let them out of my sight until I had a chance to win them back.

Hanging my head, I put on my best hurt expression. "Fine, just go ahead and turn me in then."

The sisters looked at each other in confusion.

"I'm serious," I said. "If after everything we've been through you still don't trust me, then, yeah, go ahead and report me."

Now they really looked confused. "What have we been through?"

I closed my eyes. Pinching the bridge of my nose, I let out a sigh. "I didn't want to have to tell you ladies, because I was trying to protect you." Lowering my voice for effect, I continued, "But that car that rammed us when we first got here wasn't a highway robbery attempt."

"It wasn't?" Sophie asked, meekly.

I shook my head.

"Then what was it?" demanded Bella.

I stole a brief glance around at our fellow travelers. "Come with me," I said, unwedging myself from our painfully low table.

The Elliott sisters followed me out of our courtyard to an open area surrounding the town's well. It was quiet, and it was out of earshot. The night was warm with just enough of a breeze to keep it from being uncomfortable. With a thick blanket of stars overhead, some sort of prayer echoed from the top of the mosque.

Bella turned to Sophie as they bumbled over the uneven ground. "That's the muezzin, calling out the adhan."

For the first time, Sophie didn't respond. The *I don't give a shit* expression on her face pretty much said it all.

Stepping into a small pile of walnut sized camel dung, I stopped to scrape my sandal against a stone while considering my pitch to the women.

"I strongly suspect the people who rammed our taxi on the way from the train station were foreign assassins," I said.

The sisters gasped.

"Russian Mafia, most likely." I paused, trying to decide how much they really needed to know. Just enough to maintain their loyalty and more importantly their silence, I figured.

"They probably followed me here from home," I said.

Sophie started to say something but Bella cut her off. "Why?" Bella asked. "Why would the Russian Mafia be following you?"

"It's kind of a long story." I checked to make sure we were alone. "But the short version is that I've been looking for some information that they don't want me to find."

Bella's eyes widened. "Are you saying they came here to kill you?"

My expression turned somber as I nodded. "That's why I didn't want you to say anything to Waleed. You can't tell anybody."

Sophie tentatively raised her hand as if to ask a question. "You declined an invitation to join us today, and then we find you wandering in the desert dressed as a nomad. Now you tell us you've uncovered information about the Russian Mafia and that they're trying to kill you. I just have one question for you, Mr. McKenna: What subject is it that you teach?"

"I'm not a teacher."

The sisters exchanged looks, and then Bella started, "But you told us that--"

"I know what I told you." I glanced around again. "I'm actually a private investigator, and I'm here working a case."

Bella shook her head at her sister. "How do we know this isn't all just pork pies?"

Never having heard the term, I took it to mean that she didn't believe me. "Here," I said, flipping open my wallet to show them my PI identification and my SFPD retiree card.

Bella stepped back to contrast the photo with my real face while Sophie said nothing. "I need to speak privately with my sister," said Bella.

The women stepped away, and I watched their discussion from a distance. Unable to hear the debate, I could only try to interpret their animated gestures—mostly from Bella. The fact that she had been the more dominant of the two, I imagined her *don't trust him* argument would ultimately win the day.

After several minutes, they turned and started toward me. As I waited anxiously for their verdict, I watched through the archway into the courtyard where our birdwatching group stood and began to gather their things.

Headlights illuminated us as a vehicle turned off of the highway and approached on the road. I assumed that it was a resident of the village or perhaps a taxi, but as it drew nearer I saw it more clearly.

Turning away from the SUV's headlights, I hustled over to the Elliott sisters and wedged myself between them.

Throwing an arm over each of the women's shoulders, I pleaded, "Quickly! Help me into the tour bus."

It was more like a 12-seater van, and they walked me all the way to the back seat. My hope was that it would appear to an observer that I was traveling with the women and had taken ill.

I'd wanted to coach them on what to say, but the sisters got out of the van and joined the rest of the group. Having no idea what they had decided regarding my trustworthiness, I felt trapped.

The black SUV came to a stop on one side of our van as the tour group was approaching from the other. My fate was in their hands.

Ducking down, I could no longer see what was happening outside. Voices carried on the night air sounded French, which was somewhat confusing to me. The tourists had all been English speaking, and I had only heard Waleed speak an Arabic dialect.

More muffled conversation trickled through the open windows, and now it was in English. It sounded as if the men in the SUV were questioning the Elliotts about me.

"That was a member of our tour group," said Bella. "Apparently, the Méchoui lamb didn't set well on his tummy. He'll be fine."

The two men talked among themselves in French, and it was a relief to hear them thanking the ladies as if they were about to leave. I heard a car door opening and my rapid pulse began to subside.

"How many are you?" asked one of the men.

"Twelve," answered Waleed.

There was a long pause, which I hoped didn't mean that he was counting couples or camels—none of which would equal 13.

"But there are 12 of you here," said the man. "If that is so, who is the person on the tour bus?"

"We came across him on our way back from Forêt Toufliht," said Waleed.

The sisters took turns trying to sound convincing.

"He's a teacher."

"We met him on the train to Marrakesh."

The good news was that it sounded as if I had successfully won over the Elliotts; they were actually trying to help me. The bad news was that it hadn't helped.

Rapidly approaching footsteps across the gravel told me that the assassins who had followed me all the way from the United States had finally caught up with me.

Stuffed into the back of the van as I was, there were no windows wide enough for me to climb through. I was trapped there like a pig in a slaughterhouse, and there was no way out.

CHAPTER 37

"Sir! Please step out of the van."

Many thoughts filled my head at that moment: surprise that the men did not sound Russian, dread that I'd end up a rotting corpse in the desert no matter where they were from, and much farther down the line was the notion that I might still be able to get away. In the end, I realized that there wasn't much I could do but comply.

With an assassin on each side, I did the dead man walk past the Elliott sisters and through the gauntlet of their tour group. One man used his phone to video me, which from the look on his face was even more exciting than the Northern bald ibis.

Seated in the back with one of the men next to me, our SUV took off in a whirlwind of sand and dust. Strangely, we whizzed past dozens of remote spots where they could have easily put a bullet in my head and tossed me out. In addition, we were not heading in the direction of the sparsely inhabited hills, but rather toward Marrakesh.

Their ethnicity wasn't clear. The driver's skin was light brown, and he had green eyes that occasionally glanced at me and his partner in the mirror. The man next to me was lighter skinned, but he had dark eyes and tightly cropped black hair.

It took me several minutes to get up the nerve, and finally I made an inquiry. "Can I ask who you guys are?"

"Police Special Investigations," said the guy next to me. "We are taking you to a more suitable place to ask some questions."

"I'll bet you are." I sneered at my captors.

But as the lights of the city walls broke through the night, I began to second guess myself. Maybe I'd been wrong about them. Maybe these guys *weren't* here to kill me.

We passed by the Medina's main gate and followed along the city's outer wall. They finally stopped in front of an odd-looking pink building with big bold letters: La préfecture de police de Marrakech.

"Wait a minute," I said. "You guys really are cops?"

Instead of answering, which I guess they already had, they led me into the building and up to the third floor. *Special Investigations* was actually a real thing in Marrakesh, according to the sign next to the office, which made me even more eager to find out what they wanted with me.

They sat me in a chair in the middle of an office. All around me were uniformed police, going about their business as if I wasn't there. A large man in a suit sat at the desk across from me, talking on the phone in what sounded like French. Like the others, he ignored me.

Waiting patiently, I began to think a few steps ahead to the possibility that I would be jailed. Although I was not in handcuffs and they had not told me I was under arrest, it was an all too familiar scenario that I really wanted to avoid if possible. I had once spent a night in the San Francisco County Jail, and another miserable night in the Tijuana jail. More recent and even more deplorable was the night I spent in a Bangkok prison.

By the time the big fella ended his phone call, I would have told him just about anything to keep me a free man.

"I am Sous-Lieutenant Omar Khatabi," he said in a friendly tone.

"Danny McKenna." Being on the subordinate side of the desk, I decided not to attempt a handshake.

Khatabi waited for me to say more. When I didn't, he continued. "The reason you were asked to accompany my men here is because you were seen lurking in the city of Safi."

"Lurking..." I repeated back. "Doesn't that imply lying in wait with some unlawful intent?"

He smiled as he lit a cigar. "Perhaps lurking was too strong a term. Loitering then."

I watched him for a few moments. "Why am I really here?"

Khatabi blew a sideways stream of smoke. "Mr. McKenna, I'd like you to explain your interest in a warehouse in Safi this morning."

"I was interested in buying it and wondered if it was for sale."

The sous-lieutenant shook his head. "When a person lies, it only makes them appear more guilty. Now, I would like the truth."

I didn't want to piss him off, mostly because I didn't want to add a Moroccan jail to my list. And although I found it validating that my visit to the Safi warehouse had somehow struck a nerve, I was not in the best position to find out what he knew about the place.

"I'm a private investigator," I sighed. "The warehouse's address showed up during one of my cases."

"Then why did you lie to me?"

"Uh, let's see...because someone tried to run my taxi off the road when I arrived in Marrakesh? Because someone kicked in the door of my room the first night I was here? Because I'm in a foreign country and I have no idea who may be involved in this? Take your pick!"

With raised eyebrows, he sat back and lipped his cigar to the other side of his mouth. "Any other reason that you lied?" he finally said.

"Yes. The paperwork I submitted to your immigration people said that the purpose of my visit was tourism. I thought I'd be in trouble if I admitted I was here for work related reasons."

That brought a smile to Khatabi. He fanned a hand through the air, and I couldn't tell if it was for his cigar smoke or my unfounded fear of falsifying the immigration form.

"Maison El Idrissi?" he asked.

I shrugged and shook my head. It meant nothing to me.

"The boarding house in the Medina," he said. "The old woman who manages Maison El Idrissi reported a break-in two nights ago. She told us that her tenant had fled. That was you?"

I nodded, and it seemed to earn some credibility with the man.

"What's this about a car ramming?"

I told Khatabi the story of our bumper car ride from the train station, though I left the Elliott sisters out of it. They had been my lifeline, and I didn't need the police sniffing around them. He seemed perplexed that it had not been reported by the taxi driver, but moved past it as if reluctance to get involved was fairly common in Morocco.

"And you think it was the Moroccan police who did this?"

"Well, no, not exactly." I sat up straight and cleared my throat. "But the car that tried to run us off the road was similar to the car your officers drove tonight."

"It was a black Dacia Duster?"

I spread my hands, palms up. "How could I tell? It was very quick, and they were behind us."

"Tell me about this case of yours," he said.

I hesitated as I tried to think of a way of omitting Aafreen Soltani from the story. What I ended up with was a bastardization of my Bangkok case file.

"It was a missing person investigation," I said. "A young man who had crossed paths with some bad actors. They came after him, I happened to get a hold of one of their phones, and the address of the Safi warehouse had been stored in it. But the place was abandoned."

Khatabi carefully studied me. "Interesting. And the young man?"

"Oh, turns out he was in our government's witness protection. He's fine, so it's all good."

He continued to watch me in silence. There were some glaring holes in my story, and I wondered if he saw them. First and foremost was the question of why I would fly all the way to Morocco to check an address if the missing person had already been found. I would have also inquired more about the man whose phone had contained the warehouse address, and why people were after me. But Khatabi didn't ask about any of that, which was just fine with me.

"I have a question for you," I said. "How did you know I was at the warehouse, and how did you manage to get a photo of me there?"

The sous-lieutenant cocked his head as he weighed his answer. "We received a tip that Sahrawi women have been seen there, and we have officers watching the place. It's been over a week, and so far you're the only person they've seen."

I shook my head. "Sahrawi? What's that?"

"They inhabit our deserts in the Western Sahara. The situation is quite complicated, because they dispute our claims to the land upon which they live. These people are descended from Berbers, and the women, they tend to be vulnerable to abuse and exploitation."

"Huh." It was a lame reaction to something that was completely over my head. Even if North African politics had been taught in one of my classes, I'm pretty sure I would have slept through it.

"So, my officers took your photo and radioed ahead for others to stop you and find out who you are. The man and the boy who drove you there, followed your directions until they were threatened with arrest."

I nodded. "And your people are still watching the warehouse?"

"Not any longer." Khatabi shrugged. "It's the end of Ramadan and we are nearing the June Solstice holiday. I don't have the personnel to spare, especially to watch a vacant building in Safi."

"And about me?"

He looked at me appraisingly. "You can go, but stay away from the place. If we have to talk again, I assure you it won't be as pleasant."

I left the police building with the strange feeling that Khatabi had controlled the flow of information during our talk, and that more of his questions had been answered than mine. He had walked away from his investigation much easier than I would have expected, which made me wonder if I was being played.

It was 10:30 p.m., and I knew that the Elliott sisters had long since made it back to their rooms and were probably tucked into their beds by now. But since they were my only option for lodging, I started through the Medina toward their suite at the Riad Mwimbi Spa.

CHAPTER 38

The police station was farther from the town center than I'd thought, and I hadn't counted on the disorienting effects of the jumbled alleyways at night. By the time I located the Elliott's riad, it was nearly midnight and the front gate was locked.

I spent another night under the stars in my favorite palm tree grove just outside the Medina. It wasn't as pleasant as I remembered, and I barely slept. In the morning, I found an outdoor fountain, used it to splash the dirt off of my face, and wandered around the market hoping to run into the sisters.

The snake charmer and his assistant were setting up for their daily show. I watched, mesmerized by the ominous serpents, as one snake sat in the terrarium and the other poked his head out of a basket.

"I am happy to see that you are not in Nouvelle Prison."

I turned to find Hassan staring up at me. "No thanks to you and your sister's cousin," I said. "What did you tell the police?"

The boy shrugged. "They saw you at Safi, and they even had your picture. What could we say to deny it?"

I frowned as if I was angrier than I really was. "I should feed *you* to the snakes."

Hassan grinned. "If so, give me to the one in the basket."

"Why that one?"

"Its mouth is sewn," he said. "That is why the charmer doesn't ever get bit. The snake kept in the glass cage is the dangerous one. They feed him a rat, and the tourists watch his venomous bite. It tricks them into thinking the basket snake is just as dangerous and they pay more for the performance."

No longer impressed by the sham of a reptile show, I turned away. "I need to get something to eat."

The boy took me to a cart that served bread with chutney, eggs, and sweet tea. It was inexpensive and tasty, so instead of tipping Hassan, I treated him to a plate of his own. Afterwards, we parted ways and I found my way back to the Elliotts' place.

It was midmorning, and I figured the sisters were likely still at breakfast. In any case, they would have to pass through the front gate at some point during the day. So, I sat against the adjacent wall and waited for them.

The women did not return right away, and I worried that they had checked out of the spa. But since they were my only hope for lodging, I continued waiting as I thought about my situation. Then I waited some more.

The trip to the police station had been puzzling. Khatabi had never really made clear what he suspected me of being involved in. Were these Berber people antigovernment troublemakers? Did the cops think there was illegal immigration going on, or perhaps some sort of human trafficking? And from a police logistics perspective, it confused me that he had expended the resources surveilling the warehouse and following me through the desert, only to discard the whole investigation because of the holidays.

There was also the question of who had rammed our taxi on the way from the train station, and who had kicked in the door to my room. My read on Sous-Lieutenant Khatabi was that he was shrewd, but his reactions when I brought up the two incidents seemed sincere. To me, the attacks had felt more like what happened in Bangkok. Assuming that Natalia Laskin and her Russian Mob friends were responsible, got me wondering how they had found out where I was staying the night they broke into my room.

By late afternoon, the sun had dipped behind the city walls. Light left the narrow alley, rendering me a shadowy vagrant who other pedestrians did their best to avoid.

"Mr. McKenna," said Bella Elliott as she and her sister appeared at the other end of the path. "If that is indeed your real name."

"Yes, it is." I'd decided to play it as if nothing had ever happened. "I thought I'd missed you ladies. How was your day?"

They ignored my question. "And I suppose you've come for your things," she said. "We thought the police had arrested you."

I shook my head. "Of course not. We are investigating the same case and they wanted to compare notes. Obviously, since they let me go, I pose no threat to you or to anyone else."

"Might I ask what kind of case you're investigating?" she asked. "Aside from the Russians."

"I'm afraid that information is protected by the U.S. Private Investigations Act of 2002, besides, I wouldn't want to put you two lovely ladies in any danger."

The law I'd quoted was complete bullshit, and my line about *protecting the lovely ladies* was equally as phony. But it got me out of Bella's little interrogation. Sophie, on the other hand, still hadn't uttered anything besides *"Oh my,"* as she watched with her fingers pressed against her lips.

"If I could just impose on you both to let me stay one more night, I'd be most appreciative," I said with a remorseful expression. "Thing is, someone found out where I was staying the first night here, which is the real reason that I left the other place. They probably tracked my credit card, so now there's no way for me to--"

"Yes, yes, you can stay," said Bella.

Sophie did a little *tea and crumpets* clap, which is what I felt like doing as well. Alas, I had a place to sleep.

The bathroom in their suite had a deep wooden tub, which I filled with hot water. Next to it were an array of teabags, which turned out to be filled with scented bath herbs and leaves. They felt kind of grainy beneath my backside, but they made the water smell nice and it was good to soak off the grime of the past few days.

As my mind drifted to my present situation, I again fixated on how Laskin and her people knew they could find me at the guesthouse. Remembering that I had exchanged my dollars for Moroccan Dirham only minutes before registering there, I suddenly realized that I had paid the old lady in cash.

I quickly toweled off and slipped back into my indigenous attire.

"Ladies," I said, bursting into the living room. "I paid cash for my room that first night!"

Their stupefied faces stared back.

"That means, I wasn't tracked by my credit card. It had to be the kid, Hassan. He was the only one who knew where I was."

They exchanged looks.

"What?" I asked, looking back and forth between them.

"But we also knew," said Bella.

"Huh?"

"Remember?" said Sophie. "Hassan had marked it on our map."

Bella added, "We also heard him tell you the name of the place."

I dismissed it with an impatient hand. "I'm not worried about you two. I mean, you wouldn't have said anything. Right?"

They eyed one another again.

"Just to a man from a tour company." Bella suddenly seemed less sure of herself. "He helped set up our birdwatching trip."

"Was that Waleed?" I asked.

Sophie shook her head. "No, the man we told wasn't Moroccan. The young man's name was Viktor."

"Viktor," I repeated. "Short hair, slight build, soft features?"

"That's him," said Bella.

I rolled my eyes. "He was a she. Her real name is Natalia Laskin, and she's a highly-skilled assassin who's trying to kill me."

123

CHAPTER 39

"Okay, let me get this straight." I said, pacing the living room like Perry Mason. "This Viktor person asks if you know anybody else who might like to join the tour, and you give him my name?"

"He seemed quite legitimate," said Sophie.

"Uh-huh." I spun back to Bella. "And you also decided to tell this supposed tour guide where I was staying?"

"He was very persistent," she said. "He promised to give you an exceptional discount."

"Again, he's not a *he*, he's a *she!* And the only thing *she* wants to give me is a bullet between the eyes!"

I played out the timeline in my mind. Whatever database they had hacked when I left New York, had alerted Natalia Laskin that I was flying to Morocco. She and her crew had to have been waiting for me at Mohammed V Airport and then they followed me from Casablanca to Marrakesh. I realized that they were probably on the same train and must have seen me talking with the Elliotts. That was why Laskin had posed as a tour guide and targeted them in order to find me.

"What are you going to do?" Bella asked.

I thought for a minute. "Disinformation."

They both looked lost.

"The intelligence agencies all do it to each other," I said. "It works best when your opponent believes they've gotten over on you."

"Like Viktor," said Bella.

I nodded. "She thinks she can get to me through you, because you still believe she's a male tour guide, right?"

The ladies nodded their agreement.

"We want her to keep believing that. So, you pretend to go along with *Viktor the male tour guide,* and once the trap is set, we feed her false information."

Their eyes grew wide. "We?" said Sophie.

Her sister finished the thought. "Are you suggesting that Sophie and I actually engage in espionage on your behalf?"

I grimaced. "It sounds a lot worse the way you say it."

About to launch into a long-winded, off-the-cuff appeal, I caught a look in Sophie's expression that gave me pause. I had taken her wide eyes as trepidation, but now I wondered if it was something else. The quieter of the two, she was more difficult to read.

Sophie suddenly blurted, "That's rubbish!"

I wasn't sure if she was talking about my disinformation idea or her sister's affront to it.

"Excuse me?" said Bella.

"Mr. McKenna is obviously in trouble, and I for one am not going to turn my back on him." Sophie's pink face was set in defiance. "Clearly, he's not some kind of *nutter*. And he has obviously sorted out whatever issues he had with the police."

Bella's face was red too, but hers was from shock. "Maybe you should have a glass of sherry and lie down for a bit," she told Sophie. "You don't seem well."

Sophie shoved a hand toward her. "I've never felt better. As for Mr. McKenna, yes you may stay the night with us. In fact, you may stay as long as you please. And yes, we will help you." Then, turning to her sister she said, "We came here looking for an adventure of a lifetime, Bella, and I don't give a camel's arse about birdwatching or the history of the Bab Doukkala Gate. I have spent my entire adult life as a stay at home mother, and I waited hand and foot on Clive for almost 40 years. Now that my children are raised and Clive is gone, I am going to live *my* life the way *I* see fit. Starting with this vacation!"

Bella looked like *she* needed the sherry and a nap. Finally, she let out a long sigh. "Well then, I guess that's that."

Realizing that I was still dripping wet, I went back into the bathroom to towel my hair. When I returned, the sisters were deep in hushed conversation. Apparently, they had worked everything out between them because their discussion had transitioned to dinner plans.

"Where did you find Viktor, anyway?" I interrupted.

"He, I mean she, approached us near the marketplace," said Bella. "Should we run into him again, what do you want us to say?"

"Uh, I don't know. Maybe that you and your sister want to book a trip into the Atlas Mountains." Admittedly, I hadn't thought that far ahead, and what I'd come up with wasn't much of a disinformation campaign. My primary intent was to throw the scent in the opposite direction of Safi, which is where I planned to return.

The sisters invited me to dinner with them, but I couldn't risk showing my face around the Medina any more than necessary. I asked them to bring me back something to eat.

"...and some liquor if you can find it," I added. "With what I've been through, I can sure use it."

Bella frowned, but Sophie grinned. At least it was something.

They returned with chicken rfissa with lentils and fenugreek. It was enough for all of us, and the topper was the two bottles of wine they had bought.

"Fun fact," said Bella. "Morocco is the world's 35th largest wine producer. I turned to the index on the back of my map and Bob's your uncle—a wine shop just there in the Medina."

The three of us sat on the balcony, listening to the sounds of the city while we enjoyed our dinner. The wine was an unexpected bonus.

The orange sky darkened, and we stayed outside under a canopy of lights. It was after a few glasses that Sophie's face abruptly turned to distress.

"We forgot to tell Mr. McKenna about Viktor," she said to Bella.

"Oh yes, we saw him near the marketplace, and he asked if we had seen you."

The turmeric in the chicken rfissa started working itself up my throat, making it hard to swallow. "What did you tell him? Her."

They glanced at each other, and I wondered if they had blown the whole thing.

"We hadn't expected to see him, and it caught us off guard," said Bella. "We couldn't remember what we were supposed to tell him."

My shoulders dropped. "I've got to be honest with you ladies, this is kind of a buzzkill. Just tell me what you said."

I gazed over at the door, half expecting to see Laskin and her hit team crashing through at any second.

Sophie finally copped to what she'd told Viktor. "I said that you had shown up unexpectedly during our camel tour and were taken away by the police."

Chewing on that for a minute, I felt my anxiety begin to ease. "Telling her that was actually a pretty good idea," I said. "Laskin probably knew that much already, and hopefully it convinced her that you don't suspect anything."

Sophie flashed a satisfied smile at her sister.

The carefree night had taken on a more serious tone, and the wine was nearly gone anyway. We bid one another goodnight, and each of the sisters retreated into their respective rooms.

I lay stretched on the couch in my t-shirt and boxers, thinking in the darkness of the living room. Mulling over the facts as I knew them, it occurred to me that I had lost track of time since leaving New York.

The old blind man had told me that the young Berber women came to the Safi warehouse in the middle of each month. Suddenly, I found myself counting backwards trying to figure out when that was.

The impulse to return to Safi dominated my thoughts as I stared up at the ceiling fan, and the plot began to take on exaggerated importance. Despite Sous-Lieutenant Khatabi's ominous warning that I not return, I knew that the answer may be waiting for me inside that warehouse.

I tiptoed to Sophie's door hoping she was still awake. Wanting to ask her what today's date was, I listened at her door for a few seconds. It was quiet inside, so I tapped lightly.

"Sophie, It's me, Danny." I whispered. "Sorry to bother you, but I need to ask an important question."

"Come in, Mr. McKenna."

CHAPTER 40

The room was dark, lit only by the Medina's glimmer through the open window. The fan over Sophie's bed was also turning, and it gave me a negligible reference of her proximity to me.

"Do you know what today is?" I nervously asked.

From the bed, I heard her answer. "Your lucky day?"

The breath caught in my throat, and out of it came the sound of a slight gasp. "Please, Sophie...Ms. Elliott. I'm afraid there's been some sort of a misunderstanding. I just came to ask--"

"You don't have to ask," she said. "We're consenting adults, and we're both as free as jaybirds to do whatever we like."

I felt my wobbly legs backpedaling toward the door.

The bedroom light suddenly came on, illuminating Sophie's body like a searchlight. She was splayed on the bed like a giant gingerbread cookie, yet as earnestly as I tried, I was unable to look away.

Her sister's voice boomed from behind me, "What in the bloody hell? I should have known he was on the pull!"

"I just knocked on the door to ask a question," I said. "This is totally innocent. Not at all what it looks like." I turned back to Sophie who had now grabbed a robe. "I'm so sorry."

Bella was yelling so loudly that dogs began to bark in neighboring yards. "I'm absolutely gobsmacked!" she said to Sophie. "I come to check on you after your earlier outburst, and find you *starkers* on the bed with this punter standing over you. Had I been a minute later, he would have whipped out his *John Thomas*."

The sisters began arguing; Bella with wild accusations and Sophie doing her best to defend herself. "I don't have to run my plans by you as if I'm asking permission," she said.

I had to hand it to the old gal. She hadn't said two words until today, and now it seemed the floodgates had opened. Though her offer had been one I wasn't eager to accept, it did tickle my ego. So much that I wondered how much of Bella's anger stemmed from the fact that I was in her sister's room and not hers.

I realized that no matter who won their argument, I was still the odd man out. Bella will hate me for trying to sleep with Sophie, and Sophie will hate me for turning her down. I needed to repair this before I was back sleeping under the palms.

As I stood there in my boxers, I tried my best to calm the situation. "Please, ladies, we're all going to be kicked out of here if you don't quiet down. Now, as I said, this was all just a big misunderstanding. An unfortunate mistake. I only came to Sophie's room to ask her if she knew today's date."

"And why was that suddenly so important?" asked Bella.

"The case I'm investigating...it involves a warehouse in the town of Safi."

Bella glanced at her sister and then back to me. "Go on."

"I really didn't want to involve you ladies, but I guess there's no other way..."

A heavy knock on the door startled the three of us, and nobody said a word. We all looked at one another as the knocking turned to pounding.

Sophie whispered, "Do you think it's the hotel management?"

"Could be, but we can't take any chances." I glanced around, but there were no closets in which to hide. Then I spotted a wooden wardrobe against the wall. "Grab my things," I said to Bella.

I opened the wardrobe and eyed the interior dimensions. It would be a tight squeeze, even if Sophie's clothes hadn't been hanging in it.

Bella handed me my things, and I slipped back into my sandals and kaftan. "No matter who it is or what they say, don't let them in. And whatever you do, *don't* admit that I've been staying here with you."

The sisters nodded, but they had panic in their eyes. I gave it better than 50-50 odds that one or both of them would crack under pressure.

They left me alone in Sophie's bedroom, closing the door behind them. The pounding stopped and I heard voices conversing at the front door. The Elliotts were making excuses for the noise, though I couldn't make out anything else.

The voices became clearer, and I realized whoever had been at the door was now inside the suite.

It sounded like two men, and I had a fleeting prayer that it was the night manager and the concierge. That ended when I recognized a third voice as that of Natalia Laskin—formerly known as Elaina Teagan—more recently a tour guide named Viktor.

Managing to wedge myself into the wardrobe, I noticed that there were no knobs on the inside and I had to hold the door closed with my fingertips. The airless confines smelled musty, like a combination of old wood, mothballs, and Sophie's effusive perfume.

My bad knee was killing me, so I cracked the wardrobe door to unbend it. At the same time, I listened as best I could.

From the sound of things, Laskin was now Laskin, which was bad news for me. Dropping the façade of her alias meant she no longer found it necessary to conceal who she really was. Essentially exposing herself as an assassin meant she was nearing her endgame, which was getting rid of the one living loose end—me. And now, the Elliot sisters were probably on that same list.

The women were doing an admirable job of denying that I'd been there, but it didn't seem like their interrogators were buying it. And when Laskin commented on the three wine glasses on the tray, I knew the jig was up.

The door to Sophie's room flew open, and I heard purposeful footsteps marching across the floor.

I'd been in a similar situation on a boat once, so the terror of being shot up like Swiss cheese was not new to me.

My clutching fingers ached as I struggled to maintain my grip. Then I heard Laskin's voice.

"You might as well come out of the wardrobe, McKenna. There's nowhere for you to go."

I readjusted my grip and closed my eyes.

A sudden gush of air caused the window curtains to billow out as Laskin and her henchman yanked open the wardrobe.

Other than a slight squeak from Sophie, the room fell silent.

CHAPTER 41

"Where is he?" Laskin demanded.

With my legs wrapped around a drainpipe, I gripped the terrace railing and hung suspended in the shadows. I had fled the confines of Sophie's wardrobe at the last minute, through the double doors and onto the rooftop patio where we had moments earlier been sipping wine.

Clinging there in the darkness, the ground two floors below seemed like a treacherous drop—especially with my failing knee. Meanwhile, the debate above me seemed to rage on for an eternity—Laskin insisting that the sisters had harbored me in their room, and the Elliotts denying it.

They moved on to search Bella's room, giving me time to readjust my footing and get a better grip. A minute later, I heard them step onto the patio from Bella's room, presumably glancing around but obviously not spotting me hugging the pipe at the opposite end of the landing.

Finally, Laskin and her henchman left the suite and the sisters hustled out to help me up. Together, they hoisted me back over the railing like a sturgeon onto a boat.

"You were right," said Bella as I struggled to my feet. "Viktor was a woman."

I rolled my eyes, but didn't respond.

"And whatever it is you are investigating has certainly thrown her into a lather, because she seems quite intent on finding you."

No shit.

"You never did tell us," Sophie said as she clutched the lapels of her robe together. "What is the significance of today's date?"

They had both earned my trust, having stood tall against Laskin's onslaught of hot seat accusations. I owed it to them to come clean with the whole story.

Beginning with Laskin's plea to help find her missing brother and ending with tonight's raid of our hotel room, the tale took the better part of two hours. Dozens of spinoff questions about Aafreen Soltani, Leo Kingsbury, and Bangkok tourist sites I could recommend to them had slowed the story down, yet all of their inquiries were answered with honesty.

I even allowed them a peek behind the curtain of my disastrous marriage and my efforts to maintain a relationship with a teenage daughter. In the end, Bridget was viewed as an angel and I wasn't too far behind her. Doris was seen as a selfish wife who didn't know how good she had it. That, of course, was the only fallacy of my narrative, as I knew better than anyone how badly I had bungled my home life.

"So, who are these young women that come to the warehouse?" asked Sophie.

"The blind man called them Berbers," I said. "And he told me they arrive at the warehouse around the middle of each month."

Bella perked up as she thumbed through her tourist booklet. "The Berbers are native North Africans," she said, reading from the guide. "They call themselves *Amazigh*, which means free people."

It made sense; Khatabi had said something about a land dispute. That reminded me of another part of the conversation.

"The police lieutenant mentioned that young Berber women are often exploited or abused," I said.

Bella ran a finger down the page. "It says here that Berbers are considered lower class, primarily due to their unique dialects and their arid and unproductive land--"

"I need to know the date!" I said, cutting short her history lesson.

"Well!" Bella set down her handy-dandy guide. "If you must know, it's Monday, June 13th."

"Actually," said Sophie, glancing at her travel clock. "It's 2:13 a.m., Tuesday morning."

"The 14th," I said. "I need to get to Safi, today!"

Anxiety kept me awake the rest of the night. Some of it was due to my upcoming expedition back to Safi, and the rest was out of fear that Sophie might pop in at any time for a little midnight madness.

I was also concerned that the Elliotts could now be so invested in the case that they would want to join me. It was dangerous enough that Laskin suspected them of sheltering me, and I really didn't want to put the ladies in harm's way. As it was, I felt certain that Laskin's people would now be keeping an eye on the sisters.

Tossing and turning until 6:30 a.m., I finally decided to sneak out of the suite. Like the Elliotts, the rest of the riad was soundly sleeping. Shrouded in serene darkness, the stairs and hallways were lit only by a few fragrant candles. I found the kitchen, where two Moroccan women worked silently at a brick oven making *khobz*—an umbrella term for all types of bread. It smelled great, and though I wanted to stop for a quick bite, I continued past them to a service door.

Emerging into an unfamiliar alley, I realized I was beneath the window of our suite. I had avoided the main entrance in case Laskin and company had staked out the front of the place.

As I started down the alley, a light came on in the room above me. "Mr. McKenna!" Sophie called down from the window. "Where are you going at this early hour?"

I turned to quiet her, but it was too late.

Apparently, one of Laskin's men had been posted there, watching the back of the riad.

"Hey!" yelled a grizzly bear of a man with a voice to match.

Not about to stop and find out what he wanted, I took off running in the opposite direction. The man hollered again, but I couldn't tell if it was at me or if he was alerting a nearby partner.

At the end of the alley, I made a sharp yet cautious turn onto the larger road as I thanked God I had remembered to put on my brace.

I had a decent lead on the guy, but the maze of roadways left me worried that I'd end up running in circles around the riad. I needed to find my way out to the marketplace where I could either blend in or hide.

As I emerged from the tangle onto the open square, I heard a shot zing over my head. A few sellers had begun setting up, and they all stopped to gaze around in wonderment. When another gunshot came, they began to run; the rug maker, the tea seller, the snake charmer, and a handful of others, all fled in panic.

Using carts and tents as cover, I made my way to the far end of the marketplace. There had been no other gunshots, but I could hear my pursuer clanging and clashing through the *souks* behind me.

I was winded, my knee ached, and I felt myself slowing down. Then a sudden bolt of pain shot through me as my shin caught the corner of something hard. It caused me to stumble badly, yet I was able to remain upright.

Looking back as I limped away, I saw that I'd tripped over the snake charmer's terrarium. Terror swept through me as I imagined the venomous cobra slithering out of the upended enclosure. About to go back and right the thing before the serpent escaped, I heard another shot whistle past me and I changed my mind.

Somehow, I'd become tangled in ropes securing one of the tents. I had to back through a collection of hanging garments, wasting valuable time and allowing the man chasing me to close the distance between us.

Pushing aside a smelly sash, I stopped abruptly. The man from the alley stood before me, less than a dozen meters away. Up close, it was clear that he was not Moroccan.

The man's square face smiled slightly as he raised his pistol dead center at my chest. One of his meaty hands steadied the gun as the other clenched the grip. As the man's finger began to pull the trigger, I heard his thick Russian voice say, "Goodbye asshole."

CHAPTER 42

I stood waiting for the bullet's impact, and after a couple of seconds I opened one eye to find out what was taking so long.

With a face frozen in terror, the man's eyes stared downward at the upturned terrarium. The 30-inch cobra lay coiled on the ground in front of him, it's flared upper body wavering back and forth as it readied to strike. This one's mouth had not been stitched.

A frantic volley of gunshots followed, though none were aimed at me. One after the other they came, deafeningly loud and throwing chunks of dirt and snake guts into the air.

As the man emptied his entire magazine into the poor reptile, I reassessed my own situation. I knew that once he reloaded, it would be my guts splattered all over the marketplace.

Through the ringing gunshots, my ears had picked up a weak but familiar voice.

"Mr. Danny, this way!" It was Hassan, calling to me from a nearby metal worker's stall. "Come quickly!"

I ducked behind another cart and ran toward Hassan. Traversing a sea of a thousand brass teapots, I followed him through the souk and out the back into a meandering network of stalls, tents, and alleys that seemed endless.

The other end opened to a yard with over a dozen steaming tubs— apparently a textile dyeing facility. I had thought that Laskin and her man would have become lost and given up the search by this time, but it was not in my cards. There she was, in a ball cap and dark glasses, peering through the crowd of tourists. Hassan saw her too and grabbed the sleeve of my kaftan.

Suddenly, I was holding a wooden stirring rod that resembled a boat paddle. Following the boy's lead, I joined him at one of the colored tubs and began stirring. With our backs to Laskin, I hoped we would not stand out.

Although there were other workers tending to the vats of dye, several tourists began taking photos and videos of me and the boy. Perhaps it was because Hassan was the only kid there, but for whatever reason we had become the center of attention.

"Let's get out of here," I said.

Without glancing back at Laskin, me and Hassan took off again.

In my haste, I had fumbled the big stir stick and managed to splash a bright swath of cobalt blue dye across my tan gown. Not only did it ruin my only outfit, but it did nothing to help me blend in.

"The *hammam*," yelled Hassan. "Follow me!"

As I struggled to keep up, so did my mind. As far as I knew, the *hammam* was an Islamic holy person who led religious services in the mosque. I had my doubts about getting help there, not only because I was a westerner, but also that I now appeared to be dressed in an Israeli flag.

About to express my reservations to him, the fleet-footed Hassan motioned to an austere building ahead. "In here," he said.

I caught up to the boy at the front door, slowing him with a grip of his shoulder. Nearly out of breath, I asked, "This is a mosque?"

With a puzzled expression, he took my hand and led me inside. "This place is for local men only, so we will be safe here."

My reluctance intensified when I saw that most of the occupants of the supposed mosque were in various stages of undress.

Then, somewhere between stripping down to nature's own and getting into a hot bath full of guys, I realized that the word for holy man is *imam*, and that a *hammam* is a public bath.

You might think a grown man and a young boy going into a bathhouse hand-in-hand would raise some eyebrows. But my mind was back on the streets of San Francisco, and here, it was apparently commonplace and in no way improper.

"How much is this going to cost?" I asked Hassan.

"No cost. My cousin's brother works here."

"Of course he does." I shook my head, wondering why Hassan's cousin's brother wouldn't be Hassan's cousin as well.

Once I relaxed a little, I found the experience to be quite soothing. The large bath was surrounded by smaller dipping pools of differing temperatures. Side rooms with wide openings, some partly covered by curtains, concealed massage tables upon which men were being elbowed, slapped, and kneaded. There were no women anywhere, and everything seemed to be on the up and up.

Though I don't usually go in for that sort of thing, I made a mental note to try out one of those tables in the future—should I ever again find myself in a Marrakesh hammam.

Between the two of us, me and Hassan decided that my stained kaftan was permanently out of service. He left with a handful of my dirham, to buy me some suitable clothes and also check the area for Laskin. After 20 minutes he returned with black nylon warmups—zippered jacket and drawstring pants with white striping on the legs.

I strolled out of the *hammam* looking like a member of the Moroccan track team, though probably more of a shot-putter than a sprinter.

Hassan had reported seeing a flurry of police activity at the Jemaa el-Fnaa, but no sign of Laskin or her men. We cautiously made our way toward one of the southern gates, thus avoiding the marketplace.

As we neared Bab Ksiba gate, my eyes were drawn to a van parked just outside. It was the same company van that had driven the Elliotts to their camel tour.

"Mr. McKenna, is that you?"

Bella's shrill voice took the air out of me and sent a shiver up my back. I turned to find the sisters standing in a small queue waiting for the *Palais Royal* tour. After a brief conversation that covered my early departure, my new clothes, and their sightseeing plans, I gave them the *see-ya-later* salute.

Sophie stepped out of line and called after me. Whatever she had to say, she did not want her sister to hear. Hassan picked up on it and waited just ahead of me under the gate entrance.

"Mr. McKenna," she said, her face only inches from mine. "There was a row in the market this morning. Apparently, one of the snakes got loose and had to be put down. Evidently, there was gunplay."

I nodded, not wanting to get into it.

After glancing back at her sister, Sophie continued in a hushed tone. "Bella thinks otherwise, but I suspect you had something to do with what happened. I saw a man running after you in the alley this morning, and I believe you are in some sort of danger."

Of the two women, Sophie was definitely becoming my favorite. "Is there a question in there somewhere?" I asked.

"No, Mr. McKenna, just a statement."

I nodded for her to continue.

"I want to assist you," she said. "I want to help solve your case, whatever it is."

About to thank Sophie and decline her offer, I saw Laskin and her henchman approaching. They were still a good distance away, so I couldn't be sure if they had spotted me.

"Thanks anyway Sophie, but I gotta get the hell out of here."

As I started toward Hassan, I saw that he had already seen Laskin and was picking up speed toward the parking lot.

"The van!" I yelled. "Get to the van!"

Weaving around people and taxis, I prayed that the driver had left the keys in the ignition.

Hassan got to it first and jumped into the driver's seat. The kid's head barely reached above the dashboard, but that concern ebbed as Hassan turned the key and the engine started up.

"Can you drive?" I yelled, climbing into the passenger seat.

He nodded and shrugged at the same time, which didn't instill much confidence. My driver was fourteen, and we were stealing a tour bus. It was a toss-up which of the two problems concerned me more.

I gazed out across the lot, expecting to see Laskin and probably hear more gunshots. Instead, I saw Sophie.

With arms pumping and bosoms bouncing wildly, she loped out of the gate and toward the van.

What the hell?

Then, out came Bella. In a quasi-gallop, she followed her sister's path about 20 meters behind.

Son-of-a-bitch!

There was no way I was going to let them get into the van with us. But three-point-turns weren't Hassan's specialty, and the sisters made it to the open side door before I could register my protest.

"They're coming across the car park," wheezed Sophie.

When I glanced back, Laskin and her partner had cleared the gate. Having finally spotted us, they were also in hot pursuit—both of them with pistols in hand.

Oh shit!

CHAPTER 43

My mission, initially a force of one, had become a foursome; myself, two elderly English women, and a Moroccan boy who doubled as our driver. The auto theft notwithstanding, I still had a few things going for me. For one, I had managed to get out of Marrakesh alive. Having exited through the southern gate, I was pretty sure that I had secured a decent lead on Laskin. If her intent was to follow me, she would need to return to the main gate a half mile away for their black SUV. By then, I'd be well out of the area.

"Where would you like to go today?" asked Hassan, as if he was an actual tour bus driver.

The sisters were sprawled on the seats behind me, gasping for breath as they fanned themselves.

I was about to answer Hassan when the back window blew out, showering all of us in a torrent of shattered glass.

"Get down!" I yelled, trying my best to dive over the seat and shield the women.

Two additional cracks rang out, followed by more shattered glass from my passenger window. I turned to check Hassan, but could no longer see him. The driverless van bounded out of the lot and veered across the road in a wild arc.

The Elliotts screamed and hugged each other, but did not appear to be hurt. Climbing back onto my seat up front, I now saw Hassan slumped below the dashboard.

I grabbed for him. "Hassan! Are you all right? Were you hit?"

"Yes, and no." I am all right, and no, I was not hit. He sat up and took the wheel again.

"You were on the floor, and I thought--"

"You said to get down." The boy's deep brown eyes stared back at me, then a frown formed as he looked toward my seat. "There's blood, Mr. Danny."

The women had quieted down and were now cautiously leaning over the seatback to take a look. "Good heavens," said Bella, "you've been shot."

I'd had so many aches and pains that I honestly felt nothing but a slight burning in my thigh. The blood on my seat wasn't excessive, so I was fairly certain the bullet hadn't struck a blood vessel. It also helped me to pinpoint where I'd been hit.

Reaching down the front of my warmups, I gingerly felt around the jewels for an exit wound. Thankfully, the bullet had stayed inside and had not caused any additional damage.

"Head west," I told Hassan. "I have to get to Safi."

The boy swallowed hard, but said nothing. At that point, I didn't really care about his skills behind the wheel. He had gotten us out of the parking lot under a barrage of gunfire, so as far as I was concerned, he'd passed my driver's test.

Bella leaned up. "But Mr. McKenna, you're injured. Climb back here so we can have a look."

I wanted to keep up the stoicism, but my hip was starting to ache pretty good. Reclining my seat, I was able to slide back to the second row. With a sister on either side of me, it was a tight fit—made all the more difficult by having to rotate myself facing away from them.

Suddenly, my warmups were down around my ankles as my bare ass was being unveiled like a buttermilk biscuit fresh from the oven. A really big buttermilk biscuit.

"You've been shot in the bum," said Bella. "Does it hurt?"

Sophie took her sister's place inspecting in close detail. "Of course it hurts. We'll need to get you to a doctor."

"No doctor," I said. "Hassan can drop me at Safi, and I'll take it from there."

They didn't think I noticed them all exchange looks of trepidation. We were on the main highway, and the hot air whistled through the van's missing windows as we picked up speed.

The ladies found a Kleenex box under the seat and did their best to dress the wound. Trying to recreate how it happened, I surmised that it was the last shot that got me as I was climbing over the seat to help the Elliotts.

"Do you think they will follow us?" Hassan asked quietly.

I shook my head. "They have no idea that I even know about the Safi warehouse. I think we're okay."

I'd been wrong before, but I figured why scare the kid? Like the Elliotts, he had been through enough already because of me.

My plan was to have them drop me off, while they returned to Marrakesh. For all I cared, they could blame me for taking the van. My plan wasn't much of a long game, as I was putting all my eggs in the warehouse basket. If I mistimed my arrival or if it turned out to be a dry hole, I knew I'd be pretty well screwed. Even if I timed it right and found the place full of Berber women, I'd still have no idea what it meant.

Coming out of my thought fog, I saw that we were passing the once-a-week shopping mall. In contrast with the last time I saw it, the marketplace was completely empty.

Still, an unsettling weight pressed into me as I scanned the empty souks and deserted animal pens. Peering back through what was once our rear window, I expected to see a black SUV right on our tail. But thankfully, behind us was only a barren ribbon that snaked through seemingly endless sand drifts.

As the seaside town of Safi came into view, I tried to reassure myself. The police had abandoned their warehouse surveillance, and Laskin's Russian Mob had no way to know I was there. Better still, they were unaware that I even knew about the place. In theory, it all meant that I could safely investigate to my heart's content.

It turned out fortuitous that Hassan had come along, since I'd never have found my way to the warehouse on my own. Meanwhile, the Elliott sisters sunk deeper into their seats as the area outside turned from a bustling commercial port to a district full of empty buildings covered in graffiti. You could literally feel the eyes of a hundred people watching as we wound our way through the dusty neighborhood.

The van surged up a small incline and then stopped. Parked in front of the old building, the four of us listened intently for anything that portended danger. Only the sound of dry, salty wind whistling through the shattered windows was heard.

"Okay my friends," I said with forced determination, "I suppose this is goodbye."

From beneath the brim of his ball cap, Hassan looked from me to the blood on my seat and back again.

Bella extended her hand, ready to shake and be done with me. But Sophie, who had come into her own, sat back in defiance—arms crossed and face set in a frown.

"What now?" she asked.

"Well, now Hassan will drive you and Bella back to Marrakesh."

"And what of you?" she asked. "What will you do now?"

"No worries, I can manage."

"You've already nicked a tour bus from the car park in Marrakesh, where Russian criminals opened fire on you and made a hash out of your backside. Forgive me for saying so, but I think you'll manage better with us along to help."

"We've already come this far," said Bella in quasi-agreement.

"I'm afraid not, ladies. Though I sincerely appreciate your offer, I'm not going to put the three of you in any more danger."

Sophie took a breath. Ready to counter, she stopped suddenly. "What was that noise?"

I told her that I'd heard nothing. Bella said the same.

Hassan scanned out the front toward the warehouse. "No, I heard it too. It sounded like hammering."

The four of us sat in silence, listening to the wind. And then we all heard the pounding.

I said, "It's coming from inside the warehouse."

CHAPTER 44

From outside, the warehouse appeared to be abandoned. No people, no cars, just a nondescript masonry building with a rusted padlock on a set of double doors.

I got out of the van and the clanging sound stopped.

"Stay in the car," I said, motioning with a hand. Then I walked the last 50 feet up the incline to the front of the warehouse.

With a dry throat and a heart pounding double-time in my chest, I inched toward the front doors. My hair trigger senses were off the charts; watching, listening, and sniffing the air for any sign of a trap or an ambush.

Sudden footsteps in the gravel behind me caused me to jump. Whirling around, I found Hassan, Bella, and Sophie trailing me—all crouched in a single file line.

"Christ on a crutch!" I said, gripping my chest.

The three of them stared back with various expressions.

"What does that mean?" asked Hassan.

"It means you scared the living shit out of me."

The kid's face looked even more confused.

Turning back, I listened at the door like before and then bent down to peer through the old keyhole. Unlike before, the view inside was blocked. I squinted into it, hoping to make out some contrasting object. And then the realization struck me that I was staring directly into someone's eye on the other side.

Jerking my head back, I released another string of curse words. The banging started back up, and I jumped again. The psychological effects of being shot were starting to get the better of me.

I squatted in front of the keyhole and forced myself to look into it once more. This time, my view was unobstructed. A dozen or so young women huddled on the other side, one holding a shoe like a hammer.

"There are girls," I said. "They're locked inside the building."

Even though the blind man had told me that young women paid monthly visits to the warehouse, I suppose I'd still had my doubts. Maybe I believed they were day workers, ferried into Safi to can fish or whatever. But having actually found them there, padlocked inside the building, with their young faces full of fear and despair, it was shocking.

"We need to bust off this lock," I said. "Hassan, see if you can find anything in the van!"

"Let's have a look," said Bella, nudging me out of the way. She gasped when her eye focused through the keyhole. "Good heavens! Some of them are mere children!"

By the time Sophie took her turn peering in and spewing her own indignant reactions, Hassan had returned with a tire iron. We tried to pry the lock but it was too thick. Then, recalling a similar barricade during a previous case, I slipped the rigid bar under the metal hinge piece and pried the whole thing off of the wooden door. The hasp fell to the dirt, screws and all, as the heavy door swung open.

Backlit by the sun, the four of us stood staring into the shadowed chamber. The girls were crouched in a cluster, shielding their eyes from the light. It told me that they had been there awhile, at least long enough for their vision to acclimate to the darkness.

I began talking to the young women, trying to calm and reassure them that we had come to help and that they were safe. The Elliott sisters chimed in, and suddenly there were three of us jabbering over one another.

"No, stop," said Hassan. "The girls do not understand anything you are saying. These Berbers speak *Tamazight*."

I pinched the bridge of my nose. "Okay, then tell them that we are here to help them and that we mean them no harm."

"I don't know any *Tamazight* words," he said.

"Why not?"

Hassan shrugged. "Same reason you don't."

I glanced at the Elliotts and they frowned back at me.

"Never mind," I said, turning back to Hassan.

He had walked past me into the building, and slowly approached the young women as he spoke to them.

When he stopped talking, I said, "I thought you don't speak their language."

"Languages in North Africa are more like dialects. I know a few Berber craftsmen who work in Marrakesh, and they have taught me some *Riffian* phrases. It is one of the Berber dialects. I asked the girls if any of them speak it."

A light skinned girl about the same age as Hassan stepped away from the others. In a voice barely loud enough to hear, she rattled on without taking a breath for at least a minute. Whatever language or dialect she spoke, Hassan appeared to pick up the gist of it. At the conclusion of her monologue, her blue eyes flashed and she stepped back with the others.

"They were brought here two days ago," said Hassan. "She says they were promised a day's work cleaning laundry at a local hospital. The girls were assured that their employer would treat them kindly and pay them well."

"Where are they from?" asked Bella.

Hassan asked a question, which the same young girl answered. "Borders don't mean anything to Berbers because they live mostly in the deserts. From what I can tell, they are not all from the same area. Some are probably from Algeria in the east, and some from northern Mauritania and Western Sahara."

"What about their parents?" asked Sophie.

"I think they are also from the same places," said Hassan.

"No, no," said Sophie. "That's not what I meant."

Before she could rephrase her question, the blue-eyed Berber girl spoke again.

When she was finished, Hassan turned to us. "She said that their captors were two men and a woman. Very white skin, not Moroccan and not from North Africa. They promised that they would return today with food and water."

"Laskin," I said. "And probably her gang of Russians. We need to get these girls out of here before they return."

Hassan motioned to the girls and they followed him out of the warehouse. The Elliotts assisted them into the van, mothering the girls and cooing as if it were a dialect of its own.

As Hassan started the van, I hobbled back and closed the front doors. Haphazardly, I reattached the lock to make it appear as they had left it.

A siren suddenly pierced the quiet of the industrial neighborhood. I whirled around to see a cloud of dust rising above a building across the way. The commotion was coming from the direction of where the main road transitions from pavement to dirt.

"Go!" I yelled to Hassan. "Get them to safety!"

I hadn't fully trusted Sous-Lieutenant Khatabi, and for all I knew he was being paid off by the kidnappers. At the very least, I had been warned not to return to Safi. To be found in the company of kidnap victims inside a stolen tour bus shot full of holes would undoubtedly raise a few questions and likely spell prison for me.

Hassan drove around the back of the warehouse, onto the narrow drive where we had first spoken to the blind man. It was in the opposite direction from the approaching police cars, and I hoped it would give the kid time to get the girls and the Elliotts out of the area.

Meanwhile, I unfastened the jury-rigged lock and slipped back inside the warehouse. It was dark and it smelled like piss, but it was the best I could do under the circumstances.

Peeking through the cracked door, I saw several police cars and a black SUV climbing up the road toward the warehouse. That forced me to move deeper into the building.

As my eyes began to adjust, I saw a sliver of light from a high window illuminating a wide pillar in the center of the building. It was a structural beam imbedded into the dirt floor.

Crouching behind it, I knelt down and used my hands to shovel soil onto my face and exposed arms. All I could do was pray that if someone looked inside the warehouse, it would appear empty.

It sounded as if the police cars had continued past the building in search of the van. I could tell that some of them had, but at least one car was now stopping in front of the doors—probably to check out the broken hasp and dangling lock.

Willing myself into paralysis, I tried to become one with the post in front of me. My eyes were tightly closed as I heard the door creak open. A few tedious seconds passed, during which I felt as if I'd blown an aneurysm, and then the door squeaked closed again. I might have thought it was a trap to get me to come out, but when I heard the car start up and take off with sirens blaring, I knew I had eluded the cops.

I waited in the dark a good five or ten minutes, just to be sure. And when I realized with certainty that I was still free as a bird, I got up and went to the door. With my eye screwed into the keyhole, I saw that the front of the warehouse was clear.

Allowing myself a huge sigh and a cleansing breath, I stepped out into the sunlight and quietness of the seafaring town. As warm as it was, a light breeze from the ocean made it bearable, even pleasant.

Stretching a little bit to assuage the worsening pain in my butt, I wondered if Hassan and the Elliotts had managed to get the harem to safety.

It was quiet. Almost too quiet, I thought. And then a bone chilling voice suddenly seemed to come out of nowhere.

"So, we meet again, Mr. McKenna."

I froze, not chancing a look at the person who had come up behind me. My eyes dropped to the tire iron at my feet, and I wondered how quickly I could arm myself with it.

"Don't even think about it," said the voice. "Now, get on your knees and keep your hands in the air. One wrong move and you're a dead man."

146

I remembered the broken-down Audi that I'd noticed on our first visit to Safi. It was still there, partially covered in the windswept sand, and I realized that they must have been hiding behind it.

Rapid footfalls sounded in the gravel behind me, and suddenly my whole world went dark.

CHAPTER 45

When I turned eight years old, my favorite birthday gift was an action game called Rock 'em Sock 'em Robots. The two plastic figures would trade punches until one of their heads popped off.

I found myself thinking about that game as I started to come to. My head felt as if someone had literally punched it off of my body. With no idea where I was, my eyes saw only darkness. Through brain haze, I detected a sound like a motorized lawnmower, and a smell that reminded me of San Francisco's Fisherman's Wharf. I must have blacked out again, because the next time I opened my eyes, the lawnmower had stopped.

Voices above me were in a foreign tongue, but I was too groggy to try and figure out which. From the bobbing motion, I sensed that I was aboard a boat and that the lawnmower sound had been the boat's engine. A fishing boat, judging by the smell.

I tried to rub my head, the back of which was still pounding, but realized my hands were tied behind me. The overhead hatch slid open and I stared up at three dark shapes. Blinded by the sun, I felt like the poor girls who'd been trapped in the warehouse.

"Boys, meet Danny McKenna," she said. "Now get him up here."

The two henchmen leaned into the hold and roughly lifted me out. A little wobbly, I stood facing my diminutive nemesis as they cut the ropes off of my wrists. Caressing the residual red welts, I regarded the woman for the first time since Thailand.

Elaina Teagan had captivated me with her emerald eyes and talcum fine skin when she came to me two months prior asking for help. Since then, the calculating bitch had tormented me and ruined the lives of people I cared about. Now, I saw only ugliness as I stared back at Natalia Laskin—assassin for the Russian Mob.

"What did you do with our...*workers*," she asked as her two thugs held me in place.

I tried to show confidence or indifference in the face of what I was certain would be my death.

Laskin nodded. "No matter. We have more of them."

"Where are you taking me?" I demanded. It was a question that I immediately regretted asking. The answer was never going to be *"home,"* or *"to a phone,"* or *"we're dropping you off at the nearest Howard Johnson's."* It was always going to be what it was.

"We will take you far enough from shore that nobody will hear the gunshot."

I didn't have to ask which gunshot.

"Unfortunately for you," she said, "we have arrived."

Looking back toward shore, I saw the town of Safi so distant that it could have fit on a postage stamp.

I wondered if anyone would even know where to look for me? The Elliott sisters, if they hadn't been caught by the police, would most likely return to England with exotic stories of their trip of a lifetime. My little friend Hassan would probably keep quiet about his role in the van theft and parking lot shooting. I would have done the same when I was a kid.

The more likely scenario was that Sous-Lieutenant Khatabi's men had caught up with the stolen van, arrested Hassan and the Elliotts, and turned the Berber women back over to the kidnap gang. I'd read about these human trafficking rings before, operating with impunity in countries where lack of resources, poverty, and bribes are fairly commonplace. I'd also seen it with my own eyes in Bangkok.

I glanced around the old trawler, hoping to avail myself to a last-minute advantage—a knife, a fishing gaff, a MedicAlert button, but the deck was clean.

"One question," I said with a touch of urgency. "How did I become such a threat to you?"

Laskin thought for a moment and then signaled her men to let me loose. I knew they were all armed, so it was only a temporary respite.

"Like the others, you got in the way. You should have dropped it after Bangkok. *Ended on a high note*, as they say."

"The others, meaning Leo Kingsbury, Aafreen Soltani, and Nate Leclaire?"

Laskin grinned. "Them, and others..."

"What others?"

"Not that it matters to you now." She looked around, then shared a smirk with her two bruisers. "We still have a couple of *loose ends* to tie up."

They all laughed.

Staring back at her, I felt the Irish boiling up inside of me.

Laskin tossed her head back. "Technology, my friend. We have imbedded ourselves into your intelligence systems, and we are alerted when someone is searching, who they're searching for, and where they're searching from."

I gave a defiant shrug. "Figured as much."

"That means your friend in Customs, and that woman in your office."

Brooks and Shanay were next on her hit list. "If you so much as touch either of them--"

"You'll do what?" She nodded to the henchmen. "Put a bullet in the fuck and toss him overboard."

As the man on my right removed a pistol from his waistband, Laskin crossed her arms as if this whole episode was as meaningless as taking out the trash.

I knew that I was as good as dead, but I didn't want to go down begging. "It was worth it," I said.

"What was worth it?"

I forced a smile. "At least you can say goodbye to your plan to kidnap those young girls. They are free now. That was worth it to me."

She looked at me ruefully. "They were but an acorn from a giant oak. You are going to die having no idea how big this really is."

I'd heard that metaphor somewhere before, but I had no memory of where. At the moment my mind was preparing to shut down for good, and I couldn't think of much else. No jokes came to mind, and no snappy remarks.

I felt the cold steel of the gun barrel pressed against my temple, and held my breath.

CHAPTER 46

"In the name of the Royal Moroccan Navy, I order you to drop your weapons. If you don't do so immediately, you will be shot."

The stern order came blasting over a loudspeaker. We all looked to the south as a white fantail cut through the waves, heralding the arrival of some kind of race boat. It carried the Moroccan flag, and that's all I cared about.

The command was followed by instructions in French and Arabic. Even without any understanding of the languages, they were the sweetest sounding words I'd ever heard.

"Can we outrun them?" asked one of the meatheads.

Laskin rolled her eyes. "In a fucking fishing boat? They are in an Interceptor—the fastest vessel in their fleet."

"Maybe we can make it to the--"

Laskin's head whipped around toward him. "Zatknis'!"

Whatever the word meant, it sure shut the dude up in a hurry.

Trying to steady my shaking knees, I was thankful I hadn't pissed myself. The closer the Navy got, the faster I regrew my balls.

Laskin stared me down as she and her boys laid their weapons on the deck, and I stared back.

"Don't get too cocky, McKenna. This is far from over," she said.

The sleek speedboat pulled alongside the trawler.

"It's over for you," I said.

She just smiled.

There were six seats in the Navy racer. The first four were empty—their gunmen, wearing white with blue, were lined up at the taffrail in position to board us. The two men in the rear seats wore solid blue uniforms, and I instantly recognized one as Sous-Lieutenant Khatabi.

My legs turned to spaghetti again as my worst fear had come true. They were all in this together, and Khatabi had come out to personally put the bullet in my head.

It all finally added up. It was why Laskin had hinted at a much bigger picture. She was the acorn and the *giant oak tree* was Khatabi. And it was why he had threatened that I should never return to the Safi warehouse; Khatabi wanted me out of the picture when his little slave girls arrived. Hell, he probably had the entire Moroccan Navy working for him.

Once his Navy men had collected the weapons and cleared the fishing boat, Khatabi and his underling came aboard. By then, Laskin and the two musclemen were in handcuffs along with the trawler's pilot—a grizzled old guy with white hair and mustache.

The Sous-Lieutenant passed by all of them and stood right in front of me. Lighting a cigar, he puffed a smoke ring in the air between us.

"I see you didn't take my advice," he said. "Now look what you've done."

"What have I done?" I used my hand to flap away the smoke. "Did I disrupt your slick little operation?"

"As a matter of fact, you did."

"By freeing those little girls from your rancid warehouse?" I said sarcastically. "Oh, I'm so sorry that now they're of no use to you."

"So am I." He took another puff and blew it sideways, his eyes still locked on mine. "Now what do we do?"

I took a breath and slowly let it out to settle my quivering voice. "Just get it over with," I said.

A funny look came over Khatabi's face. "Get what over with?"

"Just go ahead and kill me, and be done with it."

The man studied me for a moment with a blank expression. Then he turned to the other officers and motioned with his hand. They quickly muscled Laskin and her henchmen over the gangway onto the Navy boat, leaving the old fishing captain to go free. Apparently, he'd been paid to drive the boat, nothing more.

It confused me that he did not release Laskin and her goons. Also, Khatabi's face now looked more amused than angry. Not like a man who is about to kill another man.

"I think you misunderstand the situation you've put me in," he said calmly. "I have no intention of killing you."

My blood started flowing again. "No?"

"No," he said, gesturing toward shore. "My officers have been investigating these people for several weeks. We were waiting for the Russians to return to the warehouse while the Berber girls were there, so that we could follow them. We needed to identify how they were being moved, and where they were moved to after the warehouse. *That* was the 'slick operation' that you disrupted."

"But the girls were in danger."

"Not so much," he said. "We had plans to move in and free the girls once we knew how the Russians transported them. But that is all for nothing now."

"It's not for nothing," I said. "You still have Laskin in custody. "She's the big cheese of this network as far as I can tell, and she's also a wanted person."

"Natalia Laskin likely coordinates operations," he said "but she is not the head of the dragon. We believe that someone else at the top gives her the operational orders. We can charge Laskin and hold her for 24 to 36 hours, perhaps a bit longer if we can get the judge to agree, but now our one shot at catching her in the act has been blown and we have no real evidence against her if it goes to trial."

"But I know for a fact that she has framed innocent people," I said. "The woman blew up a federal safe house back in D.C., for Chrissake. And she's responsible for injuring and killing people there. That, I can prove."

"We have no extradition treaty with the United States," he said. "If we don't have a solid case against the woman here in Morocco, she will end up going free. It is as simple as that."

The solemn shake of his head made me feel like the biggest chump on earth. Nothing pisses off an investigator more than someone stepping all over their operation, and I had completely trampled on theirs. The cop in me wanted to make it right.

"Maybe I can help."

Khatabi gave me a painful grimace. "I think you've done quite enough already, Mr. McKenna. It is time for you to leave Morocco."

All the while, he kept glancing at the mottled bloodstain on my pants. The injury had stopped bleeding, but it still throbbed. I turned the stain away from him.

"It's nothing," I said. "Just scraped myself on a nail."

He shook his head in disbelief. "You really need to leave the…" Khatabi paused abruptly. Gazing over my shoulder, he stared further out to sea.

I turned and followed his line of sight to a large freighter anchored a few miles farther out. Our little fishing trawler had been on a direct path toward it when Laskin stopped to kill me.

"*Le mer,*" I said under my breath. "*The sea!* That's what the blind man was trying to tell us—the girls were taken out to the sea!"

Khatabi plucked the cigar out of his lips as his mind worked in tandem with mine. "The girls," he said. "They were supposed to be on this fishing boat."

I finished his thought. "Because they were going to be transferred onto the freighter. That freighter," I said, pointing to it.

The Sous-Lieutenant stared at his cigar as he rolled it between his fingers. "But why would they still be heading out there when there were no girls onboard this fishing boat?"

He was right. It didn't make sense. "There would be no reason for Laskin to hire the old sea captain to pilot the trawler all the way out to the big ship, unless..."

My brain was finally starting to fire on all cylinders. The phone records, the port cities, Laskin's oak tree metaphor—an implication of a much broader network. It was like the fog was being wiped from a window, and I could now see everything more clearly.

The dead Russian's phone log showed calls to or from harbor towns near larger international shipping ports. That's how they did it, I realized. The young girls were kidnapped and held in warehouses in small fishing villages. Then, like clockwork, they were ferried out to the transport ship as it left the larger container port nearby.

"There are other young girls being held on that freighter, I said."

CHAPTER 47

"How do you know this?" asked Khatabi. "How do you know there are other victims being held on the ship?"

"I don't have time to explain it all, but trust me…when you search it, you'll find more young girls."

He shook his head. "We're already a good ten miles offshore, and the ship is another three or four miles out. We can't board a sovereign vessel in international waters."

"What about your Navy guys?"

"Same thing," he said. "The country of Morocco is powerless to intervene once they are twelve nautical miles offshore."

"So that's it? You guys won't do anything?"

Pinching the remaining inch of his cigar, he flung it down and ground it into the deck with his boot. "I am sorry, but there is nothing we can do."

I had come so close to figuring it all out. I'd flown all the way across the world and risked my life. I'd been shot, and nearly thrown in jail. Now the whole investigation was slipping through my fingers like the desert sand.

I wondered what more I could do. Laskin and her enforcers were about to be set free, and a ship full of kidnapped girls was beyond the reach of law enforcement. The vessel will pull up anchor and leave, and the young women will be gone forever.

I'd learned that human trafficking was big business, but I was only one man against the Russian crime syndicate. They had tried to kill me more than once, and my odds of surviving another assassination attempt were dropping into the single digits.

Then the image of Natalia Laskin's smug grin suddenly popped into my mind, and the reminder that she had successfully framed Aafreen Soltani for murder. Laskin was now threatening to go after Shanay and Sarah Brooks, and the worst part was that she'd be free to do it. Shanay and Sarah were like family to me, and I owed them my best effort. More than that, I owed them my life.

I turned back to Khatabi. "I need a big favor from you."

He eyed me suspiciously as he lit another cigar. "Go on."

"First, I want you to put the fear of Allah into that old man driving the fishing boat. Then I want you to release Laskin and her buddies."

Khatabi's eyes widened. "Right now? They'll dump you overboard before I even make it back to Marrakesh."

"No, I didn't mean now. I'll need a little bit of a head start, so I want you to take them back to Marrakesh and then set them free."

He chewed his cigar before answering. "Okay, yes, I can do that. But only under one condition. Whatever it is that you are planning, I don't want it happening here in my country. You must give me your word that you will leave Morocco."

"Agreed." We shook hands. "By the way," I asked, "did your men ever catch up to the tour bus?"

He nodded. "Of course. In fact, we are in the process of returning the girls to their families and the British ladies to their hotel. Only the little hooligan boy will be punished."

"Then I have one more favor to ask."

Khatabi's face twisted, as if it pained him to even think about letting Hassan off. But when I explained how much the boy had helped me, he reluctantly agreed to drop the charges against him.

The police commander signaled the Navy boat to follow us back to the Port of Safi. When we arrived, he made a visual show of seizing the fishing boat and taking me and the pilot into custody. But as soon as Laskin and her thugs were hustled away in the waiting police car, Khatabi released us.

Once we were alone, Khatabi turned to the old boat captain and spoke to him in Arabic.

"What did you tell him?" I asked.

"I told him that no matter what happens, no matter what you say, he is not to bring you back to Moroccan soil."

I laughed, he laughed, and then Khatabi's driver held the car door as he climbed in.

"Whatever mission you are about to embark on," he said, "I wish you the best of luck." He rolled up his window and then they headed off toward Marrakesh.

"I'll need it," I said under my breath. Then, turning to the old captain, I said, "We'll wait until dark to head back out."

He gazed at me in a daze, and I realized he didn't understand a word of English. Turning back toward Khatabi's car, I desperately tried to get his attention, but they had turned onto the main road and all I saw were taillights against the setting sun.

I looked back at the captain who was preening his mustache like a squirrel monkey.

"WE WAIT FOR DARK!" I said. But the added volume and wild gestures didn't help his understanding.

156

Once the sun had settled below the North Atlantic, I took the old geezer by the arm and walked him onto the fishing trawler. Then I pointed out to sea.

He was either playing dumb or he really didn't get the charade game. In any case, I knew my way around a boat and had logged some time in a wheelhouse. So, instead of more pantomiming, I fired up the motor myself and started back toward the big freighter.

The crescent moon served our needs quite well. It outlined the anchored ship, yet left us concealed in the inky seas.

Navigating a wide arc around the ship's aft, I slowed to a stop when I spotted its name: MS Versand. The same container vessel had come up during a murder investigation in San Francisco. The case had been my first as an SFPD homicide inspector, and my last with the department.

As I stood aboard the bobbing scow, more lights came on in my head. The case had involved Latvians, one of whom was a bigwig in the Latvian Consulate. The man had since been deported and was later found murdered somewhere overseas—an airport bathroom in Germany as I recall. A tingle rippled throughout my body and into my bones; *this cannot be a coincidence.*

Closing my eyes, I tried to fit it all together. There were too many pieces, and they seemed to go in all different directions. The people running the trafficking ring were Russian, not Latvian. And from what I remembered from the Soviet Union collapse, the two do not get along. And furthermore, my case had to do with hijacked liquor not hijacked humans.

I opened my eyes to find the old fisherman sitting on a tackle box, waiting for me. I motioned him up and then I searched the box for anything I could make into a weapon, but there was nothing useful.

Dropping the engine back into gear, I motored slowly to the far side of the ship where a network of cables and rope ladders hung.

Though the seas were relatively calm, the bobbing motion of our little boat made it too risky to draw any closer.

"Right here," I said. "This is where we say goodbye, Skipper."

The man thumbed his wiry mustache as I pointed to his chest, then back toward shore. "You...go!"

Then, I gave the old guy a mock salute before climbing over the bow and dropping into the frigid water.

CHAPTER 48

By the time I climbed the 300-foot hull, I felt like I had run a double marathon. Clinging to the top of the rope ladder, I rested for several minutes until I caught my breath.

It was dark, and the steel cargo containers towered above me like rusty skyscrapers. Trying to acclimate myself, I saw that I'd come up on the port side in more or less amidships. To my left was the bow, or front, and to my right was the stern. Also to my right was the nine-story superstructure that held the bridge, navigation equipment, and a bunch of other functions of which I was unfamiliar.

The deck of the ship looked like a big city, but I figured that somewhere beneath its monolithic stacks of containers were cargo holds and sleeping quarters where the young women were confined. I'm not sure what I'd been thinking, but the task of finding more victims aboard the monstrous vessel now seemed impractical if not absurd. Searching the entire ship could take weeks, and maneuvering around while dodging the crew wasn't going to be easy. I would likely be caught long before I ever found the girls.

Now that I'd drenched myself, I had the additional problem of trying to get warm and dry.

I'd been on the go since early morning, I'd managed to get myself shot in the ass, and I was exhausted from the climb onto the ship. All I really wanted was to find a warm place to sleep, but I didn't have that luxury. I had to somehow familiarize myself with the ship's layout, otherwise I'd just be spinning my wheels and this entire effort would have been in vain.

Peeking out from my hiding spot under an iron staircase, I saw that the ship was not configured as I had imagined. The area just inside the hull was a deep, hollow well that took up three quarters of the deck. It too held columns of the huge cargo boxes that extended several levels below the deck as well as above it. I guessed that there had to be at least 10,000 containers on the ship.

As I sat shivering beneath the steps, I realized that I couldn't even begin my search until I warmed myself. I found a door marked FIRE LOCKER just a few meters down the catwalk, but inside were only fire extinguishers, barrels of sodium carbonate and hazmat suits. No blankets.

The hooded hazmat suits were thick and dry, which convinced me I'd be warmer in them than in my wet clothes. But they were black with bright yellow reflective strips across the front and back, which would undoubtedly draw unwanted attention. Rummaging around, I found a roll of electrical tape and used it to cover the yellow bands. It was a crude job, but I had no other options.

Stripping out of my wet warmups, I considered staying inside the warm closet. Other than a fire, I doubted the crew would have reason to come in. As much as I wanted to stay in the closet, part of my plan was about to move forward and I needed to be outside to witness it.

As I stood naked in the locker, I heard a man's voice on the deck. I listened at the door, imagining him coming in and finding me. *Naked stowaway arrested on container ship—News at eleven.* Boy oh boy, Doris and her dimwitted boyfriend would just love that one!

I couldn't make out the words at first, but it sounded like he was on the phone. "She's coming aboard at 10 o'clock," he said. "We can get underway then."

A few seconds went by as the man continued past the fire locker. I knew in my gut that the "she" they spoke of was none other than Natalia Laskin. *She,* was on her way to the ship.

After thwarting her scheme to bring the Berber girls aboard, I was banking on Laskin returning to the ship with or without them. In my mind, she would need to be present to supervise transport of the other girls who were already on the ship. What other reason could she have for returning?

I was thankful that Khatabi had agreed to take Laskin back to Marrakesh before releasing her. It gave me the time I needed to get myself aboard the ship before her. Now, I hoped to watch her board the vessel and lead me to the human cargo.

Estimating the time to be around 8:30 p.m., it left me an hour to reconnoiter. Careful not to encounter any of the crew, I left the fire locker and climbed the rail into a dark space between the stacks.

I had always thought the boxes were piled flush against one another, but that wasn't the case. Narrow pathways cut between each row, all of which were held in place by a scaffolding type of framework running at right angles across the width of the vessel. Each container was lashed down at several points, both fore and aft, allowing sparse room to move about between the rows.

Traversing the ship through the cargo maze, I got to the end and climbed to the top of the scaffolding. It was like being on the roof of a ten-story building, except during an earthquake. As the tower of boxes rocked to and fro, I imagined what it was like when the ship was cutting through wind and waves.

I clung to the thick lashing while scanning eastward toward shore. My hip had begun to throb and my hands ached from gripping so tightly. With no sign of a boat, I remained perched there like a crow.

While there, I realized that container ships were nothing like the crowded Navy vessels on which my dad served. I'd only spotted two men on deck since I had come aboard, and I guessed that once the containers were loaded, a paired down crew could monitor them while in transit. Another thing I realized was that my phone—the one with the dead Russian's data card—had been drenched during my little swim from the fishing boat to the rope ladder. Stupid me, now I had no way to tell the time or connect with the outside world. If I wasn't already out on a limb all alone, I had now sawed it off.

Suddenly the chug of a boat engine drifted up to my little roost. Squinting out at the dark sea, I knew the boat carrying Laskin was on its way. In a perfect spot to watch her come aboard, I waited up there, invisible to the rest of the world.

After about 10 minutes, a small gray blot could be seen against the dark water. Its running lights were off as the engine throttled down, quieting its approach and causing me to reevaluate my theory. When the boat took an indirect path around the ship's aft, I realized I'd taken up the wrong position to see Laskin's arrival.

Climbing down, I hustled to weave my way back through the network of passages. It occurred to me that Laskin had masked her approach in the shadows of the big ship just as I had, rather than where the lights of Safi might illuminate her. That, combined with cutting off the fishing boat's lights and engine, told me that not everyone on the Versand knew about the illegal cargo hidden aboard. She was also being discreet.

Slowed by a bad knee and bullet wound, my trek back to the other side took some time. I emerged amidships, and then looked both ways like a kid about to cross a busy street. A little farther aft, I spotted a deckhand helping Laskin over the bow. She had apparently climbed the same rope ladder that I had, but without the physical exhaustion. The woman bounded onto the deck, followed by one of the thugs from Marrakesh. I hoped that the other had been bitten by the cobra and had succumbed to its venom.

As the crewman quietly spoke with the two of them, I realized he was the same man I'd heard outside the fire locker. He was stout, with a shaved white head, and wore an orange jacket with the name Büren stenciled on the back. Though I couldn't expose myself by moving any closer, I had at least identified a member of the crew who was clearly involved in their plot.

The boat motor suddenly started up, and I assumed their ride out was departing. As Laskin and her group were focused on hauling a sack up and onto the ship, I hurried toward the rail to get a look. Pulling away from the ship was the same fishing boat that I had taken. Whatever threats Khatabi had made to its captain, they hadn't kept him away. The greedy little shit weasel had undoubtedly told Laskin that I had also come aboard.

Creeping back into the dark recesses of the containers, I watched Laskin as she unloaded the cargo sack they had just lugged onboard. I saw the shape of a rifle stock, the barrel being screwed into place, and then the outline of a scope being tightened onto it.

That confirmed she knew I was somewhere on the ship.

CHAPTER 49

I had mistakenly thought I could simply follow Laskin, and she would lead me right to her captives. But I should have known it wasn't going to be as easy as that. It never is.

The crewman led Laskin and her goon aftward before quickly disappearing into a stairwell on the superstructure. I was certain they weren't going up to the bridge, since it was pretty clear their presence on the ship was a secret. But the high-rise tower was the guts of the vessel, and from there Laskin could access below deck passages, food, shelter, and probably a million other places on the ship.

Other than the high-powered rifle, she had given no outward sign that they were hunting me. In fact, they barely even glanced around before leaving the deck. I wondered if I'd misread the situation, and that maybe Laskin didn't know I was aboard.

I kept looking back toward where I'd last seen them, wondering where they had gone and if they would reemerge. A dim light caught my attention, high on an exterior catwalk over the bridge. Leaning out onto the deck to get a better view, I saw a silhouette moving silently across the top of the superstructure. When the figure began to climb the signal mast, it finally dawned on me. The mutt who had come aboard with Laskin was acting as a sniper.

The man took a position on a small landing about 50 feet above the wheelhouse, where he had a commanding view of the entire cargo deck.

I had searched for suspects many times as a cop, and I knew how it was done. Laskin figured that I was hiding among the containers, and they were going to try to flush me out. Once I was exposed, the sniper would take care of the rest. There was no way to know which direction they would start combing; back to front, front to back, or side to side.

A heavy vibration suddenly began to shake the ship, accompanied by what sounded like artillery fire. I realized that the massive chain holding the anchor was being raised, and that we were about to get underway. It was the point of no return for me, because I would now be stuck on the vessel indefinitely. And given that Laskin knew I was on board, and that she and her people were there to kill me, I felt trapped. That's probably because I was trapped.

As I hunkered in the middle of the stacks, a thought occurred to me. The deckhands operating the giant winches that raised the anchor had to be on the forward deck where the anchor is deployed. And since I hadn't seen them come past me, I realized they had arrived at the bow via a passageway beneath the deck.

I immediately began weaving my way through the dark narrows, trying to reach the front of the ship. Once the crew finished hoisting the anchor, they would leave and I would be able to find my way below deck and away from Laskin's search party. It seemed like a decent plan, until I got to the frontmost row of containers.

As I waited and watched the crew secure the giant chain, I heard the men radio up to the bridge before going below. I had also spotted the companionway they used, and I planned to wait a few minutes before following their route into the stairwell.

Thankfully, I was still concealed among the cargo when Laskin and the crewman came out from beneath the foremast at the front of the ship. They each split to opposite sides, about 20 or 30 feet apart. In classic grid search formation, they were only seconds away from beginning the fox hunt.

I carefully backed my way around the first row, and once I was far enough from them, I took off as fast as I could toward the aft of the ship. The searchers were evenly spaced and had begun advancing in synchronized lockstep.

If I ran too fast, I'd trip on a cleat or guywire. If I didn't move fast enough, one of them would spot me and call out to the other. They would surround me like hyenas around a lone wildebeest. And if they didn't kill me outright, they would flush me into the open where the sniper would pick me off.

I could hear the searchers calling to one another in the darkness behind me. I was quickly running out of deck, and would soon emerge at the base of the bridge castle upon which the sniper was perched. I began zig-zagging, and got turned around in the maze of containers.

Somewhere near the middle of the ship I spotted a stenciled sign that read: NO. 3 PORT HATCH. It was a large opening in the deck, with a sliding cover that had been left partially open. The dark innermost recesses of the ship called to me, and I answered by climbing over the raised lip and down the steel rungs into the hatch.

The noise was deafening, and every sound seemed to echo off the metal hull and reverberate through me. After climbing 15 or 20 feet down, I saw a passageway built right between the ship's double hull. I knew that I'd be risking running into a crewmember, but decided to take my chances against one of them rather than Laskin's man with the sniper rifle.

163

The bulkhead lights led me onward, but the passageway was long and dark and had been built for a much smaller man. I felt like a hamster in a Habitrail. There wasn't enough space to pass another person, but thankfully it never came to that.

At one point, I stopped to give my hip and knee a break. Unsure of where I was headed, I also wondered why I was in such a hurry to get there. My pursuers were presumably still combing the deck above me, and it seemed unlikely they would look for me in such an obscure passageway in the ship's hold.

I took out my phone and opened it up. Though it didn't appear to be as wet as I'd thought, it still didn't work. Trying to blot it off as best I could, I laid its parts out the grill over one of the hallway lights to dry.

Sliding against the hull to a seated position, it felt good to stretch my legs. The thrum of the ship's motor vibrated like a massage chair, and I felt myself giving in to it. As hungry as I was, I felt even more tired.

I should probably get up and keep moving. It was the last thought I had before falling asleep.

CHAPTER 50

I awoke like a hibernating bear—my stomach empty and bladder full. The coveralls I wore felt sticky. Blood had seeped from the injury, and I realized that all the climbing and running around on deck had wreaked havoc on my wound.

The passageway in which I had fallen asleep was empty. The ship's movement told me we were still at sea, but I had no idea how long I'd been out or whether it was night or day. My first priorities were to find a bathroom and food, in that order.

Watertight doors were spaced at intervals along the passageway, facing inward toward the ship's interior. I passed several before picking one at random. As soon as I cranked the wheel to open it, the pounding sound of an engine vibrated through me. My initial instinct was to close the door, but then I realized the racket might help to mask any noise I might make.

Finding myself in the generator room, I counted four big diesel engines—two on the port side and two on the starboard, all operating at full tilt. Nobody was in the room at present, but I assumed it was someone's job to monitor and maintain them.

Searching for something useful, I culled through a bucket of used hand towels and tucked the least greasy of them down the inside of my pant leg to help sop up the blood. I also found a half drunk mango Snapple, which I poured out and used the jar to pee in. The room itself was otherwise spotless. I couldn't find so much as a crumb of food to eat, so I kept moving.

Climbing a staircase to the level above me, I emerged onto an interior hallway. Across from me was a door marked CREW MESS, inside of which I heard talking and laughter. I slithered past it to the officers' mess, which was empty. There was no real food to sink my teeth into, only a basket of condiments in the center of the table. I quickly grabbed what I could; a catsup bottle, some packets of Swiss Miss, and a shaker of parmesan cheese.

On my way out, I passed an upright water dispenser. Dropping to my knees, I opened the spigot and gulped down as much as I could in the scant time I had. Dashing back across the hall, I took the same door and stairway back down to the generator room where I made quick work of my less-than-nourishing meal.

As I sat against the far wall with the clamoring engines pounding in my head, I tried to focus my mind on the mission—to find the girls being held in captivity. But I couldn't see to their safety unless I was first able to locate them. The answer to where they were hidden was like a riddle I had to figure out first. The ship was just too big, and there had to be a way to narrow my search parameters.

Closing my eyes, I tossed my head back and concentrated. If it was a secret that Laskin and her man were onboard, it had to also be a secret that the young women were onboard. That meant they were in a hold somewhere in the belly of the vessel, probably near the ship's engine or the generator room to camouflage any noise they made.

"Huh," I said to myself as a thought came to me. If the ship is underway, that means its engines are running. And if the engines are running, why is the generator also running? It seemed that the only use for a generator would be when the ship is at anchor and the engine is not in operation. But that wasn't the case, yet the generators were pounding away right in front of me.

I was onto something, but a pain in my stomach was suddenly taking center stage. The Swiss Miss, catsup, and parmesan banquet had hit my gut like a torpedo, and I felt it starting to make its move. Heaving into the bucket of rags, I was surprised the ship's captain didn't hear my retching all the way up in the wheelhouse.

It wasn't the best place to continue hanging out. So I climbed back into my narrow passageway in the hull. Feeling badly about what I'd deposited in the diesel mechanics' bucket and their Snapple bottle, I reasoned that I'd be forgiven by the man upstairs once I helped the kidnapped victims to safety. Saving the girls was still a big *if*, and I knew I would have to do better than I'd done so far if it was ever going to happen.

There had been no windows in the hallway, so I hadn't been able to get a sense of time. With the exception of a couple of voices in the crew's mess, the place seemed pretty desolate. I had definitely come away with the impression that it was late at night or very early in the morning. Both of which seemed like a good time to do some more prowling around.

I waited another hour or so before sneaking back through the generator room and up to the hallway where I'd gone before, and this time I found both mess halls empty. Steering clear of the condiments, I drank more water before continuing deeper. On the opposite side of the hall were two other rooms, labeled OFFICER LOUNGE and CREW LOUNGE. The doors were closed and both were quiet, so I continued past them.

Not unexpected was the galley right next to the crew's mess. The door was closed, but I knew there would be plenty to eat inside. Listening and hearing nothing, I cracked the door and squeezed half my head in. The pleasant scent of baked bread took me back 24 hours to the kitchen at the Elliott's hotel in Marrakesh. I had passed it up then, but I was not going to leave this galley without a real meal.

My eyes scanned the empty kitchen, spotting doors behind which I knew were fruits, vegetables, meats, and both canned and dry goods. Stepping all the way inside, I saw an industrial sized coffeemaker and made my way toward it. Filling a cup, I stood there reveling in the bloom of dark roast.

A storage closet opened behind me, and before I could turn around, a voice asked, "Can I assist you with something, sir?"

CHAPTER 51

Turning slowly to face her, I expected to find Natalia Laskin gazing back at me from behind a rifle.

"Uh...no. Thank you, though. I was just in need of some coffee." I stared back at the thin Filipino woman who wore a chef's apron and a nametag that read *Noelma*.

She eyed me back. "You are new here?"

I smiled. "How could you tell?"

"Because you would know that there is always a pot brewing in the crew's lounge." She gave my outfit the once over, stopping halfway down. "Are you hurt?"

The blood had seeped through my coveralls, and I quickly turned my hip away from her. Too quickly, I think.

"I think you are not with the crew," she said.

"Right, no, an officer, actually...in training...to be one...an officer, that is."

She had the kind eyes of a grandmother, but a shrewdness that comes from working around merchant seamen. "I know this is not the truth," she said. "Maybe you are a stowaway, maybe not. But my business is only to cook food for people aboard this ship."

I stared into a face that was difficult to read. Unsure where she was going with the line of questions, I hoped she wasn't about to pull the plug on my entire operation.

"I get you something to eat," she said, opening a walk-in cooler. After a few seconds she came out with a crate of eggs and a slab of bacon.

I watched her slip several pieces of bread into an industrial size toaster as a half-dozen eggs and the bacon began to sizzle on a long griddle. By all indications, I had stumbled upon a saint, a pearl inside an oyster.

She pulled a stool up to the wide workstation in the center of the room and slapped my breakfast plate down in front of me. Overcome with gratitude, I wanted to throw my arms around her and plant a big kiss on her tightly pressed lips. Instead, I gripped both of her hands in mine and thanked her.

"Now, you eat." She took a step back and crossed her arms. "And then I report you to the captain."

I had just taken my first bite, and it suddenly stuck in my gullet. Washing it down with a gulp of coffee, I let out a long sigh. There was no way to know who, if anyone, I could trust out here. My plan was to trust nobody, but that had gotten me nowhere thus far.

"Okay," I said. "Noelma, is it?"

She glanced at her nametag and nodded.

"My name is Danny," I said. "Danny McKenna. And you would be right to report me...under normal circumstances, that is. But I didn't come aboard this ship for a free meal, or free passage, or to sneak across a border. I am here to investigate a crime. Something very bad. So bad that somebody already shot me because of it."

Noelma's eyes dropped to my bloodstained coveralls.

"These people are also aboard the ship," I said. "And if they find me, I'm as good as dead."

The woman thought for a minute, digesting all that I'd told her. "The captain will radio ashore to the police," she said. "It is best to tell him what you know."

I shook my head. "I don't know who is involved in this thing. And if the wrong people find out, we may all be in danger."

Her eyes grew wide. "Please tell me, what is this thing that was done to make you come here?"

"Human trafficking." I let that sink in a few seconds. "Young girls from the countries whose ports the ship has visited."

"Little girls? They are here? On this ship?" Noelma was already shaking her head. "No, no, this is a mistake. There are no girls on the ship."

"You can't see them," I said. "They are being hidden somewhere below deck, in one of the cargo holds or something."

She looked at me like I was crazy, and it felt like I was losing her. The whole idea sounded a bit farfetched, especially the notion that they were being kept below. That would mean that other crewmen knew about them; mechanics, engineers, deckhands, and whoever else had occasion to go into the lower levels of the ship.

As the cook considered my story, she mindlessly ambled over to close the refrigerator that she'd left ajar. I watched her as I scooped the last of my eggs onto the toast and shoved them into my mouth. Then I abruptly stopped chewing.

"The walk-in cooler," I said, pointing to it. "How is it powered?"

She shrugged. "The generators, I guess."

"And what about refrigerated containers? Are there any onboard the ship?"

Noelma frowned. "Yes, always."

"How many?"

"I don't know. Not as many as the regular Conex boxes. A smaller percent, I think."

"And how are they powered?"

Again she shrugged. "Probably the same way, by the generators."

I was finally getting down to the meat and potatoes. I could feel it. "How do you know this?"

"My friend, Raul. He is chief electrical engineer in Cargo Control. It is his job to do this."

"Cargo Control? Is that where they keep records on all of the containers, Conex boxes, whatever you call them?"

Noelma nodded.

"I need to find a list of the ones connected to the generators."

Her look of apprehension turned to horror. "These girls...you think they are inside one of the boxes?"

"I think so. In fact, I would bet my life on it."

CHAPTER 52

"The Cargo Control Room is on this level," said Noelma. "Down the hall, just next door to the infirmary." She dried her hands on a towel. "I will show you."

It wasn't exactly the help I needed, and I would have settled for her simply not ratting me out to the captain. But off we went.

"Will anyone be in there?"

She waved a hand. "Too early, it's only 4:45 and they don't start until 8 o'clock—unless if an emergency happens."

The room was long and narrow. On the left was a worktable and two desks with computer terminals. The opposite wall held a long bank of dials, knobs, gauges, monitors and screens. On the back wall were two windows that looked out onto the dark Atlantic.

A corkboard was mounted over one of the desks, and pinned to it was a computer-generated sheet.

"Here," said Noelma, pointing to it. "A diagram of the ship's holds and all the boxes."

It was overload. There were so many numbers, colors, codes, and symbols that my head felt like I'd eaten a popsicle too fast. I needed to find a legend of some type to explain the mass of material I was looking at. A clipboard hanging on a hook next to one of the desks gave me some help. It held 26 Excel pages categorized by box size, type, ship's hold location, destination port, etc.

"It says there are 771 boxes on the ship," I said. "And 215 of them are listed as Category-R, which I think stands for refrigeration."

"For what reason would these animals want to keep the little girls cold?" she asked.

"I don't think that's what they're doing. At least I hope that's not the case." I glanced around the room for more information. "My guess is that the box the girls are in has been set at a constant temperature and is equipped with some sort of air ventilation system. The control settings for all 215 refrigeration containers has to be around here somewhere, otherwise how would the engineers be able to monitor them during transport?"

The cook looked like she was trying to keep up but would much rather be in the galley baking scones. Poking her head out the door, she gave a quick look up and down the hallway. "Maybe what you look for is inside the computers?" she said.

Noelma was probably right. Details such as temperature settings, box contents, shipping customer and such, had likely been digitally uploaded and were locked inside their system. I wouldn't know where to start looking even if I was able to get through the password page, which I didn't bother wasting my time trying.

Unclasping all of the pages from the clipboard, I ran them though a copy machine on the worktable. When I was done, I held the copies for Noelma to see.

"I'll have to check every single refrigeration unit by hand," I said. "All 215 of them."

She looked at her watch. "You should find a place to go and hide; the officers will be down for breakfast soon."

"Promise you won't tell them about me."

"If you promise to find those little girls." She made the sign of the cross. "And catch those animals who did this to them."

I gave her my word, but the bundle of papers in my hand made me wonder how I could accomplish it. The mountain of cargo boxes was bad enough, but I was still unfamiliar with the ship's layout and its operations. Even if I found the unit containing the girls, I wouldn't know how to open it. Or get them all out and down the scaffolding. Or help them off the ship to a safe place.

"I need to get back to my kitchen," said Noelma. "You are not the only hungry man on this ship." She flashed a wrinkled smile, and I realized it was her attempt at humor.

"Wait," I said, feeling like I was being left alone on my first day of kindergarten. "Do you think it can be done? I mean, finding the right container, you know, without being seen?"

"About that," she said. "There is both good news and bad news." She glanced at her watch again, and I knew time was of the essence. "It will not be easy. The number of people at work on the ship is small; only 17 crewmen, and five officers. But they are very busy, and they will know if you are on the main deck. I think it will be better to wait until night when there are fewer men on duty."

My shoulders slumped. "What's the good news?"

"That was the good news."

"You mean it gets worse?"

Noelma nodded. "Did you notice the weather code posting in the hallway?"

My shoulders dropped lower as I shook my head.

"We are at Weather Condition Yellow now, meaning the crew must radio to the bridge when going on deck. If we get to Red, the entire cargo deck will be secured and off limits to crewmen."

I could barely muster the words to thank her as she scurried back down the hall toward the galley.

As I passed the weather placard on the wall, I stopped to read it. Voices from the end of the hall startled me, and I tore the paper from its backing and stuffed it in my pocket. I tried to cut through the generator room on my way back to the hidden passageway, but a crewman was inside working. I heard cursing and clanking of tools. Maybe he had found my Snapple jar.

More voices from the crew lounge threw me into panic mode. I spun donuts in the hallway, trying to figure out where to hide. A door opened behind me and two officers stepped out, each holding a coffee mug. They turned and headed down the hall in the opposite direction, never looking back at me.

A round of laughter sprouted from the crew's mess hall, and it sounded like they were headed my way. I dove for the first door I came to and closed myself inside. It was a bathroom with two urinals and two toilet stalls. Secreting myself in one of them, I flipped the latch and sat there trying to figure out what to do.

Pulling the wrinkled weather report from my pocket, I held it at arm's length as I tried to decipher it in the absence of my reading glasses.

WEDNESDAY, JUNE 15, 0355 HRS. WESTERN EUROPEAN SUMMER TIME (WEST)
A GALE-FORCE, NON-TROPICAL LOW PRESSURE SYSTEM IS CENTERED BETWEEN THE MADEIRA ISLANDS AND THE AZORES. THE SYSTEM HAS BECOME MORE ORGANIZED IN THE PAST 24 HOURS, AND ENVIRONMENTAL CONDITIONS ARE CONDUCIVE FOR DEVELOPMENT. THE SYSTEM IS EXPECTED TO PRODUCE STRONG WINDS AND HEAVY RAINS, AND HAS A 70% CHANCE OF CYCLONE FORMATION IN THE NEXT 12 HOURS.

I slumped back in the stall. "And the hits just keep on coming!"

CHAPTER 53

Finding my phone on the light in the passageway where I'd left it, I sat against the bulkhead, looking over the paperwork and trying to figure out how best to proceed. My phone now worked, but we were too far off shore to get even the slightest signal.

I hadn't seen or heard Laskin or her people since they began searching for me, but I knew they had to be out there somewhere. If I was lucky, I'd spot them before they spotted me and then I could use them to find the container full of victims. Less desirable, of course, is that they have been watching the container in the hopes that I'll show up.

The ship seemed to be rocking with more intensity, and I could hear waves crashing against the hull. This *low pressure system* was starting to get real.

Suddenly, I was overcome with the realization that the girls were bouncing around out there inside a metal box. It seemed more urgent that I quickly figure this thing out. But the sheets I had copied did more to confuse me than help. The powered boxes were not all stacked in one hold, as I had hoped. Instead, they had been arranged based on destination port—presumably to simplify off-loading. That meant that all 215 containers were scattered throughout the ship, mixed in with the regular containers.

Tightening my hood, I backtracked down the passageway to where I had first entered. The wind whistled down the hatch, and the rain pelted my face as I climbed the steel rungs to the main deck. The clouds were so thick and dark that it felt like nighttime, even though it was still early in the day.

I held the ream of papers in my wet hands, trying to figure out the layout of the holds. There were seven listed, but for whatever reason, they were numbered 2 though 8. I was somewhere in the center of the ship, and the stenciled number painted on the deck told me that I was in the #4 hold—as good a place to start as any, I thought.

A grouping of six refrigerated containers were in that hold on Deck A, according to my papers. I descended a metal staircase to a catwalk deep within the bowels of the ship. Several levels below the main deck, I followed a bundle of thick power cords to the six containers. Using my elbow, I rapped on each one. Nothing.

A digital readout at the end of one container read -18°C. Unable to convert Celsius to Fahrenheit in my head, I knew enough to realize that the set temperature was well below freezing. Moving on, I found two more on the deep freeze setting, while the remaining three were set at 3.5°C. Though not as cold as the others, I reasoned that if zero Celsius was freezing, 3.5 was probably a normal refrigerator setting. Too cold for humans.

With six containers down and 209 to go, I began climbing up to the next grouping on Deck C—still a few levels below the main deck. I was taking it slow, making sure to avoid running into anyone. But my search wasn't moving along very quickly. I'd been at it nearly an hour, and I was still barely getting started.

The boxes on Deck-C were much the same as the six I had just examined. All were set to normal refrigeration temperatures, and none appeared to have any type of air exchange mechanism.

I was checking my paperwork for the next group in the #4 hold when an alert horn suddenly sounded, pulsating from every level of the ship and nearly startling me off of the catwalk. For a moment I thought I had tripped a security alarm, but then it stopped and an announcement came over the ship's speakers: *"This is First Officer Hans Vogel with a weather condition update. We have now moved to Level Red, repeat, this is a Level Red weather code alert. All cargo holds must immediately be secured and will be off limits to ship's crew until further notice."*

The first officer repeated the announcement before signing off. The wind was quickly picking up, and I felt the spray from waves sloshing over the main deck and cascading into the holds. As I clung there, I realized that anyone now out in the open would easily be spotted from the bridge and would probably be identified as non-crew. But the same would hold for Laskin and her people, who would also be easier for me to spot.

I had been below where the ship's rocking motion was less noticeable. As I climbed higher, the steps became slippery and the pitch of the ship more violent. The wind slapped at my coveralls, flipping my hood back and blowing me against the steel bulkhead. The whistling wind filled my ears, drowning out all other sounds.

Somewhere out of the tumult came a *ting* as sparks jumped off of the steel girder next to me.

"What the hell?" I yelled, diving to the floor. Gazing up at the mountains of containers rocking to and fro, I saw a muzzle flash followed by another ricocheting bullet. Laskin had found me, and with the high ground advantage, she and her men had me pinned on the catwalk.

Backed under an external stairwell, I was temporarily behind cover. But it would take only a moment for the shooter to readjust to a position with a better angle. For me, there was no such option. I was a sitting duck, and I had to figure something out quickly.

I was four levels up from the floor of the hold, and the shooter was somewhere several levels above me. Standing on a square landing about the size of a kitchen table, I knew any movement I made would be visible from above. My only hope was to climb under the railing, which would leave me dangling 50 feet in the air.

Slithering beneath it, I kept to the far back end of the platform. Gripping the metal stairs, I hung there afraid to look down. Then, I swung hand-over-hand down one step at a time, careful not to lose my grasp on the freezing, wet stairs. I was carrying quite a bit more weight than the last time I had played on the monkey bars, and I made a promise to myself to get back on some sort of diet if I managed to live through this.

The landing below me was protected by a scaffolding beam, and once I reached it I was safe. Kicking a leg onto it, I hoisted the rest of me over the lip and onto the platform.

Now I had two choices; I could either go back into hiding, or I could crawl up topside and get a look at who was trying to shoot me. Not that I didn't already know who *they* were, but their location might be a clue to the container's whereabouts.

The stinging rain was somehow finding its way into the below deck hold, and the ship bounced like a seesaw in the waves. The wind felt like it was coming from all directions, and now there were flashes of lightning. Climbing atop a pile of metal containers was about the last thing in the world I wanted to do.

CHAPTER 54

The claxon alarm sounded again, this time followed by a siren. "Ship Security Officer to the bridge ASAP! Gunfire reported on the main cargo deck. This is a level 3 security alert! All hands are to follow illegal boarding protocols and immediately secure hatches and entryways. This is not a drill, repeat, this is *not* a drill."

Well, I guess the cat's out of the bag, I thought as I shimmied between container stacks. My plan was to pop up in a completely different area and try to zero in on the shooter's location.

I had assumed that me, the shooter, and maybe Laskin would be the only people topside. But the announcement ordering the ship's security officer to the bridge made me wonder. Whoever or whatever this security officer is, might also be armed and could mistake me for one of the gunmen.

Trying to be even more cautious, I started climbing up another scaffold. The stenciled number on the floor told me that I had somehow crisscrossed to the #7 hold. It was a race against time, and I was quickly running out of it. If I were captured by a crewman, they would take me into custody and nobody would ever believe my story about the girls. And if I were captured by Laskin, it wouldn't matter anyway. I'd be shot and tossed overboard.

Wiping the rain from my eyes, I started up the scaffolding between the oscillating stacks. Pausing on the first landing, I pulled the papers from my pocket to check which, if any, refrigerated boxes were in the immediate area. A lightning strike directly over the ship caused a sonic boom that reverberated through me. There was an immediate gust that ripped the papers from my hands. Carried by a whirlwind of rain and battering sea air, they fluttered in all directions until I could no longer see them.

"Son-of-a-bitch!" I yelled at the top of my lungs. Now I was really pissed off. And the higher I climbed, the angrier I became. After zig-zagging my way up another half dozen levels, the sound of another shot barked from above. The echo made the shooter's location impossible to pinpoint, but at that moment I didn't care. I had been running from them long enough, and I was ready to end this thing.

I hollered into the wind, "You assholes are going down!"

During my frenzied outburst, I had climbed another few levels to the top of the containers. It was so high that I felt I could touch the black clouds swirling overhead. Gripping the guy wires for dear life, I flattened out as the world swayed around me. *This*, I thought, *this is exactly why I hate to travel.*

Another alert tone came over the ship's speakers, calling again for the ship's security officer to immediately report to the bridge, which I guessed was because I was now in full view of those in the wheelhouse. The poor security guy was probably sleeping it off somewhere, oblivious to all that was happening.

Sleeving the rain from my eyes, I once again forced myself to open them. When I got a load of how high I was, I wished I'd have kept them closed. News photos I had seen of containers tossed about like dominoes, many falling into the sea, suddenly came to mind. I saw myself on the E-ticket ride of my life, plunging 15 stories down into the water.

The wires and cables holding the boxes in place were groaning like an old man with hemorrhoids, as they stretched to their tensile limits. With each massive wave or wind gust, the stack I was on top of shifted erratically in another direction. It was getting to the point that I was going to give up, get sick, or both.

Seemingly out of nowhere, I noticed movement between two containers across from me. An open chasm separated us, at the bottom of which were low, flat rack containers full of construction equipment. Focusing through the torrent, I saw two figures clinging tightly to lashing cables as they maneuvered over the hold I had been in earlier. They appeared to be so fixated on where I had been, that they did not notice that I had moved.

I was completely exposed on my perch at the top of the boxes, and only one glance in my direction would reveal myself to them. Spread flat like a flying squirrel, I remained still. As I watched them, I realized that one was Natalia Laskin. The other carried the rifle, and appeared to be the same size and build as the chump she had come aboard with. I scanned the deck below for their man on the inside, Büren, but he was staying out of sight.

My pulse pounded as I clung there wondering if they had climbed the containers to check on their special cargo. Besides trying to find and kill me, I imagined their financial interests were motivation enough to put themselves in such jeopardy. I made a mental note to double-check those containers for the girls if I lived long enough.

I wanted to check my six to make sure Büren hadn't climbed up behind me, but my face was pressed like a pancake against the top of the metal box and it was all I could do to hold on.

When I wiped my eyes again, I looked across to the other stack and saw Laskin squinting through the squall. She had spotted me, and was pointing me out to the sniper.

I thought if I could possibly flatten myself more than I already had, the target would be too small to hit—especially with the wind and the ship's rocking motion. But this guy was as good as they come, and had already hit the mark with me once.

There was nothing I could do. Gripping the securing cables in my wet hands, I didn't want to see what I knew I was going to see: a muzzle flash, and then lights out for good.

I started to inch my way backwards across the top of the box, using the tips of my shoes and my elbows to drag the rest of me in reverse. It was an inch-by-inch process. Meanwhile, the gunman was getting into position.

Pressing my toes into the container's corrugated grooves, I felt my way backward, hoping that any second they would reach the edge. Even then, I wasn't sure I could lift my body enough to climb over in this wind.

When my eyes focused across the open space again, I saw the rifle aimed directly at me. Laskin's shooter had moved to the leading edge of the container to rest the rifle's forestock on its lip. I watched as he wrapped his arm in the sling, tightening it for stability. With his right arm tucked against the rifle stock, I knew his finger was slipping through the trigger guard onto the trigger. He cocked his head slightly, lining himself up behind the scope.

I knew from experience that he had done his textbook best to create a stable shooting platform. He was just about as ready as a sniper can be, and with both hands gripping the rifle, my end was near.

A lightning strike suddenly lit the sky. A loud boom quickly followed, just as the ship crashed through a gargantuan wave. In one respect, it was like the perfect storm. With no free hand to grip the vessel, the sniper started to slide forward. The rifle came loose, but it's sling was still tangled on the man's arm. It dangled over the edge like a wind chime as the sniper clawed for traction.

Managing to grasp the rifle barrel before it fell, the man swung it around so Laskin could grab the other end and pull him to safety. He held it there as the weight of his body slipped a centimeter at a time toward the edge of the box.

I expected Laskin to reach for him or even grab a pant leg, but she did neither. Finally, when the sniper had slipped so far that he was straddling the leading edge, he let go of the rifle altogether and used both hands to claw for purchase on the wet container.

Laskin showed no emotion, and only watched in fascination as her partner skidded over the edge with the pitch of the ship. He tumbled in the air like a kind of running man dance, all the way to the bottom of the hold.

Staring at where the sniper's body had disappeared into the chasm below me, I realized that wasn't quite what I meant when I threatened that he was *going down*. But his demise meant one less opponent for me, and was a drop of luck nonetheless.

By the time I glanced back to the summit across from me, Laskin was gone. And so was the sniper rifle.

CHAPTER 55

She has to be down here somewhere, I thought as I slowly monkeyed my way down the mountain of boxes.

Laskin had seen which stack of containers I'd climbed up, and she was smart enough to know whatever goes up must come down. She had also recovered her partner's rifle before his swan dive, leaving me at an even greater disadvantage.

I cautiously stepped off of the scaffold onto the main deck, watching for any sign that Laskin was lying in wait for me there. Assuming that her sniper friend was dead, I figured that his high dive and subsequent landing would have been difficult to survive and that she and Büren were my two remaining adversaries.

The rain was still coming down in sheets, making it nearly impossible to hear anything else. Having to depend only on my eyes, I saw that nobody was visible on the deck.

As I stealthily made my way around the corner into the open area that had been directly below me, the unimpeded rain pelted me with more ferocity. It washed over the entire deck creating an odd cranberry colored puddle at my feet. I followed the stream to its source—an earth mover being transported on one of the open top, flat rack containers.

The sniper had plummeted the equivalent of a six-story building, landing on a bulldozer covered in sheets of thick vinyl wrap. It had padded the guy's landing somewhat, but not enough. He lay there, bent like a Gumby character and gasping for breath. Having broken a lot of bones, the man was in considerable pain.

I hoped the fact that he was clearly going to die and that his pal Laskin had made no effort to save him, might give the man an incentive to tell me where the girls were hidden.

Lowing myself onto my good knee, I leaned down toward him. "Tell me where they are." I shouted.

But before he could even answer the question, the man's head exploded as if he had swallowed a stick of dynamite.

Diving backwards, I scrambled to find cover from wherever the gunfire was coming from. Realizing from the shot's placement that Laskin was firing from somewhere above me, I dove beneath the crated tractor and used its thick engine block as protection.

Laskin's headshot had put her partner out of his misery, but I knew its intent was only to shut him up. The next shot would be meant to shut me up—permanently.

Instead of another blast, the clattering sound of metal on metal barked its way through the driving rain. The rifle careened down a stack of containers, landing on the deck near the dead man.

I waited, wondering if it was a ruse to lure me out from under the tractor. Inch by inch, I slowly emerged while scanning the tower of boxes overhead. As I searched for where the rifle had landed, the sound of a motor cut through the downpour and drew me to the starboard railing. Natalia Laskin was at the bottom of a rope ladder, trying to step onto a waiting speedboat.

She was my only suspect. The woman had framed Aafreen for Kingsbury's murder and then killed Nate Leclaire when he got too close. She was responsible for the trafficking of untold young girls into who knows what kind of servitude, and she had also shot me. Now the bitch was trying to get away.

The wild waves made Laskin's disembarkation effort look almost impossible, yet I knew this feral cat had nine lives. I ran back toward what was left of the sniper, hoping to find his rifle and get a shot off at Laskin. She had beat me at every turn, but I was not going to let her get off the ship alive.

I found the rifle lying on the deck a few yards from its owner, scratched but in one piece. Snatching it up with gusto, I spun back toward the railing. In a pathetic moment that I would have given anything to do over, my feet slipped out from under me and I went down hard on my bad knee.

The pain felt like I had fallen on a tractor from 100 feet up. As I floundered there, writhing in agony, the sound of a motorboat speeding away drifted up and over the railing. I couldn't even catch my breath enough to curse.

Using the rifle to brace myself, I tried to stand.

"Drop your weapon!"

I glanced up to find myself surrounded. Some of the men wore the uniforms of ship's officers and others appeared to be the crew.

Following their orders, I let go of the rifle and came to a wobbly stance with my hands up. "It's not what it looks like," I said.

Before I could explain further, I was smacked from behind. The force propelled me forward into the side of a container. With my body being restrained by what seemed like a thousand hands, I felt the cold sting of wet metal against my face. As much as I wanted to tell my story, even I could see that this wasn't the right time.

My arms were bent awkwardly behind my back, and I felt plastic zip ties being tightened onto my wrists. They searched me and found only my phone, which they took. The ship rocked, and I nearly lost my balance. Without my hands to break my fall, it could have cost me a few teeth. Luckily, I managed to stay on my feet.

"Turn him around," said one man in the group.

Someone spun me, and with a man on either side, they braced me upright before him. I guess I had expected the ship's captain to look the part; crisp uniform on a well-built body, and chiseled features that looked like they'd seen a bar fight or two.

"I am Captain Jimmy Wolff," he said.

The only thing captainly about him was his scowl. Otherwise, the dumpy redheaded man in a sweater and slacks could have been my insurance agent. He eyed me through round glasses, fogged by the rain.

"You terrorists have the arrogance to attempt a takeover of my vessel?" Captain Jimmy strutted in a slow semi-circle around me. "I ought to have you shot right now, and feed your carcass to the sharks."

When he paused, I thought it might be a good time to try again.

"Look, captain, we didn't really get off to a good start." I tried to straighten up a bit. "I'm an American. A private investigator, and an ex-police officer."

"Passport?"

I cleared my throat. "Well, you see, that's the funny thing of it. It's with my money and police ID back at this hotel in Marrakesh. I was staying with these women, the Elliotts, and--"

He cut me off with a hand in the air. The captain then turned to a subordinate. "You radioed authorities in Sines?"

"Yes sir, but they are delayed." The kid shifted his weight from one foot to the other. "Apparently they are not able to take the chopper up in this weather."

The captain glanced skyward but said nothing. He gestured, and the group followed him toward the superstructure—me being muscled along by a couple of meaty crewmen. We stopped halfway across the deck, in front of a door marked BOSUN STORE.

We entered the storeroom, which was a sizable, well-lit space containing a bunch of chains, ropes, and tools. For a few minutes, I thought they were going to use them to string me up. And who could blame them? I had nothing to support my story, which had come out all jumbled and deranged.

"I wasn't with that man," I said, pointing with my chin toward the deck. "In fact, he was trying to kill me."

The captain smirked. "We watched you from the bridge, saw the both of you climbing up together, getting into position with your weapons."

"No, no," I said. "That wasn't me. I was across from them in the #7 hold."

The officers looked at one another. "Oh," said the captain. "You have done your homework. You are familiar with the cargo holds."

"It's not like that." I took a breath to calm myself.

"Why did you shoot your own partner?" asked a ship's officer. "Afraid that he would implicate you if he got caught?"

"Of course not. The man fell. It was the other person that shot him. A woman. She's the one you saw climbing to the top of the containers with the man who's now dead."

A round of chuckles percolated up from the crew. "I see. So now there is a woman on the ship."

"Unfortunately no, she's already gone. Went over the rail and climbed into a speed boat to make her escape. She's wanted by the police, and there's an Interpol lookout for her. That's why I came aboard in the first place."

More chuckles erupted.

I tried to ignore them. "I hate to tell you Captain, but you have a rat in your crew. They have someone on the inside, and I saw him. His name is Büren, it was on his jacket."

Now there was outright laughter.

"Like this?" said the captain, turning one of the men so that his back was to me. He was a dark Indian man wearing a jacket with identical markings. "Büren is the name of the shipping company," said the captain. "The entire crew wears them."

The door opened and another man came in out of the rain holding two cellphones. He nodded to the captain as he entered.

"Ah, there you are," said Captain Wolff. "This man says he has no connection with the dead terrorist."

"His phone says otherwise," said the newcomer. "I have both of their cell phones, and the call histories show that they have been in contact with each other."

My head fell back as the air sputtered out of my body. "That's not my phone," I said, sounding like every perp I'd ever arrested. "Well, it's my phone, but it has another guy's SIM card in it. He's a Russian Syndicate man who died in Bangkok. It's a long story, but there are people who can confirm what I'm telling you. Call Sous-Lieutenant Omar Khatabi in Marrakesh. He knows all about my investigation into women being trafficked."

The captain's eyebrow lifted, as if he couldn't wait to hear my next story. "Now there's not just one, but more women onboard?"

I nodded. "Lots of young women."

There was a mixture of cheering and laughter from the crew. This whole thing was a freak'n joke to them, and it was painfully clear that no one believed anything I was saying.

The captain held out his hand, and the man handed him the cellphones. Then the captain turned back to me. "This is the ship's security officer," he said, nodding toward the newcomer. "He will secure you below until the maritime authorities from Sines arrive."

The stout security man dropped his hood as he unbuttoned his rain jacket. His shaved head left me no doubt that he was the same crewman who had helped Laskin and the sniper aboard.

"There's your rat right there," I said. "He's the inside man who's working with them."

Now the ship's captain was laughing along with everyone else.

CHAPTER 56

"Take the terrorist to the dry goods storage room on Deck A," said Captain Wolff. "We'll hold him there."

The men were still laughing as the so-called *security officer* led me to an elevator in the superstructure. Once it began descending and we were away from the rest of the crew, the guard dropped his indignant expression.

"You and I both know what you are," I said as we stepped off. "How much are they paying you to move those girls?"

He glanced around the hallway to make sure it was empty, then slammed me face first against the wall. Rearing back as if he were about to throw a couple of body punches, he suddenly stopped and yanked me upright.

Noelma stood at the open galley door. "Everything all right, sir?"

The security man grunted, and continued shoveling me down the hall. I caught Noelma's sorrowful eyes as we passed, and I gave her a wink to convey that everything was okay. In truth, it was not okay. In fact, things couldn't have been much worse.

When Noelma disappeared back into the kitchen, the man bounced me across the hall toward the crew's mess. Two workers looked up from their meal and the security man yanked me back and continued down the hall to find a vacant room. I could feel a good ass kicking coming on, which I might have been better able to handle if my hands weren't cuffed together.

The asshole bulldozed me through another door into the empty officer's mess, and at last we were alone. I tightened my muscles in preparation for the beatdown, and then just stood there waiting.

The security man closed and locked the door behind us.

"How do you see this playing out for you?" he asked, calmly.

I relaxed my abs and started breathing again. About to take a stab at an answer, the guy began talking over me and I realized that it had been more of a rhetorical question.

"Because let me tell you what I see happening," he continued. "There are really only two options, and I'll even let you choose which one you want."

"I'm listening."

He leaned back against the counter and I saw the condiment tray behind him. My stomach almost retched at the sight of it.

"Option number one is I pitch you overboard and tell everyone that you broke free and dove in of your own accord. You won't live, but it will be much quicker than the second option."

"Which is?"

"You be a good little boy while we wait for the Portuguese authorities, and don't cause any more problems for me."

"Seems kind of like a no brainer," I said. "I'll take my chances with that option. Because once I tell my story to them and they recover those little girls from the container, you'll be the one who will wish he'd been pitched overboard."

He grinned. "Except they will all be dead."

"Who will be dead?"

"The girls inside the boxes." He shook his head with feigned regret. "You didn't think we would leave that to chance, did you? If they are dead, there are no witnesses left to testify. Without any witnesses, it's just your word against the plain and simple facts."

"Which are?" I didn't really want to hear them, because I knew they weren't going to sound good.

"You and your partner smuggled yourselves onboard illegally, brought a weapon to protect your investment, and when it looked like you were going to be caught, you killed your buddy and then pulled the plug on the girls. Every soul on the ship will testify to that, even the captain."

I knew it wasn't going to sound good.

"We even have your phone calls back and forth to prove you two were working together."

"Back up a minute," I said. "What did you mean by that?"

"Yeah, I know. It was the Russian's phone."

"No, not that," I said. "The part about pulling the plug on the girls. What the hell does that mean?"

"That was *her* decision," said the security man. "She did it just before she caught that speedboat out of here."

"Laskin, you mean?"

He flashed a *no shit* look.

"What was her decision?" I asked. "What did she do?"

"She shut down the containers. Turned off the temperature control, filtration, fresh air intake, all of it. They'll be lucky if they last 12 hours in there."

"No!" I yelled. "You can't do this. These are innocent women. Some are just kids. I will tell the cops. I'll convince them to check every single container if I have to."

He smirked again. "Nobody will believe it. And even if they do, they'll find a couple of containers full of corpses and they'll blame you. I hate to say it, but you will be villainized all over the world as a child smuggler and then you'll die a lonely death in a foreign jail."

I couldn't lift my head off of my chest.

"C'mon," he said, grabbing my arm and hauling me out of the room.

At the end of the hall was the storage room. It was a large space with metal racks full of dry goods in sealed containers. He cut my plastic straps only to reattach new ones after looping them through a steel girder in the middle of the room.

"Are you sure you don't want to reconsider that first option?" he said with a laugh. Then he flipped off the light as he walked out and closed the door.

CHAPTER 57

I sat in the dark for the better part of the morning, waiting to explain my side of things to the Portuguese police. But the violent sway of the ship convinced me that the foul weather had not subsided and that it would be a while before their helicopter made it out to us.

I was tired, hungry, and I needed to use a bathroom, but my thoughts kept going back to the imprisoned girls. With their air supply shut off, the clock was ticking. I had already wasted a couple of hours in the food locker, and I knew that each second that slipped by was critical for them. As bad as I had it, their situation was worse. With every roll of the ship, I pictured them crammed into their box. *Boxes!* The corrupt security man had used the plural, which meant they were held in more than one container. *How did I miss that?*

I struggled, tugged, and twisted, but neither the plastic ties nor the steel girder would give. Kicking into the darkness, I stretched my body as far as I could until I felt something solid. I cocked my foot back and slammed it into the object. It rang hollow in the cold and sterile room, but I did not stop. Again and again I kicked, until a harsh crash filled the room and caused me to curl up for cover. The clatter seemed to go on for minutes, but in the end I was still fastened to the post. Then someone opened the door.

"Noelma?" I asked, squinting into the light. "Is that you?"

"Mr. McKenna, what have you done?" She asked, turning on the light.

I had knocked over one of the metal racks, which had toppled into another rack like dominoes. Plastic tubs full of pastas, beans, rice, teas, oats, and every manner of spice had come crashing onto the floor. It was a cleanup crew's nightmare.

"I'm sorry for the mess," I said, "but I really need your help."

"There was shooting on the main deck earlier," she said, her breath laboring with the very words. "They warned us over the intercom. Please tell me if that was your doing."

I shook my head. "You saw me earlier; I have no gun. It was the other people. The ones I told you about. They were trying to kill me."

"Then why are you locked in here and not them?"

I wished I could free my hands, if only to massage the headache pounding in my temples. "There were two, a woman and a man, and both of them are human traffickers for the Russian gangs. The woman escaped on a boat after the shooting, and the man is dead. He fell from the containers."

She made the sign of the cross over her heart, and I felt a tinge of guilt that my own heart was so full of anger and hatred.

"What is it that you need from me?" she asked.

I struggled against the bindings. "I saw wire cutters in the bosun's storeroom. Can you get them and bring them to me?"

"I am not allowed on the main deck or in any of the cargo holds. If someone sees me, I will lose my job."

"Nobody is up there on deck because of the weather conditions. Just hold tightly to the rail, and watch your footing." I knew what I was asking was above and beyond reason. But if the end justifies the means, then saving the kidnapped young women would make her minor transgression worthwhile.

Noelma's gaze took in the jumble of dry goods all over the floor and she shook her head, turned out the light and left.

After 15 or 20 minutes, I began to worry that she had been caught or had simply decided that my story was too full of holes and I wasn't worth the risk. Then, the door opened and the light came on.

Noelma stood in the doorway with no wire cutters and only a shamed expression on her face. When I saw the man behind her, the last bit of hope drained from my body.

He was short, with dark, leathery skin—a crewman, judging from his utility coveralls and Büren jacket. The man's round face showed neither anger nor glee as he studied me with discerning eyes. I noticed that he was carrying the wire cutters, which told me that Noelma had been caught red-handed and had sung like a bird. In my experience, there is always a deal to be cut, and in situations like these, saving one's own hide usually trumps all. Who could blame her? The woman didn't know me from Ted Bundy.

"This is my friend, Raul," she said. "The man I told you about."

Friend, you say? Maybe I had been looking at him through the wrong lens. Perhaps Noelma had brought help. After all, Raul did have the wire cutters.

"Danny McKenna," I said. "Nice to meet you, Raul. I'm hoping you've come to help."

"You could say that." He gazed around at the mess I'd made. "I'm here to help Noelma."

190

I swallowed a lump of *shoulda known better*, and slumped back against the post.

"I found her on deck," he said. "Rummaging around in a tool box. I'd hate to see my friend get duped by someone like you, and then find herself in trouble."

"Did she tell you why I'm here? What I'm trying to do?"

He nodded. "Yes, she told me the story you gave her."

"But you don't believe it."

Raul shook his head. "A bunch of little girls locked inside one of my containers? No, I'm afraid not."

My containers, he'd said. It was a proprietary reference, maybe even paternal. He felt like they were his babies. Raul's position in Cargo Control clearly meant a lot to him, and my guess was that he was a devoted and trustworthy employee. Bad in one way, because he would likely put the company first. But good, because I might be able to use his sense of integrity to my advantage at some point.

"What about this ship's safety officer?" I asked. "Because I'm telling you, that guy is as crooked as Lombard Street."

He and Noelma gave each other a confused look.

"He's in on it," I said. "That asshole is the gang's inside man."

Raul shrugged it off. "I don't know him that well. And anyway, bad workers are the captain's problem to deal with. Not mine."

My stomach rumbled. "Can I at least use the restroom?"

The man scratched his head as he considered it, then came around behind me and cut the plastic bindings. He helped me to my feet and then reattached them in front. Noelma looked upset as she walked with us toward the bathroom.

When I came out of the stall, Raul was leaning against the open bathroom door and Noelma was waiting in the hallway with an apple.

"It's not much, but I thought you'd be hungry," she said.

I smiled. "Anything is better than catsup and Swiss Miss."

We started back toward the storeroom.

"That was you?" she asked.

"What was me?"

Raul flashed an amused grin. "It was all for nothing," he said to Noelma.

She let out a chuckle as we passed the mess halls, though I had no idea what they found so humorous. As we neared my pantry jail cell, I wanted to make another plea on behalf of the poor girls who were up there somewhere in Container City.

Stopping at the doorway, I turned but said nothing as I tried to think of the most effective way to present my plea. They exchanged anxious looks.

"It's nothing," said Noelma, "Some condiments went missing from the officers' mess and I set a trap to catch the thief."

"Had we known it was you, we wouldn't have gone to the trouble," said Raul.

"Oh." I tried to force a chuckle, but still didn't see any humor. "I was actually going to ask you to reconsider letting me go. People are going to die if you don't."

Raul reached past me and pushed open the door. "Take a seat against the post. We'll let the authorities decide what to do when they get here."

"I know you care about the cargo on this ship," I said while Raul looped another plastic binding around the girder. "And if someone had tampered with it or was using the containers to do something illegal, you would take that personally."

He paused for a second while an internal debate took place, but then he shook his head and made for the door. "Like I said, the police will figure it all out."

Noelma went out first, just as Raul flicked the switch and the room fell dark. As the door started to close and the last wedge of light illuminated my spot on the floor, Raul turned to Noelma. "I'll help you disconnect the camera."

The door clicked shut as something else clicked in my brain.

"Hold on a minute!" I yelled. "What camera?"

CHAPTER 58

Bathed in light again, I stared up at Noelma and Raul. "You said something about a camera just as you left the room. What camera are you talking about?"

"It's like a nanny cam," said Noelma. "But don't worry, Mr. McKenna. We know that you only took the food because you were very hungry and needed nourish--"

"Where?" I cut her off. "Where, exactly, did you and Raul place the camera?"

Raul said, "It's on the shelf above the microwave. Why?"

"Because your ship's security officer shoved me in there this morning. Does your camera have audio?"

They both shrugged. "I never used it before," said Noelma. "It was a gift from my daughter. She wanted me to put it by the window of my stateroom so she could see the different ports we visited."

"Yeah, sweet of her. Go get it and see if it captured me and him in there this morning. It was just after the shooting on deck. Probably sometime between eight and nine o'clock."

They left me there, lashed to the girder. Thankfully, they had at least kept the light on. Seconds turned to minutes, and minutes turned to...I don't know, lots of minutes. The wait was giving me a peptic ulcer, and I couldn't figure out what was taking them so long.

The sound of footsteps trudging down the hallway brought my anxiety to a peak. Had they even been able to retrieve the camera? Did it have audio capabilities? Had it captured the security guy's admission?

By the time the door finally opened, I thought I would die. In walked two men I'd never seen. They looked different than others on the ship; in uniforms that somehow seemed more officious.

"I am Comandante de Mar e Guerra Emilio Ferreira," said one of them, pausing as if I was supposed to salute.

"Danny McKenna," I said.

"You are under arrest for crimes against human life," he said, "Specifically, Article 132 of the Portuguese Penal Code; Aggravated murder."

Here we go again, I thought, as they cut my plastic cuffs and replaced them with real ones. It crossed my mind to shoehorn my side of the story into the introduction, but the circumstances were bleak enough already.

Walking me through a gauntlet of crewmen, I craned my neck in search of Noelma and Raul. But only the working stiffs crowded the hallway to watch me. Not even the security man or the ship's captain were there.

I thought he would take me up the elevator to a helicopter pad at the top of the superstructure, but I was led out onto the main deck instead. A group of investigators were gathered around the dead man, collecting photos and forensic evidence. I couldn't see Raul or Noelma anywhere, and worried that the camera hadn't yielded anything useful. Or worse, the security man had gotten to them.

Comandante Ferreira marched me past the action to the accommodation ladder—a portable stairway lowered down the side of the ship. At the bottom of it, an inflatable launch bobbed up and down in the waves. Moored about 150 yards off our port bow was a Navy patrol boat flying the Portuguese flag.

"Comandante, please wait a second," a voice called from across the deck.

The lanky man with a neatly trimmed beard approached with his hand extended. "I am the first officer, Hans Vogel." The two men shook hands. "The ship's captain asked me to thank you and your men for your assistance. He also would like the favor of your company on the bridge for a few moments while we look into this man's absurd claims."

He had dipped his head toward me when he said *"this man."*

I held my breath as the navy man considered the captain's request. It wasn't just my life that hung in the balance, it was also the lives of the girls. About to make my appeal, I thought it better to hold off until I heard the comandante's answer.

"Yes," the man finally said, "we will wait."

The first officer escorted me and the comandante up to a small conference room adjoining the bridge. Captain Wolff introduced himself to Comandante Ferreira and they shook hands.

I noticed the shaved-headed asshole was there too, seated on the other side of the table wearing a smug grin. I eyed him back malevolently, but since I was in handcuffs and he was not, my insolence came off a little underwhelming.

"This man is in charge of our ship's security," Wolff said to the Portuguese officer, motioning to the security man.

The captain removed his eyeglasses and wiped them with the tail of his sweater before turning to me.

"Tell us again why you came aboard my ship."

I gazed around the room at the stacked jury; Captain Wolff, his first officer, his security officer, and the Portuguese comandante. None of them looked all that interested, and their interrogation seemed little more than a formality—not to mention a violation of my right against self-incrimination.

But rather than cry foul or demand a lawyer, I went ahead and retold it. "I've been investigating this case since the beginning of April. What started out as a missing person in California turned into a criminal conspiracy that took me to Thailand. It involves money laundering, organized crime syndicates, human trafficking, and murder."

The security officer rolled his eyes and yawned.

"We unknowingly got close to identifying those at the top of the food chain, and they started a campaign of assassinations and frame jobs. They've already taken out a high-level U.S. Marshal and a U.S. Attorney's investigator."

"Not to be impertinent," said the first officer, "but how does all of this involve you and the man killed on our vessel?"

"Excellent question, Hans." I swung around to face him, wishing my hands were free to gesticulate more fully. "I tracked one of the primary suspects all the way to Marrakesh; Natalia Laskin, a shot caller for the Russian Mob, who is also wanted by Interpol. She and her henchmen had kidnapped a group of young women in Morocco and were holding them in an old warehouse awaiting transport out to your ship."

"That's absurd," said the first officer. "Nobody can board the ship without the security officer's knowledge and permission."

Captain Wolff placed a hand on Hans's arm to quiet him.

"Continue," said Wolff.

"I managed to find the girls and free them in the city of Safi, although I was shot in the process."

They all frowned.

"And this was how long ago?" asked Wolff.

The days were all jumbled in my mind. "It happened the day before yesterday, I think. Yeah, two days ago."

He cocked his head. "Where is this injury?"

I motioned toward my buttocks. Then, afraid they'd make me drop my drawers, I pulled out the hand towel I'd used and held it up for them to see.

Captain Wolff examined the bloodstain without touching it, then nodded for me to continue.

"Anyway, Laskin captured me and was taking me out to sea so they could shoot me. That's when I spotted your ship at anchor and realized that's where she had intended to bring the kidnapped girls that I'd already freed. So, I got a fisherman to bring me to the ship. I boarded without anyone seeing me, and I waited for Laskin to show up."

"It's a bunch of crazy talk," said the security man. "Kidnapped girls, Thailand, Russia... You have quite an imagination."

The ship's captain cut him off. "How does this Khatabi person fit into the story?"

"He's a sous-lieutenant in the Marrakesh police. He stopped Laskin from killing me, and he knows all about what I'm doing. His men have been working on this trafficking case for a while and were just about to close in on them."

My last comment about Khatabi was a stretch, since he hadn't really had a clear idea about the activities in the Safi warehouse. The security man tried to call me on it.

"How long are we going to listen to this nonsense, Captain? The man is deranged. Wouldn't everybody on the ship know if we had a couple of containers full of girls onboard?"

"Perhaps," said the captain.

"Did I say there was more than one container?" I interjected. "Huh, I don't recall mentioning how many there were."

It wasn't the smoking gun by any means, but it gave the captain another thing to ponder. He and the first officer huddled in the corner, embroiled in what looked like an impassioned discussion. After a few more seconds, the captain glanced at the Portuguese comandante and shooed him with his hand. "You can go ahead and take the prisoner."

The security man grinned.

"And we'll conduct a thorough search of the cargo holds when we get to our next port in Hamburg."

"Germany?" I tugged away from the comandante. "It will take at least a few days to get there. Those girls will be dead by then."

Captain Wolff gave an uneasy nod. "There are no girls aboard my ship," he said. But the worried expression on his face belied his strong proclamation. "Take him away."

CHAPTER 59

I frantically glanced around the table looking for a friendly face. But I was an outsider, and it had become clear that nobody in the room was going to take my word over that of the ship's security officer.

A crinkling sound drew my attention to the far end of the table just as the comandante took hold of my arm. The security man was unwrapping a piece of gum. He grinned up at me as he popped it into his mouth, then sat back contently with his arms crossed.

The conference room door opened as I was being led out, allowing me a quick glimpse into the wheelhouse. I paused there to look out through the massive glass panes. The sea of cargo boxes was nearly level in height to the bridge. Stacked row after row, they stretched for an eighth of a mile all the way to the ship's bow. Hundreds and hundreds of them. And somewhere among the multitude, two of them were full of kidnapped girls. Their fresh air intake and temperature regulators had been disconnected, leaving them to die a slow death.

As I was being manhandled out to the elevator, I realized that there was no longer anything I could do to help them.

In the hallway, just outside the navigation bridge, stood Raul and Noelma. I tried to read their eyes, but they both saw the perilous predicament I was in and hurried past us into the bridge. If there was any clue to their purpose, it was not apparent. Their hands were empty. No mini camera. Not even a memory card or a compact disk. I had no more cards to play.

"This man is innocent!" Noelma protested as the rest of the group, including the captain, beheld the ship's diminutive cook.

Raul leaned around her and addressed the captain directly. "There *are* kidnapped women on the ship, and we have proof."

The security man nearly choked on his wad of gum.

Comandante Ferreira shoved me onward, but I pulled away, thrusting myself back onto the bridge. Observing expressions and body language around the room, it felt as if the dynamics had suddenly been thrown into a cocktail shaker. The ship's cook may not have had much standing, but the captain now gazed back and forth between his chief electrical engineer and his security officer. It was between them now, and I was nothing more than a pawn.

Captain Wolff eyed the two officers before raising his palm toward the comandante, temporarily stopping him from whisking me away. "What is this alleged proof?" Wolff asked Raul.

I wanted to ask what took them so long, but apparently the process of uploading the data from the camera's chip wasn't an easy task. Raul told the captain how he had helped Noelma set up the spy cam in the Officer's Mess in order to catch a thief.

Wolff motioned impatiently. "What has this to do with human trafficking?"

The first officer tossed in his two cents. "Are you going to tell us that the women were hiding under the dining table all this time while we ate our meals?"

"I've transferred the video onto our system," said Raul. "I think it will speak for itself."

The worry on the security man's face was unmistakable, and I knew he'd have to make his move before the tape started rolling.

He suddenly erupted, "Why are we wasting our time with this nonsense, Captain? Raul is obviously part of the terrorist plot to commandeer our ship. I am certain that he's colluding with this guy. They should both be taken to jail immediately!"

The rest of them must have recognized the curious timing of his impassioned retort. To the captain's credit, he fired right back. "Last time I checked, Alan, you are not in command of this vessel. This decision is mine to make, and its consequences are mine to suffer. To that point, if there is even a 1 percent chance that women are being trafficked on the Versand, I will turn this entire ship inside out to find them!"

With that, the captain swiveled his laptop around toward Raul. "Show me." Then he glared at Alan, who had casually moved toward the starboard wing bridge door. "And you can sit your ass back down until such time as you're dismissed from this inquest."

Inquest. I liked the sound of that.

The first officer had removed a pistol from the gun locker, and held it to his side as he strolled around the table, taking a position directly behind the security man, Alan.

I couldn't help but grin at the chump. "My, my, how the worm has turned," I said.

Captain Wolff flashed a pointed finger at me. "And you, shut the hell up before I toss your ass in cold storage."

My clever quip had cost my team a point or two, but it had been worth it.

Noelma and Raul worked quickly to call up the recording of the earlier exchange in the Officer's Mess. Finally, the grainy image of the empty room filled the screen.

Alan's voice could be heard asking me how I saw the situation playing out, even before we entered the field of view. Then his back took up most of the frame as he leaned against the counter where the camera had been set up.

Captain Wolff shot him a look at the part where he threatened to throw me overboard.

Though the view of me was blocked by Alan, I could hear my voice saying, *"Once I tell my story to them and they recover those little girls from the container, you'll be the one who will wish he'd been pitched overboard."*

Alan's eyes bulged and his fists tightened with the anticipation of his next line.

Wait for it... I thought.

"Except they will all be dead."

It was the *ah-ha* moment that I had been waiting for, and I might even have said the words if not for what happened at that second.

Alan suddenly jumped up and drove his shoulder into the first officer, knocking him back against a radio console. In that flash of a moment, the weapon slipped out of the first officer's grasp and clattered to the floor. Both men dropped below the consoles and displays, as they wrestled for control of it.

My years of training and muscle memory kicked in and I felt myself grasping for my own sidearm, which, of course, was back on *Wanderlust* at the Buena Vista Yacht Harbor in Alameda.

The struggle over the gun was like watching each grain of sand fall through an hourglass, though it actually took only seconds.

When Alan came up with the pistol in his hand, I knew that I would likely be his first target. Without waiting for confirmation, I dove to the ground—handcuffs and all—landing hard in a sort of belly flop and knocking the wind out of myself in the process.

As unpleasant as that was, it took a backseat to the sound of a gunshot that rang out at the same moment. Someone in the room had been shot. And even though my knee ached and the bullet wound in my buttocks hurt, I was pretty sure it wasn't me who'd been hit this time.

CHAPTER 60

The cast of characters flashed through my mind as I wallowed on the floor, hands cuffed behind my back and trying to suck in the air that had been knocked out of me.

I figured, if Alan had shot the captain we were all in a world of shit. The second officer hadn't impressed me much, and my guess was that he might side with the ship's security officer against me. If the Portuguese comandante was the one hit, it could spell more trouble for yours truly, since I would be the most likely beneficiary and would somehow be blamed. Then I realized that the gunshot might have hit Raul or Noelma, which gave me a sickening guilt. After all, they wouldn't have been in the line of fire if I hadn't gotten them involved in this.

Peeking upward, I saw all of them standing, unimpaired and in good shape. No one had moved, with the exception of the first officer who had picked up a radio mic and was making some type of distress call.

Comandante Ferreira had a stunned expression on his face, which I couldn't figure out until I saw the smoking gun in his hand. To my surprise, it was he who had done the shooting, not Alan. Which meant that Alan was the one who had been shot.

The security officer, now on the floor, had a growing bloodstain radiating from the center of his chest, and I knew there was little hope he would survive.

I knelt next to him as he struggled for breath. "Where are they? Which containers are they in?" I asked.

An invisible hand wiped all expression from his face except steadfast resolve.

"C'mon, Alan," I said. "It's not too late to do the right thing." Again, all I could visualize were those poor young girls, hungry, scared, and quickly running out of air inside heaving containers. "You can save them. Just tell us where they are."

The man's head lifted off the floor, his pale face and bluish lips laboring to speak. I leaned closer, trying my best to listen to what might be my one and only chance at saving them.

He held his face to my ear long enough to whisper a breathy, "Fuck you." Then the asshole slumped back, dead.

Closing my eyes, I knew that his death spelled the end for the captives. Laskin was in the wind and nobody else knew which of the cargo containers they were in.

Ferreira's radio wasn't getting reception this far out, so he had Captain Wolff page his detectives over the ship's loudspeaker. A pair who had been collecting evidence on deck from the earlier incident, quickly responded to the bridge.

"You can remove the cuffs from this man," Wolff told Ferreira. "The video clearly shows he did nothing wrong. While your men tend to the shooting of my corrupt security officer, the rest of us have a much more difficult task at hand. There are 771 boxes onboard that need to be searched. The captives could be in any of them."

As the comandante set me free, I felt a gust of wind beneath my wings. "Now that we're all playing nice in the sandbox, I'd like to make an observation..."

The captain and first officer exchanged looks.

"The kidnap victims will be dead long before you get through checking each container," I said. "There is a way to narrow the number of boxes we have to search."

"How?" asked the captain. "There are so many of them."

Captain Wolff may have known how to steer the ship, but his baffled expression made me wonder how much he really knew about his cargo.

The man was Raul's boss, so Raul tried to toss the guy a bone. "The captain is right. The standard boxes come in all sizes and types, though the 20-footer is most common, followed by the 40. But there are also open sided, high cube, open top and soft top, doors at both ends, and flat rack, which is what you saw the man fall onto this morning. We even have specially designed cubes and a secured section for pharmaceuticals."

"Most of those we can disregard," I continued. "If they *'pulled the plug'* as Alan claimed they had done, logic would dictate that we're looking for something other than a standard Conex box. Something that actually has a plug."

"Reefer," said Raul. "There are 215 of them on this voyage."

"Right, but I would think that most of those are set to keep the contents cold—close to freezing, and in some cases well below that. How high can the reefer containers be set?"

Raul thought for a second. "Somewhere in the range of -30 to +30 degrees Celsius. In answer to your question, on the high end, we're talking 86 degrees Fahrenheit."

"Okay," I said. "So we would be looking for a setting of what, about 20 Celsius?"

Raul nodded. "Something like that."

"Also," I said. "The box would have to be insulated and have an oxygen source; fresh air intake, air exchange, filter, something like that. I assume there are containers capable of those things?"

Raul nodded.

"And you have records that can tell us where on the ship they are located?"

"Absolutely," said Raul. "They're all on my computer down in Cargo Control."

He turned to go and I was about to follow him when I caught another look between Captain Wolff and his first officer. It was clear that they weren't fully convinced of my innocence.

"I'll wait here," I said. "Where the captain can keep an eye on me."

Calling them out on it seemed to make both men uneasy, but neither of them denied it. While we were waiting, the comandante received a radio call on the ship's frequency. He was handed a set of headphones with an attached mic. Meanwhile, I stood around like an expectant father as the captain discussed the ship's ongoing delay with his first officer. Apparently, having to anchor off the coast of Portugal while the authorities investigated one and now two deaths, was screwing up their schedule.

When Ferreira's call ended, he gave me a strange look before motioning the ship's captain over for a private huddle.

"What is it?" I asked with a tad more force than intended.

The men stopped to look at me and then the comandante faced me, head up and feet together.

"The Portuguese Navy has intercepted a boat near shore, and the woman you described has been taken into custody."

I threw a fist into the air. "Yes! That is good news. So, she'll be held in Portugal for the murders in the U.S.!"

He started to respond when Raul and Noelma burst through the door, Raul waving a computer printout. "I've gone over all of them, and there are five Class-B MACA boxes that meet your criteria."

"Wait, what?"

"Modified/Controlled Atmosphere," he said. "Fully insulated and each maintain constant atmosphere by replacing consumed oxygen using an air exchange system." He smiled as he held up the printout. "And the best part is that they are set to keep the interior temperature at a comfortable 68 degrees, Fahrenheit."

"What are we waiting for?" I said. "Let's go free those poor girls!"

Things were finally starting to turn my way, and I had a little pep in my step as we all descended to the main deck.

The five containers in question were spread throughout the cargo holds based upon their destination ports. Two of them were being shipped to the same place and were both in the same cargo hold.

Raul insisted that we work through his list methodically, starting with the closest—a single 40-foot box directly in front of the superstructure in the #5 hold. It was three levels from the bottom, which was still a few levels below the main deck.

I felt my heart race as we climbed down the stairway and out onto the catwalk. The digital displays were lit and their blue flashing numbers seemed an indication that they had not been disconnected. Still, I had hope that this was the right container.

Raul popped the door, and I felt the promising spirit drain from my body.

"Cosmetics," said Raul. "The manufacturers transport them at room temperature because they are made with gelatin, and it spoils in extreme heat or cold."

The next was a shipment of popcorn kernels, and after that was a container full of shampoos—all of them susceptible to temperature fluctuations, according to Raul.

The last hope were two 40-foot containers in the #8 hold. This had to be them, I thought. They fit the profile to a tee, and were even stacked one on top of the other. Again, I felt nervous with anticipation as we climbed up the scaffolding. But my heart sank when I spotted the massive electrical cable connecting the boxes to the ship's diesel generator. I couldn't even look inside when Raul unclasped the swinging doors.

"Potatoes," he said with an air of disappointment.

I climbed to the next level with legs so weak that I barely made it. My stomach did flip-flops as the fifth and final container was opened.

It was a scent I'd experienced before, and it took me only seconds to place it. I closed my eyes and dropped to a sitting position on the metal landing. Burying my face in my hands, I wanted to cry.

"Green tomatoes," said the first officer, a little too cheerfully for my taste. "They are scheduled to be offloaded at the next port of call."

Idiot! Who the hell cares about that?

I had been so certain that the victims would be there. As I sat on the wet landing, I wondered what I had missed.

The Portuguese comandante climbed up to join us. "Nothing?"

Captain Wolff shook his head.

"In that case then, we'll be offloading the bodies and your ship can get back underway."

The captain nodded, but said nothing. Suddenly, both men were focused on me. I sat up, gazing back and forth between them.

"An unfortunate thing," Comandante Ferreira said to me.

I thought he was talking about the fact that we'd come up empty, but I started to sense it was something else. "What is it now?" I asked.

"The woman on the boat," he stared down at his polished black shoes. "We must let her go."

"Natalia Laskin?" I was shocked. "What the hell for? You said that she would be held pending extradition to the U.S."

"No, you said that."

"But we have an extradition treaty with Portugal, don't we?"

"Yes, since 1908."

"Then what's the damn problem?"

"It does not include capital crimes," he said. "We will not allow extradition to another country if the subject faces the possibility of the death penalty or a sentence of life in prison."

I let out a long mopish breath. "Swell. Thanks a pantload for that."

Climbing down to the deck, I was at a loss of what to do next. The day had been a total failure, and I felt as if I was alone in a life raft in the middle of the ocean, and I didn't even have a compass to point myself in the right direction.

CHAPTER 61

It was late in the afternoon when the comandante and his team of investigators finally shoved off, taking with them two bodies zipped in bags and several envelopes full of physical evidence. The sky was still a patchwork of dark clouds, but the wind and rain had subsided enough that the ship's operation had returned to normal. I watched as the navy vessel pulled anchor and headed toward the Port of Sines, where I knew their plan was to set Natalia Laskin free.

As we also got underway, I wondered what would become of me. For all intents and purposes, I had come aboard illegally—essentially a stowaway—without a passport, visa, or any other identification. My stock had dropped exponentially since my failed hypothesis about finding the girls, and I could only assume that the captain still viewed me as a potential suspect. I needed a favor from him, but I doubted he would lift a finger to help me any more than he already had. In any case, I was sure he blamed me for disrupting his schedule and that he wanted me gone.

The captain had organized some of the crew in two-man teams, and was having them check the containers, beginning with those at the front of the ship and working toward the stern. It would be a long process, and I sensed that it was more of a *just-in-case* measure to cover his ass in the event a bunch of girls turned up dead later.

Noelma had excused herself to the galley where she was preparing the evening meal, but I noticed that Raul hadn't left my side.

"Coffee?" he asked, leading me toward the elevator. "Captain wants me to keep an eye on you," he said as we walked. "The crew can be...less than hospitable at times. And crazy ideas often spread quickly on a ship."

He left it at that, but I knew what he meant. Not unlike the rumor mill at SFPD, I could only assume that facts had been mingled with speculation and that somewhere along the way the truth had been swallowed up by gossip and hearsay. As we sat in the crew's lounge, angry looks from the other men confirmed Captain Wolff's instincts.

Maybe they thought I actually had tried to take over the ship. More likely, the crewmen blamed me for the shooting death of their ship's security officer.

"What happens now?" I asked.

Raul stirred a packet of creamer into his coffee and stared at it. "Captain Wolff will turn you over to the authorities when we arrive at Hamburg."

"If that was the captain's intent, why didn't he just send me on my way with the Portuguese cops?"

Not that it really mattered at that point, because I felt myself quickly running out of steam. I had done everything I could to save the girls. I had fought the good fight. I had taken my best shot and I had missed. Not only had I lost the battle, but I'd lost the entire war. I was done.

"Captain wants the medical officer to take a look at your gunshot wound first. Company liability and all that."

I nodded, not caring one way or the other.

"C'mon," Raul said. "I'll walk you down to the infirmary."

We walked in silence, and Raul sat on a chair against the wall as the ship's medic took a look at my injury.

"How does it feel?" he asked, probing my most private parts under a spotlight.

I decided not to give him one of my usual wiseass answers. "Sore, like a toothache, but not as bad as when it first happened."

"It's already starting to heal," he said. "Bullet's still in there, which makes it even more amazing that there's no infection."

As he felt around for what I assumed was the bullet's location, I couldn't shake the image of the kidnapped girls. I had been so certain that they were on this ship. Flinching a couple of times at the pain, it was more of a reminder that what the captives faced was so much worse—if there really ever were any captives to begin with. I began wondering if the Versand was just a decoy and there could have been another ship close by. Whatever the case, I had missed it. Something important had been overlooked. I could feel it.

I felt a skin prick and I lifted my head to see a hypodermic syringe in the medic's hand, the sharp end of which was stuck in my ass.

"Antibiotic," he said. "You're getting this strong first dose, and then I'll give you something to take orally. And a pain killer too, if you need it."

I grunted a shrug, figuring that the German authorities would probably seize them from me anyway. What I would have rather had was a double Scotch on the rocks.

The medic took out a ring of keys and unlocked a heavy cabinet. Donning a pair of reading glasses, he started thumbing through pharmaceutical bottles and boxes that lined the shelves inside.

"Here we are," he said. "You'll take these three times a--"

I froze. "No, no, no!" I sat up, swung around, dropped my feet off the exam table onto the floor. I bent over, yanking up my pants and flashing Raul in the process."

"That was a sight I may never be able to unsee," he said.

"What is it?" asked the medic. "Don't want to take the Cephalexin? Or is it the Percocet you don't like?"

"Neither, Doc. It's not that. I just thought of something." I turned to Raul. "It was there, in front of us the whole time."

"What was there?"

I waived him up off the chair. "We need to get moving. I'll fill you in on the way."

CHAPTER 62

"Should I contact Captain Wolff?" asked Raul as he jogged to keep up with me.

I dismissed his question with a wave of my hand. "No time," I said. "Besides, he's busy getting the ship up and running again and I've already been enough of a distraction for him." I hit the elevator button to the main deck.

"Which way is it to the secured pharmaceutical containers?" I said as we stepped off.

"What?" Raul sounded confused.

"Earlier you mentioned a specific area, a secured place on the ship where drug containers are kept. It didn't click at the time, but then the light suddenly came on when I was down in the infirmary."

"Yes, that's right." His eyes widened. "They are the only cargo on the ship not under my control."

"What does that mean?"

"Well, that it takes the captain's permission to even access it." Raul took me by the arm to turn me toward the stern. "They are aft of the bridge, protected from wind and away from the normal activity on the ship."

"It's the perfect place!"

Raul nodded.

"What else is back there?"

Raul thought a second. "Not much. The security cage is on what we call a sunken deck. There's the freefall lifeboat and some mooring wenches. That's about it."

"Show me the records," I said. "I need to see which of them are temperature controlled and what they are reportedly carrying."

"But I haven't got that information."

"What about bills of lading? Someone must be responsible for monitoring their cargo," I said, "to know what they contain and to make certain their temperature systems are working properly and set correctly."

He stopped suddenly and stared back with a slack jaw. "Alan," he said. "The ship's security officer is, *was*, the only person other than the captain with unrestricted access to the cage."

"Of course he was." I gazed up at the bridge. "It was a perfect setup. Nobody would ever ask questions about the highly secretive pharmaceutical shipments."

We came around the corner and now the superstructure stood behind us. Three rows of containers took up the space between it and the transom stern; one row of 20-foot boxes, one of 40s, and then the deck dropped down a set of stairs to an enclosure of chain linked fencing topped with razor wire. Inside the cage sat four 40-foot containers, side-by-side on the sunken deck.

My heart nearly jumped out of my chest. This time, it all fit; the security, the location, the restricted access, all of it. I felt it in every cell of my body.

Raul lifted the radio from his vest pocket.

I wheeled around. "Who are you calling?"

"Captain Wolff. We'll need his key to get inside the security cage."

Blocking his hand with mine, I shook my head. "No. Not yet."

Doubt, apprehension, loyalty, fear... I read his facial expressions like a map. He finally nodded his compliance without my having to actually say the words: *I don't fully trust that the ship's officers aren't involved.*

"We need tools," I said, examining the heavy chain and lock used to secure the gate. "Bolt cutters won't be much help with this thing."

"The steering gear room and fitter's workshop is just below us," said Raul. "Anything we need will be in there."

We returned to the security cage with a hydraulic spreader. Raul glanced around nervously as I wedged it beneath the fencing and activated the pump. It creaked and groaned as the linked chain fence slowly lifted off the deck. Once it had accordioned up a couple of feet, I slid under the space and Raul followed, dragging the spreader behind him.

All four of the boxes appeared to be outfitted with either filtration, air exchange hardware, or temperature controls, but the equipment and digital readouts were on the opposite end of the container from the hinged doors. We couldn't see if they were functioning.

In the interest of expediency, we moved directly to the first box and used the spreader to pop open its door.

Initially, I wasn't sure what we were looking at. Large dark outlines at obtuse angles filled the space, and it took a minute for my eyes to recognized them as black, shrink-wrapped boxes on wooden pallets.

I released a held breath. "Damnit!"

"EpiPens," mumbled Raul.

"Huh?"

"They're probably EpiPens. The epinephrine has to stay at room temperature, and can't be exposed to sunlight."

"Whatever." I left the door swinging in the ship's draft as I moved to the next box—another 40-footer. We were able to pry its lock open without the hydraulic wedge, but as soon as the tinny hollowness bounced back at me I knew it was a bust. There were a few pallets of cargo, but the box was otherwise empty.

Moving to the third container, I found its double hinged doors were similar to the first two boxes. But the locking mechanism was recessed beneath a stainless-steel cover that had been welded in place. Clearly more security than the other containers I'd seen, its additional safeguarding gave me an immediate buzz of adrenaline.

As the hydraulic pressure started to bow the heavy door, I felt my breathing accelerate. With the pulse of my blood pounding in my ears, the latch at the top of the door suddenly gave way. Unable to remain calm any longer, I lost my composure and began yanking on the lower latch that was still engaged.

I was a madman. Frantically, I tugged and wrenched at the door, back and forth as if the metal would somehow weaken and snap off like the top of a tuna can. When it didn't, I looked back at Raul and then dove head first into the space created by the spreader.

My torso was partially squeezed through the upper half of one of the doors, as my lower half struggled for footing on the bottom lip of the container.

The jet-black interior gave no hint as to what was inside, but my first breath unearthed a rancid odor that made me gag. As the stale air escaped over me, my watering eyes began to acclimate. The first thing I became aware of was the thick foam padding that insulated the doors I was wedged between.

Then I saw the girls.

CHAPTER 63

Hunkered behind pallets of boxes, their terrified eyes stared back. Big, brown, and thankfully flickering with life, they blinked at the daylight pouring in from the opening.

"Anything?" asked Raul.

"They're here," I said, my words crumbling into tears that I didn't particularly want him to see. Once I regained composure, I called out over my shoulder, "And don't radio anyone about this yet!"

The door was still bent out in a V shape, as I motioned the girls to come toward me. "I'm here to help you," I said to blank faces. "Does anyone speak English?"

Inching toward the light, one-by-one they tentatively took hold of my hand and allowed me to lift them through the gap. Their soiled skin added to the brownness of their complexion, and I guessed they were from somewhere in Southern Asia—possibly India, Pakistan, or Bangladesh.

It took about five minutes to free the 13 girls from the container. They had become larger than life in my mind, and I felt as if I knew them like they were my own daughters. I wanted to pick up and hug each of them, but their withered faces told me that they were hungry, thirsty, and had already been through enough. They didn't want some smelly old stranger hugging them anymore than my daughter would.

Once they were out, Raul stayed with them while I started on the last container. I walked around to the far side first, observing that the generator connection to both of them had indeed been severed. Then I went to work on the door, which fortunately opened easier than the other had.

Bowing far enough out to lift both upper and lower latches, its double doors swung open with relative ease. The second container was equally as well insulated, and its odor was equally as bad. The girls inside were lighter skinned, with more traditionally Asian looks. Some appeared to be even younger than the first group, yet they were also alive and able to walk out on their own. I counted eleven of them in the second group, none of whom spoke a word of English.

"Those in the first container are from Mumbai, India," said Raul, motioning toward them. "And these girls must be from the Port of Aberdeen in Hong Kong."

"How do you know this?"

"Because those were our only ports of call before Morocco."

Something about the Port of Aberdeen rang a tiny bell for me. Flashing back to the list of phone calls that launched me on this case's trajectory, I remembered Aberdeen was a smaller port right across from Hong Kong Harbor. It was one of the locations from which a telephone call had been placed to the dead Russian's phone.

Everything was starting to make sense now. The phone calls had all been from human trafficking pick up spots. First Hong Kong, then India. The empty container had probably been intended to hold the young Berber women, but I had thwarted that plan at the warehouse in Safi.

"What now?" asked Raul, kick-starting me out of my thoughts and back into the problem at hand.

"We need to get these girls safely off of the ship."

"The captain needs to be told," he said. "This is too important for him not to know about it."

When I hesitated, Raul opened his hands in a questioning motion.

"Something isn't right," I said. "I can feel it."

He frowned. "What are you talking about?"

"I think there's a rat in your wheelhouse." Behind him stood the girls, shivering in the cold spray as the ship raced through the surf to make up the lost time. "I'll make you a deal," I finally said. "I will notify Captain Wolff of what we've found, but you need to get them off of the boat first."

"Are you that certain that the captain can't be trusted?"

"Not sure about him. But I'm almost positive that your first officer is playing for the other team."

"Vogel? No. I've sailed with him before. He's more capable on the bridge than the captain."

"That may be, but he's been pushing the captain in the wrong direction since the beginning. And how was Alan able to take his gun away so easily? In fact, who told Vogel to get the gun in the first place? He essentially armed the suspect, and if it hadn't been for the police comandante, Alan would have escaped—possibly shooting all of us in the process."

Raul's face showed doubt, but I had left enough of a possibility in his mind that he acquiesced. "Okay, but how do I get them off of the ship?"

I motioned toward the free-fall lifeboat mounted to a metal slide above us. "I assume you have drills on how to operate that thing."

"Of course, but it sets off an alert on the bridge. The captain will know as soon as it launches."

I kneaded my bristly face. "Then let's get the young ladies aboard it, and be ready to hit the release as soon as I give you the signal."

"What signal?" he asked.

"You'll know it when you see it."

Climbing onto its track, I stuck my head inside the self-contained lifeboat and found it even more claustrophobic than the containers. But I counted 30 seats, plus that of the operator—room enough for all of the girls and Raul.

We got them loaded into the lifeboat and belted into their seats. Raul took his spot on an elevated driver's seat facing front. The other seats faced backwards in order to absorb the impact of a 35-foot drop into the sea. Once they were ready, I went to the elevator and pressed the button marked NAV LEVEL—to the bridge.

CHAPTER 64

The captain and the first officer were both in the wheelhouse when I came in.

"Nobody can just walk onto the bridge," said the first officer. "You are either summoned, or you request authorization. In either case, the captain must approve it. *In advance!*"

That's strike one, I thought.

"It's all right, Hans." The captain rested a hand on the man's arm. "What can we help you with? Mr. McKenna, is it?"

"Danny McKenna." I forced a tight smile at them both. "I'm sure I've figured out which containers the girls are being held in."

Hans rolled his eyes. "Not this drivel again."

Captain Wolff interjected, "We already have crewmen searching the cargo holds. Whatever theories you have about that will be passed on to the police when we arrive at our next port, if we haven't found them by then. In the meantime, I want to have your wound examined by the--"

"Your medic has already checked me; I'm fine."

"A relief, to be sure," he said, turning back toward the controls. "Then, if there's nothing else..."

"There is."

"Excuse me?"

"There is something else," I said flatly. "The girls are being held inside two 40-foot reefer boxes on the sunken deck near the stern of the--"

"I know where the sunken deck is," Wolff snapped. "And the only boxes aft are the secured pharmaceuticals. They are in a fortified cage, and access is highly restricted. It would be literally impossible for anyone to get to those containers, much less hide people in them."

I nodded. "And the only person with unfettered access would be?"

"Me," he said.

I shook my head. "And the ship's security officer."

"This is absurd," said Hans. "Alan has no access, for God's sake, he's dead. Unless you are trying to imply that Captain Wolff--"

"I'm not *implying* anything, Hans. I'm giving you notice that those young girls are being transported to your next ports of call in those containers, and now that their power supplies have been severed, they will be dead by the time we arrive in Hamburg."

Hans dramatically brought his palm to his forehead. "Captain, this is absolutely redicu--"

"Go check it out, Hans."

"But captain!"

"Just do it, and be quick about it." Wolff turned to me. "And this is the final goose chase. After this, you will be placed under guard and confined to the crew's dayroom on B Deck."

"Fair enough." I started for the door, with First Asshole Hans following close behind me. I noticed that the captain had not handed him the key to the cage, which was a confirmation of sorts. I took it to mean that Captain Wolff had delegated the pharmaceuticals' security to his first officer. So, either the captain was in on it or he was lazy and probably in violation of company security protocols for passing it off to a subordinate. Either way, it was a strong indicator that Hans and Alan had been working together with Laskin.

Taking the elevator down, I pondered Hans's next move. Since he was unaware that I had already recovered the victims, I assumed he would somehow try to deter me from finding them. The countdown had begun and I knew he would have to do something in the next few seconds.

Sizing him up, I surveyed his waistband for the bulge of a gun but his loose jacket made my assessment inconclusive. The man was young and fit and if there was a weight room onboard, I was sure he spent a lot of time in it. I decided to go on the offensive.

"You might as well give it up, Hans."

He glared back with eyes that burned.

"I have already gotten into the cage and found the girls," I said. "They've been taken to a safe place and all I needed was confirmation that you were the one working with Alan."

His jaw twitched but he said nothing.

The elevator door opened and we both stepped off.

"I don't believe you," he said, continuing along a catwalk that led to the backside of the superstructure.

I walked in front of Hans, which wasn't the most advantageous place for me to be. On one side of the catwalk was a long drop to the bottom of a deep cargo hold and on the other was another long drop into the roiling sea. Hurrying along, I descended the stairs to the sunken deck before he had a chance to shove me overboard.

The security cage stood before us with a warped swath of chain link fencing bent away from the ground. Hans frowned at it as he moved past me to the locked gate. With a key produced from his pocket, he opened the padlock and rolled it open.

Without even entering the cage, he could see the doors of the four containers—three standing wide open and the other one bent six ways from Sunday.

I watched Hans' twitching jaw as he surveyed the security cage. He turned to me after a long silence, and managed a tight smile.

"You have no idea what you've done," he said. "You just signed your own death warrant."

I coughed out a laugh. "If I had a nickel for every time someone's told me that."

"You will be blamed for burglarizing the containers. As far as the captain knows, the manifest lists the contents as drugs and liquor. Once I locate the female workers, they will secretly be taken off the ship and nobody will ever know they were here. Instead of being the hero that you so desperately want to be, you will only be remembered as a common thief who broke into the pharmaceutical boxes."

That's strike two.

"I take that to mean I won't be around to tell them the truth."

Hans nodded. "Correct."

He dropped a hand into the small of his back and came out with a pistol. Raising it to the center of my chest, his index finger itched to drop the hammer on me.

"Haven't you gotten yourself into enough trouble with that gun today?"

The grin returned to his face. "Say goodbye, McKenna."

That was strike three.

There was a sudden popping sound as Raul activated the release from inside the lifeboat. It rumbled down its casters as if the Big Dipper rollercoaster was passing directly overhead. The sound caused Hans to momentarily glance up, but that was all the time I needed.

An upward palm strike to his nose sent a snotty spritz of blood in one direction, and his handgun flying in the other. The splash of the lifeboat hitting the water was only eclipsed by dear Hans flopping onto the deck.

The rear door of the wheelhouse flew open almost immediately, and the captain leaned over the railing with binoculars tethered to his neck. "What in the name of God is going on down there?" he bellowed. "Who in the hell authorized launching the free-fall?"

I picked up Hans's pistol and waved back at the captain. "That would be me."

CHAPTER 65

The captain had shut down the ship's engines and we were now slowly drifting in a counter-clockwise motion. The scant light that had intermittently shown itself through the clouds had disappeared over the bow. Behind us was only the dark sea, and an occasional flash from the lifeboat strobe as it headed toward land.

A couple of burly deck hands had been sent to help the first officer to his feet. They eyed me, but said nothing, as we made our way up to the navigation level where Captain Wolff and a few other officers waited. The launch of the free-fall lifeboat had apparently triggered certain protocols, as evidenced by the feverish pace of activity on the bridge.

"I guess I should thank you," Wolff said listlessly.

He had obviously connected the dots, realizing that we had found the girls and Raul was now taking them to safety. The man's red and swollen eyes blinked through his round eyeglasses, revealing even more than his words. While his career may have survived the security officer's criminal misconduct, the additional betrayal of his first officer would be an insurmountable disgrace.

"Gendarmerie Maritime has sent a P400 class patrol to intercept our lifeboat," a man with a headset told the captain. "Their ETA is 17 minutes from Nantes."

Wolff nodded, glancing around the bustling navigation station as if it were his last time there.

Gendarmerie was French, which told me that we were probably somewhere in the Bay of Biscay. As the recovery efforts grew, I could see that the event had taken on an international life of its own. The captain had probably realized it long before I had. The scandal would likely spell an abrupt end to his career, if not a prison sentence for his gross incompetence.

Noelma appeared at the door with a pot of coffee and tray of cups. She flashed a glance at me and then to the bedraggled first officer, who was under guard on a chair next to me.

I moved toward the door and caught her just as she was leaving. "Will you do me a favor?" I whispered.

"If I can."

The captain had become distracted with a phone call, and I leaned closer to the cook. "Is there a locker room for the officers?"

She frowned. "Not that I know of. Why? What do you need?"

"I need Hans's phone." Glancing at the captain, I saw that he was still occupied. "I checked, but he doesn't have it on him."

"Might be in his sleeping quarters," she said, then scurried off of the bridge as the captain finished his call.

He turned with a handheld mic and made an announcement to those in the room and over the ship's loudspeaker at the same time. "This is Captain Wolff speaking. We are being ordered to port at Saint Nazaire. All hands are to remain onboard the ship until cleared by French Customs and the police. For those of you who are not aware, First Officer Hans Vogel has been relieved of duty. All related roles and responsibilities will be assumed by the second officer."

I figured it would be after midnight by the time we docked. Tired and hungry, I wasn't sure how long I could last without collapsing. "What do you plan to do with me?" I asked Wolff.

He looked as exhausted as I was. "Like I said earlier, you will be confined to the crew's dayroom until the French authorities arrive. Both of you will," he added with a nod toward his former first officer.

"What, me and Hans?"

The captain let out a sigh. "The crew will be undergoing docking maneuvers. I'm shorthanded as it is, and I already have to reassign a man to watch Hans. It's just simpler to have you both in one place."

"Why don't you tie him up in the store room like you did me?"

He removed his glasses and rubbed his eyes. I knew that I was making a bad situation worse for him, but I was also tired of being treated like a suspect. Besides, my complaints would put me in a better bargaining position.

"That was a mistake," he conceded. "You are not being held as a prisoner. I'm asking that you remain there for your own safety."

I acted like I was thinking it over, even though I knew I had no choice. "Then I'll be able to eat something, use the phone, and walk around to stretch my legs?"

"Within reason." Wolff turned back to the controls. "The second officer will see to your needs when he's able."

Sometime around midnight I felt a sharp and distinct vibration as the thrusters pushed the ship up against the dock. Some food had been left out for us in the dayroom, and there was a pot of coffee in the corner. A flat screen TV was mounted on the wall, and the Weather Channel played quietly as I nodded off and on. Hans had reclined on one of the sofas with a blanket over him, and hadn't spoken to anyone. Our guard sat in a chair reading from his tablet.

I wanted to find a way back up to the officers' quarters, but the captain had made it pretty clear that I wasn't to be left unattended.

"Any chance I can walk around a bit?" I asked the crewman who was guarding us. "I was shot a few days ago, and it's pretty sore."

"You don't look shot." He set down his tablet. "Walk around in here if you like, but my instructions are not to let you out of the room."

"Yeah, I get it. Well, is there a phone I can use? Captain said I would be able to make a call once we docked."

The man stood up, stretched, and walked to the window. He could see that we were in port, and I could tell by the uncertainty on his face that he didn't want to bother the captain about the phone call.

"Yeah, you can use mine," he said, handing me his phone.

I once lost my Social Security card and had to call them for a replacement. That was the most convoluted automated phone tree I'd ever encountered, until I tried to call the Portuguese coast guard.

As it turns out, coastal law enforcement is performed by several government agencies that make up their Maritime Authority System. From there, I was transferred to the Autoridade Marítima Nacional, who then transferred me to their Lisbon headquarters, where I was transferred to their office at the port in Sines. After all that, I was finally connected to Comandante Ferreira's voicemail.

"Yes, hello Comandante! You may remember arresting me and then unarresting me on the MS Versand earlier today, well, it was yesterday now."

My guard cocked his head with a single frowning eye.

"Anywho," I continued. "I've been fully cleared of any wrongdoing and, in fact, we have recovered two dozen young girls who had been held in captivity on the ship."

The guard grunted and gave me a full-faced glare.

"Well, to the point, I need a huge favor from you. If Natalia Laskin is still in Portuguese custody, I'd like you and your officers to try and document whatever you can; phone numbers she calls, visitors she gets, and the identities of anyone who signs for her release or comes to pick her up. That would be of great assistance in this investigation. This *international human trafficking* investigation. Thanks."

I had intentionally emphasized the human trafficking angle to pinch his balls a bit. If the comandante had any ideas about blowing me off, the nature and importance of the case might make him think twice. Without a phone of my own, I had no recourse but to leave the number of my office in Oakland.

Realizing that Shanay could get the callback and have no idea what it was about, I started to dial her cell to warn her.

"I said, only one call." The guard reached out with an open hand. "And you just used it up."

I returned his phone and then made one more pitch to stroll the hallways because of the pain in my hip. Not surprisingly, my request was flatly denied.

I ate a bagel with peanut butter, then stretched out on one of the couches opposite Hans. With time quickly ticking away, it seemed unlikely that I'd get the opportunity to call Shanay to let her know I'm still alive, or to search Hans's room for his phone.

CHAPTER 66

I must have fallen asleep, because it was 6 a.m. and light outside when I opened my eyes again.

Rubbing the life back into my face, I saw that our guard had also nodded off in his chair. Hans was snoring away on the other couch—his distended nose crusty and bruised after yesterday's run-in with my palm.

Tiptoeing past the sleeping crewman, I had just reached the hall when he called out to me. "Where the hell do you think you're going?"

"To take a leak," I said, though I had actually planned to make a mad dash up two levels to the officers' quarters. My aspirations of getting a look at Hans's phone were quickly becoming a dead issue.

Our guard stood at the dayroom doorway where he could watch me enter and exit the restroom while keeping an eye on Hans at the same time. There was no way to duck the guy.

"They're here," he said when I came out. "Looks like the Frenchies have sent some sort of special forces cops. They're boarding us now."

I went to the window but couldn't see anyone, only two black mini buses with flashing blue lights and the letters GIGN on the side. An accommodation ladder had been lowered for them, and it now hung off the side of the ship like a fruitless tree.

"Which one of you is Hans Vogel?" demanded a darkly-clad man who suddenly appeared at the doorway.

We both pointed to the snorer on the couch. With a wave of a hand two more came in, rousted Hans, and zip-tied his hands behind his back. As they led him out, the initial officer turned to me.

"Are you McKenna?"

"Yeah."

"Come with us."

Two other men who had waited in the hall, entered and slid the plastic ties around my hands before escorting me to the main deck. *So much for not being treated like a suspect.*

Yellow tape barricaded the catwalk to the aft, where I imagined a hoard of investigators would soon descend on the four containers. The cops had obviously intercepted Raul and the girls, which meant that the cat was more or less out of the bag.

Noelma stepped out from an interior stairway and held out a brown paper bag. "I made a breakfast sandwich for you to take."

One of the commandos snatched the bag and looked inside before passing it to me.

I was hustled off the ship and loaded into one of the black buses. They took me to an office building where I was whisked down an empty hallway and into an interview room.

Two nicely dressed investigators, a man and a woman, awaited me there. My plastic ties were taken off and I was given a cup of coffee. The interrogation was much less confrontational and less accusatory than I was used to, and seemed to focus mostly on the information that led me to recovering the girls on the ship.

"Do you need a doctor for your bullet wound?" the woman asked at the end of the questioning.

I told her that I'd been checked and that I felt okay.

"Any questions for us before we finish?" asked the man.

Something Hans Vogel had mentioned earlier still gnawed at me. "The first officer told me that liquor was found inside the containers," I said. "It didn't sound right that the traffickers would provide the girls with alcohol instead of food and water."

The investigators smiled. "No, no," said the woman. "The victims had been given water and a little bit of food. The liquor was being shipped on pallets. The girls never even knew what it was."

"Liquor shipments," I repeated, wondering what the chances were that this seemingly insignificant tidbit was also connected to my first homicide case in San Francisco. "These liquor shipments wouldn't have originated in Latvia, by any chance?"

They flipped through their notes. "Yes, as a matter of fact they were. A company in Riga, owned by a man named Sergei Petrenko."

"I'll be a son of a bitch!"

They looked at one another and shrugged.

"So, what happens to me now?"

"Tomorrow you'll be deported back to the United States," said the man. "Your Department of State is aware of the situation and will take custody of you upon landing in Washington D.C."

"Tomorrow?"

"Unfortunately, there are no other direct flights out of Nantes today. In the meantime, we have what we call a *quiet room* where you can rest. It has a sleeping cot and a private washroom."

At least it wasn't a jail cell. Turns out the quiet room actually had a door with a little sign that flipped to "OCCUPIED" when it was locked. I washed up as best I could, splashing soapy water all over myself and then drying off with a bunch of paper towels—carefully dabbing over my gunshot wound.

I felt a little better afterward, then realized I'd have to put on my old clothes—the hazmat coveralls I'd worn off of the ship. With all of the questions I'd fielded, no one had ever asked me about them.

Sitting on the cot, I leaned back against the wall and opened the bag Noelma had given me. She'd made a sandwich of bacon, egg, and cheese, which I instantly devoured. As I wiped my face with one of several napkins she'd stuffed inside, I felt the bag suddenly vibrate. Reaching beneath the napkins, I grasped a solid block at the bottom of the bag and pulled it out.

Hans's cell phone was lit up with an incoming text message, which I needed no passcode to view. Holding the phone at arm's length so I could read it without my glasses, I felt the breath catch in my throat.

DM DETAINED BY THE GIGN IN NANTES, FRANCE, is all the message said. Assuming that I was "DM", I realized that whoever sent it was alerting Hans as to where he could find me. Which meant that the person had no idea Hans had been arrested and was now out of commission.

There was no name on the caller ID, just a phone number. The message had been texted from the (415) area code. I blinked and squinted at it, trying to force my brain to absorb what it meant. It was a San Francisco number.

I sat upright on the cot all night, struggling to make this new information fit into what I already knew. Until the text, there had been no solid local connection to my human trafficking investigation. Now I realized, probably a little too late, that I should have put more significance on the circumstantial bits of evidence instead of just chalking them up to coincidence.

My mind tried to sort through it all; the MS Versand, the Russian billionaire's liquor, and Natalia Laskin having been flown out of Thailand on a jet owned by a Latvian company. Now, somebody in San Francisco was texting my location to Hans Vogel—one of the trafficking suspects. It was almost too much, and my head felt like it was going to explode. Why? Because beneath all of the indicators was the swirling sinkhole of my greatest fear: that my wife and her boyfriend were somehow involved.

CHAPTER 67

I boarded at noon and had the row to myself. The storm had passed, leaving the air clean, bright, and crisp for takeoff.

The nine-hour flight had given me time to think, but instead, I ordered a couple of mini-bottles of Scotch and watched the latest James Bond movie—compliments of the Federal Government's repatriation budget. I'd already done enough thinking, and the whole thing was starting to get to me. Besides, I was bringing with me no physical evidence to implicate Laskin and was arriving no better off than when I'd left.

I was still wanted by the feds for helping Aafreen escape from custody and I suspected that I'd be thrown in jail as soon as we landed. Things looked even worse when I was called by name to disembark before the rest of the passengers.

Two uniformed men met me at the gate and a wave of panic washed over me as soon as I got a look at their agency patches: Department of Justice—United States Marshal. Since the woman who I'd helped escape was being charged with their boss's murder, I didn't expect a welcome home hug from them.

They introduced themselves, but I wasn't listening.

"Do you have any baggage?" one of them asked.

"I have issues with my father and I tend to drink too much."

They shrugged at each other.

"Long flight?" asked the other.

"Just an hour," I said. "We took off at 12:20 this afternoon."

He frowned and then laughed. "Oh, I get it. France is eight hours ahead of us."

I rolled my eyes. "Aren't you going to handcuff me?"

He let out another laugh as we left the building. "What for?"

I guessed that these two hadn't gotten the memo.

They drove me to their headquarters building in Arlington, and into the parking garage. We got off the elevator on the 7th floor and they walked me to the door of a glass-enclosed conference room. Leaving me standing there, they turned and got back on the elevator. Inside the conference room were three men and three women. I tapped on the door before walking in.

One of the women stood up and came toward me. It took my exhausted brain a second to recognize that she was Aafreen Soltani. "You... You're here," I said.

With eyes full of tears, she threw her arms around me and squeezed tightly. "Thank you. Thank you so much!"

I felt her body shake and heard muffled sobs as I leaned my face down to her soft hair. "I'm not sure what you're thanking me for, but I'm glad to see that you're out of jail and you're safe."

"I've been cleared," she said, "thanks to you."

She had me at a loss. I'd achieved nothing that I had set out to do. But I stayed there with my face pressed against hers, enjoying the embrace too much to disengage. Finally, I felt like a fraud and gave her fragrant hair one last inhale before straightening up.

Shaking my head, I apologized. "I didn't get the evidence I was looking for," I said. "I saw the addresses in Laskin's rental car, but she went out of range and the screen went blank before I could... Anyway, I got nothing. Zero. And then I thought I had her in Morocco, and then again on the ship. But she got away on a motorboat. The Portuguese couldn't keep her because of some technicality in our extradition treaty."

Aafreen smiled back as if none of what I'd said even mattered. When I finished, she took both of my hands in hers. "We got to her rental car before they deleted the data. We impounded it and swept it for evidence, including digital forensics. All the phone contacts and mapping locations were captured; my house, Kingsbury's, Leclaire's, even the mob's safe house in Little Odessa."

"How?" I glanced at the others who had yet to speak. "How did your guys get there so fast? How did they know which car was hers?"

"Your secretary," said Aafreen. "I guess you had been on the phone with her when you lost the data? Anyway, she apparently called the Marshals right away and told them where they could find the evidence to Kingsbury's murder. Maybe we didn't capture Laskin, but it was enough to get the U.S. Attorney to drop all of my charges."

"Shanay did that?" I said. "You know, I promoted her to executive assistant!"

One of the men at the table cleared his throat and Aafreen turned to introduce them. Two of the men were Marshals investigators and the other was with the FBI. One of the women was with the State Department and the other was a stenographer.

The State Department lady smiled as she shook my hand. "We thought it best to take care of all our interviews at one time, if that's okay with you."

"Sure." I took a seat across from them.

For the next three hours, I told my story, and retold it again. At one point Aafreen gasped. "You got shot?"

I motioned toward my hip, and they all leaned forward as if they would be able to see it through my hazmat coveralls. Avoiding the exact location of the wound, I continued with the story.

The Elliott sisters, Hassan, Sous Lieutenant Khatabi, they were all included. Even Hassan's cousin's uncle and Waleed the tour guide.

Then came the humiliating part.

"May we take a look at your paperwork?" they asked.

"Unfortunately, I fled the Elliott's hotel room before I could grab my case file."

"What about your cellphone? The one you used to photograph Laskin's rental car screen."

"Unfortunately, that was taken from me on the ship. But I have Hans Vogel's phone," I said, patting my pocket. Then I felt a flash of panic at the thought of giving it up.

I abruptly asked to use the restroom.

It was just down the hall, and I was able to do my business in total privacy for once. The business I had to do was removing the SIM card from Hans's phone, which I did before returning to the glass room. Not that I was withholding information from the investigators, but the San Francisco phone number was the one piece that I had left out. If Doris was involved in any of this, I wanted to be the first to know. The last thing I wanted, was for my wife to be dragged off to jail and my daughter left orphaned.

When I returned to the conference room, they had set out an evidence envelope and pen on the table. I filled out the date, time, and chain of custody sections and tossed the phone inside—minus the data card. For all they would know, it was that way when I took it.

"What now?" I asked.

"Our embassy in Paris will liaise with the Maritime Gendarmerie for timely updates on the widening investigation. We will probably need accurate contact information for you, as you may be required to testify at some point."

"Testify where?"

The State Department woman gave a half shrug. "Any of the countries involved, and quite possibly the International Court in The Hague. We'll just have to wait and see how all of this plays out."

She already had a sizable file in front of her, and I suspected they had known most of my story before I even came into the room. There were a few things that I had yet to figure out, so I took a shot and asked them.

"Our next port of call was supposed to be Hamburg," I said. "That confused me a little. Do you know if the Versand was supposed to pick up more of the so-called *'pharmaceutical'* containers there?"

One of the FBI men tapped his phone screen. "No. That's where one of the boxes was supposed to be offloaded."

"What about the other box?"

He scrolled again. "That one was destined for the stop after that. Gothenburg, Sweden."

That made about as much sense to me as Hamburg. These were developed countries, allies of the United States. Respected in every sense. It took me a second to see the whole picture. "They must be the consumers," I said. "Cheap labor, domestic servitude, prostitution, pornography... The impoverished Asians from third-world countries are sold to the wealthy Europeans."

The State Department lady lifted an eyebrow; an indicator that my blunt assessment was less than politically correct.

The United States has to fit into this somehow, I thought. As much as I would like to have believed otherwise, I knew we couldn't be blameless in what was a worldwide criminal network fueled by greed, corruption, and exploitation.

"Where was the ship headed after that?" I asked.

"Latvia," said the FBI man. "And then on to the Port of New York-New Jersey."

"Latvia again." I shook my head.

They were finished questioning me, and their body language made it clear they were also finished with the investigation. The American—me—had been cleared of any wrongdoing, the victims would all be returned to their countries of origin, and both Germany and Sweden would face the humiliation of world opinion for their roles as consumers. As long as there would be no blowback on the U.S., it was all good as far as they were concerned.

"Is anyone planning to take this further?" I asked.

There was a round of throat clearing and head scratching. Clearly, nobody wanted to pry into the hornet's nest of our own complicity.

"One last question," I said. "New York wasn't going to be the ship's final stop, was it?"

"No." The FBI man stretched his neck. "Their route was through the canal, then up the Pacific Coast to--"

"Let me guess," I said, cutting him off. "Manzanillo, and then to the Port of Oakland."

"How did you know that?" asked the woman.

"Lucky guess."

CHAPTER 68

The investigation that had begun seven months earlier when I was with the SFPD, appeared to have come full circle. I would need to get back to the Bay Area and go through my old San Francisco file, but its connection to all of this seemed conclusive in my view. But finding answers to all of those lingering questions would have to wait.

As the suits filed out of the conference room, I was left alone with Aafreen. Her warm brown eyes and beautiful smile was all the salve my aching body needed. And she had an even better antidote for my pain.

"How about we go back to my house?" she said.

I think my whole body smiled, but then I looked down at myself and grimaced.

"We'll stop to buy something for you to wear," she laughed. You can take a shower, or I can even run a nice hot bath for you to soak in. I'm also guessing you could use a good meal, so I'm going to take you to my favorite steakhouse tonight."

"That sounds absolutely amazing." I winced as I stood up. "Maybe I should give Shanay a quick call, just to let her know that I'm alive."

Aafreen handed me her phone before leaving the room.

"McKenna Investigations, Executive Assistant Shanay Moore speak'n."

"Shanay, hi, it's me."

"McKenna? Where in the hell you been? I been call'n your phone, but some English lady keep on answering. Man-oh-man, there been some stuff goin' down 'round here."

"Like what kind of stuff?"

"Well for one, that wife of yours wanted to chew on you about a call she got from a embassy in France. Said you got busted for kill'n someone on a boat."

"No, no, that was all a misunderstanding. It's all cleared up now." My hip started throbbing again, so I sat back down. "Speaking of that, a guy by the name of Comandante Ferreira might be calling for me."

"He already did, but he was all in-the-closet about it and wouldn't tell me nothin'. So I wrote down his caller ID number just in case you needed it. I'll text it to you." She paused. "Who's phone you call'n me from, anyways?"

"Aafreen Soltani, the woman I came here to help." I stood again. "And by the way, I really want to thank you for helping me out with that rental car thing. Calling the Marshals was outstanding work. In fact, it pretty much saved the whole case."

"That's what you pay me for," she said. "So you comin' in to the office today?"

"No, I'm still in D.C. I'm thinking I'll spend the night and fly back tomorrow."

"That's what I'm talk'n 'bout."

"What's that mean?"

"You get'n yo self a little *Soltani* tonight. Good for you, McKenna."

I ended the call before Shanay knew how embarrassed she was making me.

Overshadowing that though, was what Shanay had said about Doris getting a call from the embassy in France. It had to be about the same time that I intercepted the text on Hans's phone, alerting him to my whereabouts. A chill ran through me as I considered who else might have known where I was. Sadly, I couldn't think of anyone.

My next call was to Bridget's cellphone. She answered right away. "Hey Dad, are you all right?"

"I'm fine, sweetheart. How have you been doing?"

She blew past my question. "There are a bunch of news cameras outside. They came about an hour ago, trying to ask me and Mom a bunch of questions."

"Damnit!" I closed my eyes. "Sorry, I, uh, got into a little pickle during my last case and the embassy called Mom, and--"

"I don't think it's about that, Dad. They said you got shot saving some girls who had been kidnapped."

"Oh?" Now that was a horse of a different color. Finally, a score in the plus column for ol' McKenna.

I quickly gave my daughter the PG version of what had happened, avoiding any mention that I was currently in D.C. Not that I didn't trust her, but if Doris was indeed an adversary, she would easily be able to extract my whereabouts from Bridge. And I didn't need another assassination attempt screwing up my evening with Aafreen.

My daughter told me that she loved me, which took away all of the pain in my hip and felt better than any steak dinner ever could.

Aafreen lived in a cute brick townhouse in Fairfax, Virginia. It was neat and bright like her, and had a nice view over a central courtyard. She fixed me a Scotch, which I took with me into my hot bath. After a shave and a fresh bandage on my injury, I was about to dress in my newly purchased clothes for our romantic meal.

229

There was a tap on the bathroom door, and I nearly threw out my knee as I spun around. Seeing myself in the mirror was even more of a shock. It crossed my mind to quickly get on the floor and do a bunch of sit-ups.

Another couple of taps made it clear that my greatest fantasy and my greatest fear were about to become one.

"We have some time before dinner," she said against the door. "So don't bother getting those clothes on just yet."

CHAPTER 69

As we sipped our wine at a candlelit table, Aafreen and I laughed about our comical escape from the hospital. Now that we weren't going to prison for it, the whole episode seemed more entertaining.

She was beautiful in every way, and I couldn't take my eyes off of her smile. The only problem was that I had a hard time imagining what she saw in me. I kept an eye out for buyer's remorse, vis-à-vis regretting the intimacy we shared before dinner. But she just kept looking at me with those loving eyes.

"I owe you so much," she said, reaching across to rub my hand.

It had been a long time since I'd felt this way, or been made to feel this way, and it was nice. Almost too nice.

"That isn't why you..."

Aafreen shook her head. "I've gotten to know you, and I see that beneath your sometimes awkward exterior, you are a good person. You're a good father, and you were probably a good husband."

"Not so sure about that last one, but I'm really glad you feel that way. I hope you can tell that I am completely enamored by you."

"Obviously. You went all the way to Morocco and got shot trying to save me. You're the only one who believed me when all the evidence said I was guilty."

I smiled through and through. This was a first for me.

We went back to her place after dinner, and it was probably one of the best nights of my life. Not only did we enjoy each other again, but we curled up together and slept soundly—another first for me in a long, long time.

In the morning, we took our time getting out of bed. You could tell it was going to be a warm day as we drove across the turnpike to a Starbucks. As we sipped our coffees, I found myself thinking about the case and wondering if Laskin was still trafficking young girls all around the world.

"Can I use your phone to make another call?"

Aafreen gladly handed it to me. "Now don't phone somebody who is going to make a great day into a bad one."

I smiled as I punched in Comandante Ferreira's phone number.

"Yes, who is this?" he answered.

"Comandante, it's Danny McKenna from the United States."

"Of course. I wanted to call and congratulate you on your success. An effort well worth the undertaking, I should say."

I thanked him, but he hadn't seemed like the type to give accolades without wanting something in return, and I wondered what was really on his mind.

"As you may recall, I and my men were quite instrumental in the investigation aboard the ship. In fact, I spoke to the captain when we were onboard, in private of course, urging him to follow your advice. I hope your testimony in court will reflect Portugal's commitment to the worldwide fight against the commercial exploitation of--"

"Uh-huh, yeah, of course." I paused a beat. "But didn't you tell me that Natalia Laskin would be released by your country?"

"Well, our hands were tied in that instance. But I have some good news, unexpected news, about the woman."

"Go on..."

"Natalia Laskin and the boat she escaped in were evidently found on Illa de San Martiño. They had drifted to the north, and that was where our Maritime Authority took her into custody."

"I'm not sure I'm following you," I said. "What, exactly, does that mean to me?"

"Well, Illa de San Martiño is a Spanish island, not part of Portugal. And we actually have no jurisdiction there."

"So you guys already released her?"

"Yes and no. She's been released, but to the custody of the Spanish authorities."

"Okay." I looked up at Aafreen and shrugged.

"Unlike Portugal, Spain has an *unconditional* treaty with the United States, including a full extradition agreement."

"Which means that Laskin will be transferred back to the U.S. for trial?"

"I believe so."

I thanked the comandante so loudly that everyone in the coffee shop stared at me. Aafreen had heard enough to figure out the gist of it, and wrapped me in a tight embrace. It was the perfect ending to our time together. The Russian alley cat had finally run out of lives.

We were both quiet as Aafreen drove me to the airport. It was a difficult goodbye, but one softened by our promises to spend some real time together once this whole thing blew over.

An INS agent met me at the ticket counter with documents that would allow me through the security checkpoint and onto the plane.

Aafreen stood behind the partition, watching to make sure I made it through the security scanners. Then I watched her, waving until she disappeared into the crowded terminal.

I had a lot to figure out about the two of us. She had her life on the East Coast, and I had mine in the Bay Area. I wondered if our feelings for each other would remain strong enough to bridge the 2,800-mile distance between us.

My flight back to San Francisco was delayed, so I sat in the bustling airport rotunda, thinking. Thinking about Aafreen, thinking about my daughter and how she would react to me dating someone, and much farther down the list was how Doris would react to it.

 Overshadowing these thoughts was my investigation and the loose ends that remained. They hung there just out of reach, like kite strings in a tree. In one way, I had accomplished what I'd set out to; Laskin was in jail and Aafreen had been set free. On the other hand, I had uncovered a massive international smuggling syndicate that was sending poor young women into wealthy countries. I hadn't expected to find that, but then I hadn't expected to learn it was all connected to my first homicide case as a San Francisco police inspector.

In hindsight, the clues had been there all along; Natalia Laskin, the MS Versand, the Russians, the Latvians, and probably whoever it was in San Francisco tracking my every move. I just hadn't put any of it together.

I now had two choices: I could either leave it alone, just like the State Department and the FBI were going to do, or I could continue investigating—tugging at the kite strings. I wanted to do the easy thing, and nobody would ever know that I could have done more. Except me.

My college football coach used to say, "You always know the right thing to do. The hard part is doing it." He was probably talking about shortcuts during training or taking a cheap shot on the field, but it had a much more important meaning to me now.

There was no way I could ever turn my back on this and pretend that it wasn't still happening.

CHAPTER 70

I awoke on Sunday morning, two weeks to the day after first reading Shanay's message that Aafreen had been arrested for murdering her boss.

I drove to the office, stopping for a cup of coffee and a newspaper along the way. My tiny 2nd floor suite was empty, quiet, and cold, so I turned on a space heater that Shanay had bought, and then sat at her desk while I opened my mail and listened to messages.

There was a package from Bella and Sophie Elliott, inside of which were my case files, laptop, clothes, and a note thanking me for making their vacation *an adventure of a lifetime.*

Noticing that the notepad on Shanay's desk had my doctor's name and number on it, I surmised that she'd made an appointment to have my bullet wound checked. I smiled to myself and then moved on to the phone messages.

I listened to a call from Sarah Brooks, congratulating me on the successful apprehension of Natalia Laskin. It surprised me that she had heard about it all the way out here. Another message from my old partner Linh Phú also offered congratulations. There were similar messages left by Lou Cassidy—my partner before Linh—and Frankie Moretti—another SFPD inspector. I couldn't figure out how any of them had heard. Then I opened the Chronicle and read the headlines: EX-SAN FRANCISCO INVESTIGATOR CRACKS INTERNATIONAL HUMAN TRAFFICKING RING.

Scanning the article, I saw that I'd been portrayed in a much more favorable light than when I'd been arrested for the murder of the police chief seven months earlier. I realized that memories fade fast, and that yesterday's zero is today's hero.

The last paragraph of the story mentioned that I would likely be entitled to monetary rewards from the Transnational Organized Crime Reward Program, for recovering the victims. It also said that I was entitled to an FBI reward since Natalia Laskin had been on their Ten Most Wanted list.

I had not been familiar with either of the reward programs. And though I hadn't been driven by the money, it was definitely going to help offset my expenses. It would also probably mean another well-deserved raise for Shanay.

Sipping my coffee, I sat back and felt the warmth of satisfaction blanketing me. It had been a long time coming. I wondered if Doris had seen the article, and I hoped that she had. Her idiot boyfriend, too. I also wondered if the person at the top of the organization's pyramid was aware of what I'd done—the one Khatabi described as *"the head of the dragon."*

Suddenly, the metaphor I'd heard twice now came to mind, about my part of the investigation being a mere *acorn from a giant oak tree*. I now understood. The giant oak tree was the organization, or maybe a whole network of organizations, and I was insignificant.

I knew that trafficking of this magnitude cannot exist without corrupt governments, corrupt law enforcement, high-level financing, and money laundering. And Khatabi had told me that Natalia Laskin was only an underling to someone much higher.

Whoever he was, and whoever was in San Francisco monitoring me and feeding that information up their chain, I hoped they knew that I wasn't going to give up. I was not insignificant, and I was going to work hard to find out who they were. Danny McKenna was going to come after them with a vengeance.

Taking my cup of coffee to the window, I stood gazing out at the view. Looking between buildings, I saw the tiny wedge of sparkling bay water—the peekaboo view for which I was charged extra each month. But I was satisfied.

It was the kind of morning when the sun, the gulls and the sound of a distant train held the promise of another beautiful day in the San Francisco Bay Area.

See these other Phil Ribera books:
(Available at Amazon.com)

San Francisco File
Book #1 in the Danny McKenna detective series

Ensenada File
Book #2 in the Danny McKenna detective series

Bangkok File
Book #3 in the Danny McKenna detective series

It's Only a Badge
Book #1 in the police memoir series

Barkers & Bones
Portrait of an Undercover Narc
Book #2 in the police memoir series

Malfeasance
Book #3 in the police memoir series

Sadhana
Two Lies–One Truth
Fictional family saga set partially in India

www.ingramcontent.com/pod-product-compliance
Lightning Source LLC
Chambersburg PA
CBHW060634260626
47161CB00008B/2885